ALLAH IN THE ISLANDS

ACKNOWLEDGMENTS:

The North Carolina Council for the Arts supported me for six weeks at Headlands, California, where, as I looked over the cold sea, the ideas for this novel began to take shape.

Mrs. Adair Armfield, through her generous funding of the Edward Armfield Professorship at Davidson College, enabled me to conduct some of the research necessary for the telling of this tale.

Jeremy Poynting, through his close reading and deep interest in the narrative, provided invaluable editorial advice for which I am truly grateful.

Kathrin Flanagan for the cover art.

To Malik, Kenya, and Niklas

BRENDA FLANAGAN

ALLAH IN THE ISLANDS

PEEPAL TREE

First published in 2009
by Peepal Tree Press Ltd
17 King's Avenue
Leeds LS6 1QS
England

ISBN13: 9781845231064

This is a work of fiction. Any resemblance to real persons or situations is not to be taken literally, but some people may do so anyway, alas.

Peepal Tree gratefully acknowledges Arts Council support

PART ONE

DRY SEASON

That this, after all, was how it would go
figment, scheme, fantasy
silent films of the poor
psychedelic flashes of madmen

> Kamau Brathwaite
> (from 'Springblade')

ONE

On the day Beatrice Salandy's case was dismissed, I was with Haji and Yusuf inspecting the house round the Savannah. Haji had just come back from overseas, and even before he went down Carenage to see his wife and children – the second one, that is – he tell me to drive him straight to the Zhara House.

I was a little worried about this because Haji had put me in charge of finishing some repairs on the house, and I wasn't sure Yusuf do everything I tell him to do. I had wanted to go and check things out for myself before Haji could do his inspection but I hadn't had time.

When you see the Haji tell you to do something, you have to do it right, but I had so much on my plate that I couldn't see to everything he wanted, so I take a chance and ask Yusuf to do some.

All the way back from the airport I was studying if Yusuf do what I tell him because I didn't want to get in trouble with Haji. He's a real workhorse, and when you see he give you a task to perform, you have to do it and do it well. Standards. He always tell us that we had to set standards. Santabella was so unruly with young people bringing up themselves while their parents gone away to hustle work. It leave up to us to set examples for them to follow.

Yusuf was a new member and he still had a lot to learn. Twice, as we travelling down, I opened my mouth to tell Haji that I had give Yusuf some of the projects to finish, just to protect myself, but I could see he wasn't in no mood to hear excuses.

The airport authorities had keep him back for a long time after the plane land, searching up his luggage, asking him questions about where he went and what he do there. He didn't tell me this, but I know their system, and the airport was practically empty by the time he come through the door.

He was usually first off the plane, flying through Customs without any trouble, but this time was different. Besides, I know him long enough to know when he clamp his lips down and start making that grinding noise, it's best I keep my tongue between my teeth.

Just when we turn off the highway, I see his face muscles relax, and he asks how everything went. I tell him fine and he asks if the books come from America for the school children. I tell him twelve boxes come and we lock them up in his office.

"We leave them for you to open."

He give a little smile and I begin to relax myself. So far so good. If Yusuf finish all the things I tell him to do, then I would be able to sleep that night in peace, Insh'Allah.

Yusuf was waiting at the house when we get there, and I could see he was smoking. At least the evidence was still burning in the drain where he throw it when the car pulled up. He still have a long way to go, I could see. Haji glance at the cigarette butt but he didn't say a word. He's a man don't always talk when he's vexed.

We get through the downstairs inspection all right, except for the sliding doors to the back yard.

"How many times I have to remind all-you about security?" Haji was outside of the closed door, shaking it, testing, and I start to get nervous as he pushed a hairpin through the lock and the door slide open in a flash. He stepped back inside.

Yusuf's jaw dropped open. I just start praying in my mind.

"Anybody could jump this wall and be inside this house in a flash," Haji tell us, and fool Yusuf had to put in his two cents.

"But the wall has broken bottles on top."

Haji didn't even glance at him. I cut my eyes at him to shut up. It wasn't as if he himself didn't used to jump over walls with broken bottles before he join us, so he was only talking foolishness. Haji didn't even answer him.

He turned to me. "Get Salim to help you fix this by tomorrow morning. Put some bars across the door, from the inside, then see bout installing iron frames round the windows, from the inside."

Some people slow to learn. Yusuf jump in again. "But the bars should be on the outside."

This time Haji turn and give him a look that make my blood run cold.

"Wait in the car." He say it real quiet. I know him, you know. When he's vexed, really vexed, his voice gets quiet-quiet. You almost have to strain to hear him.

Yusuf let out a long stupes. Another bad habit he had, sucking his teeth when he get reprimand, like a spoiled child. No home training. But he went outside, walking bumpity-bump like a bad-john from behind the Bridge, which he used to be before we give him sanctuary. You know what they say: you could take a man out of the gutter but you can't take the gutter out of him. Still, Haji and the rest of us was trying to do that with people like Yusuf.

About two months before, Yusuf – that's his Muslim name – his slave name was Kelvin Brown but everybody know him as Kentucky because he must have made three jails for breaking into the chicken place down on Wrightson Road, and all he ever get to thief was stale chicken.

Anyhow, he come bouncing into the compound one day demanding to see Haji. Well, is not any and everybody who could just come barging in and see Haji just like that. We have protocol to follow. The guards stop him cold before he could get anywhere near Haji's office. Some of us recognize him because we have other members from behind the Bridge who use to live the kind of life Kentucky was living before they joined us. We take him down in the back for questioning.

Come to find out he was running like a zandolie from Sandfly, the drug lord. He asked for Haji's protection. Well, we had to straighten him out right then and there. We're not in no business of protecting drug pushers. We make it plain that if he wanted protection, he would have to give up that dirty life and convert.

Well, he was so frightened of Sandfly at that point that he would agree to anything. His hands trembling like fig-leaf in a storm. We let him stay a few days in the compound, down in a back room we reserve for people like him, while we check things out because we couldn't put it pass the government to try to infiltrate us. It wouldn't be the first time.

9

We had to be vigilant. Haji teach us that: watch your back; keep four eyes in your head; and your tongue between your teeth because bush have ears. Radars.

After Kentucky pass the checks, and we detox him, was only then we bring the full matter before Haji and he agreed to give him sanctuary on condition that he had to change his name, perform certain good deeds, and beg pardon from Sandfly.

When he hear that he had to ask Sandfly forgiveness, Kentucky nearly pee himself, but he couldn't back out. Is a funny thing, but a lot of those bad-john fellars like Sandfly have respect for Haji, even though he was preaching against drugs every Friday, the very drugs they made their living from.

That's because they know full well he was after the real big criminals, the people in government, on the police force who have no conscience, who suck the lives out of the poor man like soucouyants. Sandfly was a small-time peddler even if he could make men like Kentucky quake in their boots.

I was the one put in charge of Yusuf's training, so I arrange for him to meet with Sandfly. In front of me, Sandfly warn him that the day he move out from under Haji's protection, his dog dead.

"Bring the dogs up and leave them here until you get this place secure," Haji was saying as we went up to inspect the second floor.

Right at the top of the stairs Yusuf had left his radio blasting. The news was coming on. I was going to turn it off but Haji tell me to leave it on. Top of the news was the story about Beatrice Salandy. I was glad to hear that she get off. I didn't know her personally but my Tante Melda lives in Rosehill and she was always talking about her.

She even ask me one time to ask Haji to say a prayer to Allah, Peace be upon Him, for Beatrice. I forget to do that, but when I hear that her case was calling, finally, I say a prayer for her.

According to the news, Allah had showered her with mercies, and a few lines of thanksgiving prayers run through my head. She was a tough sister; she had a right to get free.

I could see Haji was thinking the same thing because he give a little laugh when the announcer say the case against her was dismissed. "A few more sisters like her and we could turn this country inside out," he tell me.

I was grateful to Beatrice right there because just the mention of her beating the case had put Haji in a good mood. We went on with the inspection, and except for the insides of the kitchen cupboards that was still lined with old newspaper, Haji didn't find anything to criticize.

"You do a sweep of the whole place yet?" he ask me. I tell him that me and Kello had done it twice. He said he had brought some new equipment and once he put it together, we would need to do another sweep. I was wondering how the airport authorities let him pass with that equipment, and as if he was reading my mind, he say everything was under control.

"Who patrolling the Savannah this week?" he ask me.

I tell him Salim and Mousa had that job. Just before he went away, some dirty man had raped three young girls in the Savannah and the police still couldn't catch him. One of the girls' father was Haji's friend and he come to us for help. Since then, we had two men patrolling the Savannah from one end to the next every night. Not a single rape since.

I can tell you this. When Haji tell you something under control, you better believe it's under control. I scored a few points with him when we went into the bedrooms because I had put up two bunk beds for the boys. He asked me where they came from and I tell him my Uncle Neddy from Morvant build them from wood I have under the house. Wood I was keeping to put on a room on my own house. All he have to do was buy two mattresses.

"How much you pay him?" He was inspecting the carpentry. My uncle in the best carpenter in Santabella so I was confident Haji wouldn't find any notches.

I tell him my uncle do the work for free because he have a lot a respec for what we was tryin to do. Haji put his hand in his pocket and pull out some bills; Yankee money. "Give that to your uncle and tell him I say thanks."

Later, when I count the money, I had more than enough to pay Uncle Neddy, to buy back the wood for my house, and some plants for my garden. That's another thing I start because of the Haji. He was encouraging all of us to plant our own food.

A few days before Haji come back from overseas, Miss Farouka make me bring her up to the Zhara House just to make sure we was doing the work right. She bring a set of plants and show me where to plant them because she knows Miss Amena likes flowers.

I make Yusuf put the plants in the side yard because we had set down bricks in the back yard which was one of the major things Haji tell me to do before he come back.

Miss Amena, Haji's second wife, was suppose to move into the house in a few days. She's the one who have the most Muslim children with Haji.

His first wife, well, first Muslim wife anyway, because he had one before he convert, that first Muslim wife, Miss Farouka, I tell you, she's a good woman. And when I tell you how much she suffer, she suffer bad, oui. You would think I make up a story, but I was there with them all the time, so I know what I talking about. Don't doubt me.

People don't believe me when I say this, but Miss Farouka and Miss Amena get along better than a lot of women I know. I can't really talk for the third one, the Chinese lady, as we call her, because she didn't come to the compound much, since her house was down in the country, but I never hear anything bad about her relationship with the other two.

Some women say they would never do that, share their husband with a next woman, even when they know the man have a deputy in the Toco, and a next one in San Juan.

Miss Farouka and Miss Amena, they know where their husband is when he's not with them. I think it's better that way, but you have to have big money for that kind of arrangement.

You could see the care Haji was taking with the house, making sure everything fixed to the best before Miss Amena and the children move in. And Miss Farouka was helping him. Every woman in Santabella should have a husband like that, and every good man deserve to have wives like them, especially Miss Farouka.

She was a big time civil servant when she meet Haji, and I know she help him a lot, especially in the early days. She was married before and had a daughter who was at university in Canada when she meet Haji. By the time everything fall down, she would be dead too, and the poor girl didn't have one thing to do with what Haji or any of us do.

When we finished inspecting the top floor, Haji went into

another room. I willing to bet that nobody but me, Billal, Haji, and maybe Miss Farouka, could get from the bedroom to that other room.

While I was standing guard, Haji went inside to put away some things that he had bring with him in a small bag, then we went back downstairs.

Yusuf was smoking a joint. Just leaning up against Haji's car, smoking away. He didn't even put it out when he see us coming, just take a long drag, then drop the butt on the pavement when I open the car for Haji.

All the way down to the house in Carenage, Haji didn't once look at Yusuf. It was as if Yusuf didn't exist; Haji block him totally. He talked to me, telling me about the kind of water tower he wanted to build on Zhara House instead of them big black plastic tanks, uglying up the scenery.

He was saying he see some he like in Libya, shaped like turrets, made from concrete. If we started installing similar ones on the houses we building, Santabellans would have alternatives, another way for us to make money for the group, and for all the people Haji had to help in this country. On top of that, it would give people like Yusuf legitimate ways to make a living.

I could feel Yusuf steaming in the back seat, shuffling as if he had piles, stupesing every few minutes as if he something stick in his teeth.

When we reach Carenage, Haji order him to wait in the car.

I help take Haji's suitcases inside. Miss Amena was there and you could see how her whole face light up like a 100 watt bulb. She invite me to stay and eat with them but I only stay long enough to wash up, say my prayers, drink a glass of juice, and listen to what Haji tell me to do about Yusuf.

TWO

"Not guilty. You could go, Miss Salandy. But make sure you don't show your face in my courtroom again. I warning you."

It took a second or two for the magistrate's words to register with Beatrice, so deep was her concentration on the possibility that, before the morning was out, she would be carted in the Black Maria through town to the Royal Jail.

It was the rumble of excitement around her, rather than the declaration from the bench, that made her realize her fears were not going to be realized.

"Where's Mother Dinah? Mother Dinah?" Melda was shouting.

"Somebody say the 23rd Psalm because we out from the valley of the shadow of death in truth. They not locking you up, Bee. You free."

Miss Ann, Melda, Jestina, Reme, Uncle Willy, Mr. Roberts, the whole of Rosehill, it seemed, had come down to the court to hear the case, and they were shouting her name, laughing out loud and making such a bacchanal that the magistrate had given up banging on his desk for order, lifted his black robe, and left the courtroom in disgust.

"What you talking bout, Melda?" Jestina shouted as she grabbed Beatrice's arm to pull her away from the group. "Who in his right mind was going to lock up Beatrice? You mad or what? Come, Bee girl. Let we leave these mad people. Reme. Come go with me."

Still in a daze, Beatrice allowed Jestina to tow her through the crowd, down the stairs, and out to the yard of the courthouse. A photographer ran up to them and Jestina barked to the group, "All you back off, nuh. You don't see the man want to take picture of the girl? Is her case. Is she picture he want for the *News* tomorrow, not yours. Get out the way. Everybody except Reme. Come-come, Reme. Stand with your daughter."

The crowd pushed Reme through so she could lean against Beatrice. The light flashed, and another, and Beatrice closed her eyes against the glare. In the moment before she reopened them, she took a deep breath and exhaled the tension that had wound itself though her chest. She was unable to talk, her thoughts still a jumble, so Jestina acted as her spokesperson, answering the reporters' questions, demanding that they tell the truth because "I know how all you could lie, yuh know."

Reme was saying to anyone who would listen, "You think is two novenas I make? You think is two candles I light, my Jesus? I bathe the girl in saltwater. Three times down Carenage. Is a hundred candles I light on that magistrate's head, oui."

A man shouted down from the balcony, "Beatrice's free! We girl free."

He peeled off his shirt and began to wave it like a flag as two police officers watched, slight smiles on their faces. Beatrice Salandy, accused of stealing thousands of dollars from the government, had gotten away scot free.

It was a thing, in those hard times, for poor people to be proud of.

"But you know that's not really why the government tried her," one policeman told the other. "Eh-eh. They were really trying to send her to jail for killing the big-time Chinese doctor. They say she throw acid in the man's face."

"That's a wicked crime," the other policeman said. "Any woman who would do a thing like that is a real devil. And she get 'way free? Nah, man. Don't tell me that."

"That doctor was a raper man," the first policeman whispered. "They say that's why she throw the acid in his face, but the government couldn't find a single witness to say she do it, so they make a charge about how she thief money from the Ministry. Is two years now they trying to send she up for that but they couldn't make a solid case. But she's guilty like sin, man. I know that for sure, regardless of what that magistrate say."

"Then why them people treating her as if she's some hero or something?"

The second policeman, recently transferred from Tobago, Santabella's sister island, was beginning to think that his mother was right when she had warned him to be careful.

Santabellans are a different breed of people from Tobagonians, she had argued. "They not like we"; he would regret asking for the transfer.

"Don't say I didn't warn you," she had said when he still refused to listen to her. "Them Santabellans are real bacchanal people." Here, he thought, was vivid proof.

Out of the courthouse yard the noisy group was leading the girl, anointing her head with their fingers, powdering her cheeks with their red lips, demanding to know, "How you feel, Beatrice? How you feeling, girl?"

The first policeman said, "To them, yes, she's a real hero. But mark my words, this is not the last we hearing about her. People like her have trouble mark all over them. It's just a matter of time."

He turned away to re-enter the courtroom and the Tobagonian policeman followed.

Down in the yard, Beatrice knew what Rosehill wanted her to say; they were giving her the words.

But the words from their mouths could not express the meditations of her heart. Rosehill had lived only vicariously through her two months in jail, and nearly two years of walking with a load on her shoulders.

She wanted to tell them the truth. She wanted to say, "I still can't believe I'm not going to jail. It's not true. It can't be true."

But if she couldn't believe it, they had no doubts. Their exuberance was enough to shake the flowers off the poui trees up in the hills, and they fully expected that she, the centrepiece of this drama, should be exalted with them.

So she kept the truth to herself, as usual, and offered up her body to speak in unison with their language of praise and glory. In turn, they returned her hugs and backrubs and squeezes round her waist, and bent their ears to her chest to see how fast her heart was beating.

"Yes," she said with as much conviction as she could muster, "I could wine down Saint Vincent Street in truth."

The image made them laugh because everybody knew she couldn't dance worth a lick.

They were probably thinking of that image, or about the relief they could feel now that their homes were safe because the source of the money Beatrice had used to buy their land leases was no longer a question. That's probably why they did not pay any attention to the clear-skinned woman, dressed to kill in white spike heels, a white suit – clearly cut overseas – and a blue fedora pulled low on her forehead, pushing through the crowd, until standing right in front of Beatrice, she spat in her face.

"You kill him. I know you do it. Whore! You will rot in hell, just wait and see," she screamed.

So quick, so unexpected was her attack that before they could recover, the woman was gone.

If you had asked five of them what she looked like, you would have gotten five different stories. But her face was engraved in Beatrice's mind.

She had seen the woman in court each time the case had been called, dressed always in that white linen suit, her head covered in a fancy matching hat, her face lowered to a copybook, as if she was taking dictation. She had sat away from the Rosehill crowd.

Beatrice had thought she might be a reporter for *The Sentinel*, until the time she had suddenly glanced across the aisle and caught the woman's eyes cutting into her, hot needles searing her skin.

Stunned by the intensity of the glare, Beatrice's mouth had dropped open in shock. She remembered thinking, but what I do this woman for her to hate me so? For long seconds, she had heard nothing her lawyer, Ali, was saying to her as the woman's eyes continued to make her blood crawl.

She was gone now, but a taste of her words hung nasty in the air. Beatrice wiped her face with the back of her hand. Jestina gave her a handkerchief to wipe her cheek, but her face burned as if pepper-sauce had been rubbed into it.

A few people shuffled back from Beatrice as if to distance themselves from the effects of the woman's curse, and one whispered to another:

"Beatrice had better watch herself. Some women in this country would die for that doctor."

"But nobody on Rosehill come forward to say they see her kill the man," another argued. "You can't just go round saying something like that. You have to have evidence."

"Ah-hah, but she's a sly mongoose, oui. The way she hold herself up like a flag these past two years, nobody looking at her would think she could kill a fly. Umm-hum. That one? I'm willing to bet she thief that money in truth. Sonny come back from America to say otherwise, but where he get all that money to give her, eh, tell me that."

"He's a lawyer. You think he would lie?"

"Some of the biggest fowl thieves in this country are lawyers. What you telling me? I hope that woman's curse don't blight Beatrice, though."

"Hummm. Her Tante Vivian was a seer women, yuh know. You must remember she could fix things, eh, even if she's dead and gone. Yes, she could fix them from over yonder too. Beatrice will have to call her and quick-quick too."

The wind carries words and when they drop, they could be big rocks on your head or showers of blessing.

For nearly two years Beatrice had felt stones pelting her back, bruising her shoulders, but she refuse to break down in the quarry, at least not for the people to see. No, she couldn't let them see her tremble, not her, who all of them on Rosehill, the *mauvais-langue* ones and those who sang her praises, had so much to say about, beyond the nine-days when she was supposed to be a wonder. Fingers held against their lips, their tongues clicked-clicked about how she didn't cry when little Melvin died, and how she thought she must be better than some of the others on Rosehill with she neck propped on a flag pole.

She could read suspicion, doubt, jealousy in their crickets in her ears, and her temples strained to burst. That's when she would call out to Tante Vivian to come, come rub her head oh God, for the fever to go away, please. Next morning, there might be a wet hole in her pillow with teeth marks around it, and her head would be clear.

None of the Rosehill stalwarts encircling her at the courthouse that day knew what she had endured. For them, Beatrice's freedom was a hot new calypso to jump up to, so like mass on Carnival Monday, they held up traffic on busy Saint Vincent Street to carry her over to Ching Chee's snackette where they raised their elbows in praise of the gods of mercy, with black rum and Carib beer, sweet drinks and lemon juice to lips parched too long for a little bit of gladness.

Though still not sure of the ground she was walking on, Beatrice knew that some things had to come naturally. She put away thoughts of the spitter and turned her attention to Rosehill.

She praised them: "Yes, Miss Ann. For the prayers, eh. I know you made a lot of novenas for me. If you don't hold me down, is fly I will be flying."

"You is a soucouyant, girl," came the picong from Willy.

Rosehill loved that. They burst out laughing as Beatrice drowned the rest of her words in the Peardrax Mr. Roberts had placed in her hand.

He ordered the same for Miss Ann who shooed the drink away, scornfully.

"Sweet drink? This day? This day when poor people should drink champagne, you going to offer me a cheap sweet drink? Look man, I want the biggest glass of rum in this place. And you might as well bring back out them dollars you hiding in your pocket because you buying one for all the women." She gathered the women around her at the counter.

Their eyes carefully measured the three fingers of Old Oak as the barman poured, but before they could raise the glasses to their lips, Miss Ann dipped her right hand into hers to sprinkle some to the ancestors. Melda and Miss Roberts did the same.

"Here," Melda whispered to Beatrice. "Here, have half of mine. Rum does make my knees water, girl. I only doing it to please Miss Ann."

Beatrice gulped a mouthful, welcoming the heat of it on her tongue. Suddenly an arm came around her shoulder. Jestina's lips kissed her right ear.

"Don't drink any more of that cheap rum, girl, unless you want a massive headache in the morning."

Miss Ann, seeing Jestina pour Beatrice's drink into her own

glass, protested, "All the men you have and you can't buy a rum for yourself?"

"Money is not an object where my love is concerned, meh dear," Jestina laughed. "And it's not better to give than to receive?"

Leaving Miss Ann to puzzle over that, she leaned on Beatrice, begging her to show her to the toilet.

Ignoring Miss Ann's protests, they left the group for the narrow stall at the back of the shop. As Jestina lifted her skirt, Beatrice splashed water on her face, but the feel of the spit from the woman's mouth seemed to have penetrated her cheek. She washed her face again, then turned to the mirror and felt in her purse for her powder puff.

"Don't mind all these people, eh," Jestina relaxed on the toilet seat. "I not drunk, you know. I only do that to get you away from them. They're glad you win the case, is true, but they just thinking about feathering their own nest. Is money on their mind, eh Bee. Your money. Even them who talk you bad, who say that you thief the money from the government, will be waiting by your gate with their palms stretch out. You don't think you do enough for Rosehill, Beatrice, umh? You have to look out for yourself sometime. Tante gone; you don't have chick nor child to hamper you. Reme could look after herself. Go up New York. I'm not meaning you should go by Sonny. No. But the same way he could go there and become a big-time lawyer, you could too. Don't misuse what God give you, eh girl. Hand me a piece of that brown paper there. They never put toilet tissue in here. Cheap-arse."

Beatrice stepped aside from the sink as Jestina rose from the seat, skinning her face in mock despair at the roughness of the brown paper on her skin. She flushed the toilet handle, and straightened her clothes.

"You looking *bazoudi*," she laughed as Beatrice slipped her powder puff and lipstick back into her purse. "Don't let what that woman do get you down. She's a fool. Imagine cursing out somebody for that bad-bad man. Some women too stupid for their own good."

"You know her?" Beatrice asked.

"Every Chow, Dick, and Selwyn know that woman. She was

one of them ladies of the night for years, then they say she make a child and claimed it was for that Dr. Chow. The man was married. He never even *paytay* on her, never acknowledged the child. Maybe she had hopes while he was still alive, but the man dead. Time for her to try to latch on to somebody else."

"You think she telling the truth? That the child was his?" Beatrice asked.

"Yes, I see the little girl sometimes. She has his face. But he was a bad-bad man, Bee, you know that. I wouldn't want anybody to know he was my child's father, if I was her. But forget him and that crazy woman. Let we concentrate on you."

But even as she was saying, "I'm okay," to Jestina, Beatrice was thinking about the woman, and a feeling of sorrow came over her.

That woman, even if she was a prostitute, as Jestina said, had made a child, an innocent child, for Dr. Chow. Just like Melvin. The child couldn't be held responsible for what Dr. Chow had done. The woman had gotten herself all twisted, thinking she should defend her daughter's father. If Melvin had lived, would she have come to forgive Dr. Chow for raping her? No. No. He was dead. Good riddance to bad rubbish.

"Ummm-humm," Jestina was babbling away. "How long I know you, Bee? Eh? You think you could fool me?"

"You know me better that I know myself, sometimes." She tried to summon a smile but failed, then shook her head to clear it. "You ever see a bird that spend years in a cage, wishing it could get out? The day the cage door open, the bird's still hopping around, inside. That's me."

"Ummmhumm," Jestina acknowledged. "I know just what you mean. You remember the time I had that case for cutting Sharky? Three months in the Royal Jail. Weeks after I get out I still use to feel I was inside that little hole. Here, lend me your powder puff a minute. But it will pass, you know. Give it time. Let me put a little bit of your lipstick on my cheekbones. I forget my rouge home. Thanks. But hear what I telling you. Go up by the Botanic Gardens. You remember how we used to do that every time we come down town? Go up and see the flowers, girl, and say hello to them for me."

"Reme might not like that. You know how she is." Beatrice

told her. "She's waiting for me to travel back to Rosehill with her."

"Your mother is a grown woman, girl, and you're not in diapers."

Someone shouted from the other side of the door. "You all living in there or what? A person wants to pee."

Jestina ignored the plea. "Don't let Miss Ann and them talk you into going to the stores with them. I hear them talking about how they want you to buy this and that for their children. Watch yourself, you hear me?"

"How much money they think I have left? I paid for all those leases. Then for Tante's funeral. Reme get some to give that doctor in Venezuela for her belly. How much money they think I have so?"

"I'm going to pee myself out here. Woman, open the door!" a man's voice shouted.

"Go ahead. Wet down your pants," Jestina laughed, but Beatrice lifted the latch which opened the door, causing the man to fall into her, his cigarette brushing against her chest.

Jestina, muttering "Drunk", squeezed by him to follow Beatrice back to the front where Willy and the some of the Rosehill men were taking one for the road with two saga-girls from town.

"And a hip-hip hooray for we girl Beatrice," Willy shouted.

Beatrice acknowledged them with a smile and after a last round of "Shake my hand, nuh girl. Let some of your good luck rub off on me," she turned to Miss Ann who, she noticed, was casting deadly cut-eyes at Willy.

"Well I'm leaving now, eh. I'll see all-yuh up the Hill."

"Where you going off to, Beatrice?" Reme demanded. "You're not travelling with me?"

"I need to stop by Mr. Ali's office. I don't know how long that will take. You know how busy he is. You go on up without me."

"You need to go and kneel down in a church and thank God, Beatrice, if you ask me, but as usual, you never consult with me." Reme shook her head. "You round a corner but you don't know what's waiting for you behind the next bend. Only God knows, and only he can prevent something bad from happening. Don't say I didn't tell you."

"God finish with Beatrice," Jestina laughed. "He gone South Africa to help Mandela and them black people. She has to help herself now. Eh Beatrice? And you strong enough to do that too, meh dear. Tell them not to worry their self over you, eh." And she started to sing Sparrow's popular calypso:

> Don't worry yuh head over me
> Study for yuhself, not for me,
> Because I'm young, and I'm strong,
> And I ent 'fraid no man in town,
> So, don't worry yuh head over me.

The two shining women hanging on to Willy's arms picked up the chorus.

"Don't worry yuh head over me. Dah, dah, dah dah dah! Dah dah dah."

Miss Ann, muttering to Melda that the women had enough rouge on them to paint two motor cars, got up from the table to recapture Willy. Beatrice squeezed her mother's shoulders, kissed Jestina on her cheek, and slipped out the front door.

Jestina raised her glass of rum to the girl's receding back before turning to the frowning Reme.

"So tell me about that spirit man down the Main who cure your big belly, nuh girl. Look how nice you looking. A-A. He must be put a good obeah on you."

Reme shrugged off her arm and deliberately turned her back on her.

THREE

Before she left town, Reme went to the post office on Wrightson Road to buy a stamped blue letterform which she took over to a side counter, out of the way of *macomay* eyes. She found the black ballpoint pen she had remembered to tuck into her handbag that morning, and with it she wrote:

Dear Sonny,

I am praying that these words does meet you fine as they leave me safe. Sonny, praise the good Lord, Beatrice's case dismiss. Is not that I ever doubt that would happen but you never know what kind of thing people working on you in this country. But she's free now and we have God to thank for that. You too. You know I did always have doubts about you but when you come back to do what you could for Beatrice, I was satisfied that you still have some decency in you.

Sonny, I don't know what all happen between you and Beatrice since then because you know Beatrice wouldn't talk to me at all, but I don't see any letters coming from you so I have a feeling you and Beatrice break up again. I hear some talk about you marrying a white lady in America. You know bush have ears in this place so Beatrice must be hear that too but I don't know what is true from what is a lie.

I don't want to get in your business but deep down in my heart I have a feeling you still wouldn't mind helping Beatrice out. That's why I say to myself, let me write and ask you this favour. If I leave it up to Beatrice, you know how proud she is, she might never send to tell you how things going with her these days. So I take it upon myself to do it for her, and I hope you don't mind that.

Sonny, even though the baby dead and you and Beatrice not so

24

friendly any more, you could think about poor little Melvin and help her out for long-time's sake? I want Beatrice to go America. These vultures on Rosehill can't wait to break down the door begging Beatrice to help them, but I want her to use what little money she have for a ticket to go away. When she small, you remember, she used to talk about studying in New York. Like you. You get scholarship and leave, and Beatrice get mixed up in all this commess about land and Doctor Chow. Is time now she look out for sheself. With the baby dead, poor little soul, and Tante Vivian gone, Beatrice only have me here and I could take care of myself.

I'm not asking you for money, Sonny, just for the invitation letter because you know how the Embassy people is. You have to have a letter from somebody in America inviting you to stay with them. So for long-time sake, Sonny, I know how you use to like Beatrice even though she didn't treat you too nice when you come all the way back here to help her. But you know how she is. That girl have too much pride for she own good. She would never write and ask you this one little favour, but I asking you to do it for me please.

I went last week to see your father in the nursing home and he still the same. I will check up on him every week even after Beatrice leave. So Sonny, I'm counting on you. Please, for God's sake, help me get Beatrice out from Santabella before she get into any more trouble.

Sonny, as God is my witness, I will never forget you for doing this small thing for people who look after you long before you start wearing long pants. Do, please, don't forget your people. Remember it's they who have you where you is today. Write me at my madam's house so Beatrice won't know I ask you this favour. The address is: Reme Salandy, c/o The Ames, 120 Diamond Vale Road, Santabella. Hoping to hear from you soon, in God's love.
Sincerely,
Reme

She signed her name neatly, reread the letter, folded the form along its creased lines, licked the strip of dried gum inside the flap, and pressed it close. Then she slipped it into the overseas mail slot in the wall.

Riding in a taxi on her way to Rosehill, she looked out the

window at the plains planted with unending rows of sugarcane up to the base of the grey-green hills. They seemed to be bowing, waving at her. She smiled back at them.

Life, she believed, had to get better from that day on. If only she could get Beatrice to start thinking about herself for a change. Forget Rosehill. Let them bear their own crosses because when it came down to the wire, it was you alone dancing. Who made a jail? Not that Miss Ann sitting behind the counter in her parlour minding everybody's business. Not Melda nor Jestina. They had all profit from that money. Beatrice had bought out their leases, saved their behinds from getting thrown out in the road; keeping the government from taking over the land to drill for oil.

And for all that and more, what'd she get in return? Beatrice's own mother get? She raise the girl herself after Kelvin abandon them. Forgetting his promise to send for them. Not a postcard. Not a pound. She sweat in kitchens, her knees getting hard and dry from scrubbing their floors, just to send Beatrice to Bishop's High School, the best in the country, because she could see how bright the girl was.

She didn't need anyone to tell her that. Tante could see it in Beatrice when she was born. But look how she wasting her education. Making jail for a bunch of ungrateful people. That is what she devoted her whole life for? No! No! Beatrice had to leave Rosehill, leave Santabella once and for all. Go away to America. Like Sonny. This place was too small for her to make something big of herself, and these Rosehill people would drag her down, suck her lifeblood like the soucouyants they were. If Sonny could do it, she could do it too. Beatrice was brighter than Sonny any day. If he could become a big-time lawyer, she could do that too.

As the taxi sped away from the low lands planted with tomatoes, cabbages and lettuce, Reme marked the date in her mind. Two months from now. Two months to take care of business even if Sonny didn't answer her letter. In two months she would be up in the airport bright and early, waving Beatrice goodbye. She lifted her right forefinger to her lips, wet it, then made a cross with the dampness on her forehead. She, Reme Salandy, would make sure of that if it was the last thing she did on this earth.

FOUR

Oh God, somebody mash up the seeds from bird peppers on the pavement, Beatrice thought. Had to be. So much heat had penetrated the plastic soles of her black shoes, that her sweating, overcrowded toes had begun to hurt. She wished she had put a pair of sandals in her bag to wear outside the courthouse in spite of Reme's insistence that she should wear the heels.

"You have to make a good impression. You can't go in the courthouse in no sandals looking like *laddydar* people."

To please her mother, she had put them on that morning, then waited in silent agony for Clyde, whose taxi was late, as usual, to take them to town.

How she would love to shove her heels into her purse and walk barefoot despite the piping hot pavement, but she was in the heart of the city and people would think she was crazy. Or a country bookie, at least. What was normal for Rosehill would be cause for heckling in town. Listless sales-girls propping up showcases in front of their dreary arcades, begging passers-by to *come nuh, buy a half dozen wash clothes, only twenty dollars*, would tell each other that she had escaped from the madhouse, oui, because only mad people come in town barefoot.

Up Frederick Street she went, a little wobbly, as she was not used to walking in heels, and tight ones at that. Near Park Street she slowed when she heard two women arguing with a guard in front of the Electricity Board.

"I was in America whole last month," the dark-skinned one with straightened hair dyed the colour of honey, announced. "Six months I'm up there. My lights turned off. You tell me how I manage to run up a four hundred dollar bill, eh? Tell me that."

27

Her companion, short, her own hair in tight black cornrows, broad buttocks forced into Vanderbilt jeans, waved a handful of bills. "You see how they taking advantage of poor people in this country? We can't get jobs here. We have to go to America and work in the white people's kitchen and when we come back, look what happen. I'm not paying them. Let them lock me up. I'm not paying one blasted cent."

She turned left, right, shaking the bills in the air like an acolyte swinging incense in a church.

The green-uniformed security guard stared silently down at his shiny Government boots, his arms folded across his chest as if to keep from exploding.

Beatrice nodded in sympathy with the women but felt pity for the guard as well. His bosses had given him a gun to shoot bandits trying to hold up the cashiers and customers coming to pay their bills, but what did they train him to do with vex-up women like these, his own poor people demanding satisfaction, taking their rage out on him? They didn't care that he was only the guard, not the owner of the electricity business.

He had forced them leave the inside of the building for making too much noise but they were on public property now and all he could do was stand quietly with his legs apart and his arms folded across his chest to keep them from kicking in the glass.

Beatrice took it all in as she walked by, determined to mind her own business. Interfering in other people's lives had gotten her into enough trouble. Yet, she was bothered.

Who was in charge of the blasted world, she had often wondered. Poor people scrambling to stay alive; constantly under siege. And innocent children under pressure, some dying, like her poor little Melvin, for what nasty Dr. Chow had done to her.

The sins of the fathers pouring down upon their children? The innocents having to pay. The world was upside down in truth.

Three years she had poured all her love into that little boy, hoping against hope if he was really Dr. Chow's she could erase the stain on him. But it wasn't to be.

Why? Why the poor child who never do anything to anybody have to suffer so? Nobody could give her any answers.

So okay, God couldn't want anything else from her ever again, and she wasn't going to give him a chance to punish her any more. Never, never, would she bring another child into this world. She had made that promise on the sign of the cross over Melvin's grave, and not a man in this world would make her break it.

Those women quarrelling over a little light bill. What did they know about real trouble? About your heart mashing up into little pieces. About walking into the sea, wanting to swallow all the salt water that could never wash the blight from you no matter how long you stay under? About fighting that hand that keep pushing you to the beach, forcing you to turn your back on the sea, to walk back into a world full up with misery.

Praise be to Tante Vivian. She was still watching over her, coming in the night to blow cool air on her temples and to massage her forehead. And praise be for Reme with her novenas to Saint Jude for lost causes.

Nearing the Savannah, she could see the wide expanse of green ahead with seats along the sidewalk where she could finally kick off these high heel shoes, drink a coconut water, and taste what freedom feel like for the first time in years.

The vender sliced the top of a young one for her. A small boy working with him took her money. She waved to him to keep the change from the five, before raising the sweet coconut to her lips.

FIVE

Refreshed from the cool water and soft white jelly of two coconuts, Beatrice strolled west toward Queens College, north past the sprawling homes of the Archbishop, and the White House holding the Prime Minister's offices.

She smiled as she recalled playing in the back street, just behind the White House, when as a child, she had visited Tante Vivian on a Sunday. Tante worked then with some American people whose name she could not remember, but what came to mind was dashing across the street with Shirlin, her cousin, to play in the Botanic Gardens, and she was glad to remember this light-hearted time.

Light was fading; she should really be heading back down town to catch a taxi for Rosehill. Instead, coming to the gate leading into the valley of the Botanic Gardens, she pushed it open, and shoe straps around her fingers, ran down to the edge of the lily ponds. Between thick layers of broad leaves in murky water she spotted two reds and a white, regal on their long green stems.

The large rock beside the reeds called to her, so she lifted her dress over it, pulled her legs up under her, raised her face to the three-quarter moon rising even though the sun was still visible, and sang the song she and Shirlin used to sing as children.

Winkin', Blinkin', and Nod one night
Sailed off in a wooden shoe.
Sailed on a river of crystal bright
Into a sea of blue.

The hesitant croaks of young crapeaux came through the reeds laughing with her at her foolishness, and she drew a deep, contented breath.

In her reverie, Tante Vivian came, slight specks of grey peeping from the white cloth around her head, laughing, singing the song with Beatrice, then reaching to pull her up from the rock to dance. *Tante-Tante-Tante, dance with me. Tante!*

She heard herself scream. Shocked. Her eyes flew open. She sat up, suddenly desperate to find her shoes, but she couldn't see. She couldn't see because of the glare in her eyes.

"What you doing here?" A growl came from a face that seemed to be hanging in midair. She put both hands up to shield from the light and saw that she was looking at a policeman in his black uniform.

She scrambled upright, reached for her shoes, her purse, but the light still played on her face.

"You can't see the light's dazzling me?"

The beam shifted to her bare feet, stayed there while she slipped into her shoes, trying not to hurry against the inside voice that told her to just grab them and run. But why she have to run from a policeman?

The man shifted the beam to her face again. "I ask you a question. What you doing in here this time of night. You meeting somebody here?"

I'm not frightened, I'm not frightened, she told herself. But she was. There was something not right about this policeman – the way he was talking in a growl, as if he was trying to camouflage his voice?

She reached into her dress pocket to wipe her sweating palms and discovered the two benna beans Reme had pressed into her hands that morning.

"They belong to Tante. She give them to me to rub when I have troubles," she had said, when Beatrice had wrinkled her face.

"I not going to ask you again. Who you meeting in here, eh? Don't turn your back on me. Who you think you is?"

"Why I have to be *doing* anything?" She flung the words at him without slowing down. "You have to pay to walk in the Savannah now?"

He switched off the torchlight, hooked it to his belt, but kept after her.

"You know how many people get rape here last year? Women and men. Where you come from, eh? You don't read the papers or what? You from the country or what?"

They were nearly at the top of the rise, but he was still following her. Beatrice could see the dipping lights of cars as they neared the roundabout. She stopped abruptly. Flung herself round to face him.

"Yes, I'm from the country. *This* county. What give you the right to tell me where I could go or not go? Why you have to know who I'm meeting? This is my country! My Botanic Gardens! Since when I have to get police permission to come here?"

"I'm the watchman in this Savannah, you don't know that? Anybody coming here in the night have to pass through me." He started to laugh at his own joke, and Beatrice, looking away from his wide-open mouth, saw that he was not wearing a badge, that he was not wearing a policeman's uniform, just a hat and black clothes resembling the uniform.

He leapt at her.

She lashed out at him, grating his eyes with the benna beans, and as he paused to stop the blood from running down his face, she slipped out of her high heels, struck him again and again with them until he turned and ran back down the hill.

Rage overflowing, Beatrice pelted her shoes after him. Then she was running, running up the last feet of slope towards the street, her face down, pushing herself out of the gardens, straight into the arms of two men just coming through the gates.

"Oh god, Oh god, Oh god!" she moaned, as she struggled to release herself from them. *I done dead now*.

They held her, one on each side. They held her arms to keep her from slumping to the ground.

"Is okay, sister. Is okay," one of them was saying, his grip still tight to keep her from getting away. "We not going to hurt you. You okay?"

"She need to sit down," the other one said. She saw his boots, heavy black boots under pants made from green camouflage material. The other one was dressed the same.

They had to pull her over to the bench on the sidewalk and only then did they release her.

Still breathing hard, she lifted a hand to ward off the glare of their torch lights.

Cars drove by, their oncoming headlights touching her briefly before they sped past. Okay, she thought, okay. Anybody can see me. They can't do anything to me up here. She took some deep breaths, closed her eyes tightly, then reopened them. A sigh escaped her.

The man asked again, "You okay, sister?"

Sister? Who's he calling sister?

Four women, jogging in unison, passed them without a glance, and Beatrice began to feel a little silly for having been afraid. These men weren't with that dirty man in the Gardens. If they had been, she would be down in the gully, not up here on the sidewalk with joggers and cars.

"You awright now, sister?" The one on her right repeated. He had turned off his torch light, but the other man's lingered on her, the beam dancing across her chest. Before she could answer, the one who had been pressing her for a response instructed the other one to go down to the woman selling doubles a few yards away and bring back a cup of water.

"I'm okay," she murmured, suddenly conscious of her bare feet, and folding them under the bench. "You could shine that light away from my eyes, please?"

Her mind was clicking questions about how she would get home without shoes, and her purse. She had dropped her purse!

The man must have seen the panicked look in her eyes, because he said soothingly, "Is okay. Is okay."

He pointed to her feet, and she whispered that she had dropped them. Why hadn't she just gone home; why had she listened to Jestina? What had this country come to when you couldn't even take a walk in the Botanic Gardens?

The other man returned with the cup of water but she pushed it away. "I have to find my shoes," she said. "And my purse." She tried to get up but the one who had been speaking to her rested a hand lightly on her shoulder.

"We'll find them," he said. "Don't worry. I'm Mousa." He

pointed to the one with the cup. "This is Salim. We belong to the Masjid Compound. What happen to you down there?" He pointed with his chin towards the hollows in the Gardens.

"Nothing happen." Beatrice could feel the dryness in her throat but she resisted the urge to take the cup from Salim.

"Where your shoes, then?" Salim demanded.

She nodded toward the Gardens. "I drop them."

"Somebody do you something down there?" Mousa asked, and when she didn't respond, he said, "Look, is our jobs to patrol the Savannah. If somebody try something on you, tell us. He's probably still down there. We might be able to catch him."

Beatrice took a deep breath. "A man dress-up like a policeman try to grab me." She said the words so fast Mousa had to ask her to repeat them.

"He do you anything?" he looked away from her as he asked the question.

She shook her head. "I manage to hit him in his face with my shoe heel."

Mousa said, "Okay. Hold on here."

Leaving her with Salim, he went quickly down the sidewalk, then came back with one of the girls who worked at the stall selling doubles. He introduced her.

"This is Sister Fatima. She will get a taxi for you to take you home." Motioning with his torchlight for Salim to follow him, they ran back through the gates and down into the dark of the garden.

The doubles girl, as Beatrice thought of her, said, "My sister has some extra slippers. I sure they could fit you. Wait, eh." She went back to the shed. She was wearing, Beatrice noted, a long dress.

"Is bottled water, you know," Fatima said, as she watched Beatrice try on the sandals. "You could drink it. It's safe." She took the cup from the bench where Salim had rested it and Beatrice sipped a little of it.

"How they fitting?" Fatima pointed to Beatrice's feet.

Beatrice said the sandals were okay, even though she could feel her heels sticking over the back. Still, they were better than going barefoot.

"I make you out," Fatima nodded. "You's Beatrice Salandy, that girl…"

Beatrice lifted a hand to stop her. "Yes, okay, okay."

"You should be proud of yourself, girl." Fatima sat down on the bench and Beatrice shifted over to make room for her. "We pray for you in the mosque last week, for you and all the people in this country who catching hell with this government. You see how they put tax on the school books?"

What am I doing on this bench listening to this woman? Beatrice thought. *I have to get home.* She stood up, and as she did so, the woman back at the doubles shed called out to Fatima that the car was coming for the girl. She waved to her to come.

"Wait, eh," Fatima ordered. When she came back from the shed, she held out a bag with a dozen of the small flour balls, their hot spicy oil seeping though the brown paper. "Shanty say to give you this."

Before Beatrice could offer her thanks, a car pulled up to the curb and a man, dressed like the two who had gone back into the gardens, came out, opened the door, guided her into the back seat, waved to the women, and drove off.

Beatrice sat forward uneasily, her shoulders braced, her hand on the door, just in case she would need to push it open.

SIX

The next morning Beatrice rose early to open up the windows so the slight breeze coming up from the Gulf could pass through her room to cool off her sweaty body. She had spent a miserable night, tossing and turning, waking up several times from half-completed dreams of the woman who had assaulted her and Dr. Chow laughing at her behind closed fingers, and another, particularly terrifying, of a man whose features were blurred, his head covered in feathers, hiding under a bed from soldiers who were searching for him. She saw herself sitting on the bed, wanting to move, but unable to do so.

Her mind troubled, she turned on the light and began a frantic search for Tante's dream book, the one in which she had, over many years, written down dreams, her interpretations, and how they had been resolved.

Santabellans had come from the farthest corners of the country to consult Tante Vivian, and although she owned books published in China giving their own interpretations, it was her own scribbled notes upon which she had relied.

The book was nowhere to be found. She'd have to ask Reme if she had taken it, even as doubts surfaced about why Reme would remove it from the dresser drawer when she knew that Tante had left the book for Beatrice. Maybe Miss Ann had borrowed it.

Sluggish from the night's disturbances, Beatrice splashed tepid water over her body and was dressed before the last cock had crowed its welcome to morning on the Hill. She still had to see Ali, her lawyer, but the thought of going downtown nearly paralysed her.

For hours she was wrecked with indecision. Go to town? No. Yes. What had happened the day before was over. She was free; she had gotten away from that man; she had gotten home safely, thanks to those Muslims.

Still, it was nearly noon when she finally got dressed and took a taxi into town. A short stop at the bank, then straight to Ali's office. She would get her business done and be back in Rosehill before darkness fell. God willing, nobody would interfere with her.

Ali's receptionist said he was "Busy-busy preparing for a case", but "wait, nuh, and when I finish typing this I will tell him yuh here."

Beatrice took a seat in a corner and began flipping through old newspapers. The receptionist looked up to apologize that she had not had time to go out to buy that day's papers, but Beatrice was too intrigued by a story in *The Reflector* to hear her. It told of school teachers in a district not far from Rosehill who had started a programme to feed school children.

"Based on the belief that a hungry child cannot concentrate on school lessons, we decided to provide a free lunch to all needy pupils," the headmaster was quoted as saying. The school had served nearly two thousand lunches each week in the previous year, and intended to up that amount in the coming year.

Funds were being supplied by Santabella's leading Hindu organization. Asked by the reporter about the lunch programme, the Minister of Education had dismissed it as an attempt by the Hindu organization to embarrass the government which, the organisation claimed, had "enough revenue from its oil and gas to serve the needs of all Santabella's children."

In response, the leader of the Hindu organization had repeated that the country did, indeed, have a lot of gas but unfortunately most of it was coming from the mouths of government ministers.

The receptionist's telephone rang, and having answered it, she held one hand over the mouthpiece and called out to the slightly open door to Ali's office, "Boss, is the imam want to talk to you."

"Haji?" Ali's voice came back.

"Yes," the receptionist told him. "He's down the street. He want to know if yuh could spare him a few minutes. Pick up the phone, nuh."

When Ali was done talking, he came to the door to say to the receptionist, "He's coming. Send him right in."

The receptionist pointed a pencil at Beatrice. With a smile bursting over his face, Ali came over to shake her hand.

"A-A, Beatrice girl. How long you here? But Chandra, why you didn't tell me the star-girl waiting? Come-come." An arm about Beatrice's shoulders, he took her into his office.

They were together about five minutes when Chandra knocked on the door to announce, "Haji come."

Beatrice got up to leave as Ali came from behind his cluttered desk to pump the tall man's hand and exchange the Muslim greeting, words that Beatrice did not understand.

Ali, indicating Beatrice, said, "I want you to meet this lady, Haji. Beatrice Salandy."

"But I know Miss Salandy." Haji dipped his head in a slight bow. "We haven't met but I know her well, man. Miss Salandy?" He was smiling down at her in a kind of mocking way.

Confused, and suddenly embarrassed, Beatrice opened her mouth but no words came out. Should she extend her hand for him to shake? He had not extended his. Ali clapped his hands and moved back to his seat.

Haji, the smile still dancing round his lips, kept his eyes on Beatrice.

She picked up the purse she had borrowed from Tante's drawer, mumbled goodbye to Ali, and fled from the office.

Ali called out to her that he would have Chandra post her a receipt for the money but she barely heard him.

Outside, she had to dodge around two burly men dressed like the ones who had come to help her the night before. They stood guard at the door, their eyes darting up and down the street, piercing passers-by, as if they expected danger.

Anyone watching her would have worried that she would break a leg, so fast did she hurry down the street to catch a Rosehill taxi and get away from town.

SEVEN

Two men in military green and black camouflage, their heads wrapped in dotted black and white Arabian scarves, accompanied by a woman in a yellow veil, drove into Tante's yard in a jeep two mornings after the day Beatrice Salandy was declared not guilty.

While the driver kept the engine humming, the other man escorted the woman up the steps. Beatrice, still wrapped in a red bath towel after a shower, was in the middle of folding a bundle of clothes that had been sitting in a chair for days as the trial went on. She heard the noise of the vehicle's tyres on the gravel and had rushed into a housecoat by the time one of the men knocked on the front door.

"Yes?" her voice sounded muffled even to herself as she answered from behind the half-opened door.

The man bowed slightly. "As-Salaam Allah kum, Sister. We bring you greetings from the Haji." He pivoted, his heavy black boots crunching the veranda's wooden floor, then stepped to the side with military precision to take up a sentry post.

The woman moved forward. Beatrice peered but couldn't make out her features beneath the veil. Only her brown eyes were visible, and these hardly so, for from head to toe, her tall straight figure was draped in the all-covering costume adopted by local black Muslim women.

"Can I help you?" Beatrice asked, still unwilling to open the door wide enough to allow the woman to enter.

"If I could come inside a minute?" She smiled, making Beatrice feel slightly foolish. It was, after all, broad daylight. What did she have to fear from these people?

She buttoned her housecoat up to the neck and slipped off the chain, stepping aside for the woman to enter. Shifting the basket of clothes to the floor, Beatrice offered her a seat.

"It's okay, Sister," the woman waved away the invitation. "I don't need to sit down. I just come to bring you your shoes and your purse."

She passed Beatrice a basket containing the items. "I brought them yesterday but nobody was here."

Before Beatrice could express her gratitude, the woman hurried on. "Haji's men helped you the other night. You didn't know that, eh? They patrol the Savannah every night. Ever since those girls got raped last year. Haji send me to see how you doing, and to ask if he could do anything for you."

"I'm doing fine, thank you. You sure you don't want to sit down?"

"Thanks, but I can't stay. We opening a school in Petit Valley today. You know we going to open one up here? Soon, we'll be looking to hire a head mistress. But, we can talk about that another time. If you want anything at all, just come by the mosque."

She glided towards the door, the back of her dress ballooning behind her, then turned back to face Beatrice. "You would make a good Muslim woman, Sister. The Haji knows about your case with the government and he was really proud of how you handled yourself. He knows how this government could get nasty. We've been fighting them for years, as you know, so we rejoice in your victory, Ahamdullillah."

She stretched her arms toward Beatrice.

Beatrice moved forward awkwardly to touch them.

"Allah be praised," the woman said. "And by the way, my name is Sister Farouka. Come down to Juma any Friday. One o'clock." She gestured toward the basket holding Beatrice's things. "Keep the basket. One of the ladies at the mosque made it."

And with that, she was gone. The jeep backed out the gate. Beatrice suddenly remembered that she had Shanty's sandals to return, and ran into the gallery, but they were gone. Only the scent of the woman lingered.

Lavender oil, Beatrice recognized it. Sweet, comforting. Tante Vivian's scent. In an old Vicks bottle Beatrice kept beneath her bed, Tante Vivian had mixed oils of lavender, chamomile, peppermint, vanilla essence and blue with yellow Vaseline, a salve against ague, *malyeaux*, and those pulsing headaches that would come upon Beatrice suddenly.

So that was the Haji's wife. But which one? She had read that he had three or was it four, and that some of them lived together in a big house near the mosque. How could a woman like that, so elegant, a woman who could probably get any man she wanted, live in that situation?

And she was smart too. Wasn't she the one who people said had gone to university in England, married a man who was an ambassador, lived all over the world, then, after she divorced him, come back to Santabella to be put in charge of an important government office?

What was she doing with these people? Had she given up her government job?

For the rest of the morning, as she puttered around the house trying to reassemble her life, Beatrice's thoughts strayed to Farouka and her husband, who could wield such control over women, and the thousands of youths people said were joining his mosque.

Black people as Muslims. It was a strange and disconcerting sight in Santabella. Letters to the newspapers from highly placed individuals warned that this man, calling himself a Muslim cleric, an imam, was dangerous.

He was a former member of the Regiment who had gone away to America to study. Just what he had studied, nobody seemed to know, but he had come back to Santabella as a Muslim.

No, he told the newspaper reporters, he was not a *Black* Muslim; he had nothing to do with Elijah Mohammed and the Black Muslims in America except that they shared the same faith.

He had come home to help his people; to get them to see that their lives had been stifled by the powers in Santabella who kept them ignorant.

Powers? Yes. The Catholic Church in particular. That church with its riches in Rome controlled the lives of so many people in Santabella – those nuns and priests who decided who would get the best education, who should ascend to power in this country.

What had the hundreds of thousands of youths in Santabella

gained from the powerful Catholic Church? Where was the earth they were told they would inherit? He, with the help of Allah, the Beneficent, the Merciful, would change all that.

The people were behind him, he claimed – and powerful people who didn't want their names publicly associated with his, but who saw the desperate need for change in a country that was going to hell in a hand basket, yes, those people, too, were behind him.

On his return he had begun feeding the poor. In his mother's backyard he'd built a large earthen oven and twice a week he kneaded flour with his own hands. The warm loaves he took into the city to feed the vagrants on the sidewalks.

With his own money, it was said, he bought milk for babies; schoolbooks for poor children; uniforms and shoes for those who could not afford the high prices in the stores in town. He gathered about him young men who, so rumour claimed, were ready to die, if necessary, at his side. Many of them he had saved from lives dependent on cocaine which, he claimed, was being imported into the country under the closed eyes of top police officials.

The police responded with raids on his house but found nothing incriminating.

People in the streets, in the parks, in the markets, poor, struggling people, laughed at the foolish actions of the police and applauded the young man. They delighted in his triumph over the agents of a bad government, bent, they believed, on oppressing poor people.

Some newspaper reports of his Friday "sermons" and his roadside rallies tried to ridicule his claims that he had studied Santabella's history. He knew who owned what and how they had gotten it.

He reminded the people of the years of slavery when their foreparents had worked the land for the whites, for the ancestors of these same *bacrajohnnies* who controlled the Catholic Church, who held papers on their lives.

What did they give us, he asked one night to a crowd that had gathered at the bottom of the road on which he had grown up. What do our people own after hundreds of years of slavery and colonialism? You know who owns the land? I don't have to tell you who own the land. And when you own land, you own the power.

First thing, the newspapers quoted him as saying in response to questions about how he intended to solidify his movement, first thing was to get some land on which to build a mosque.

He had done his homework well. He knew about the land near the sea on which the Americans had built a base during World War II. Years after the War, after the Americans had ceased to claim it as their own, the land was granted to the Muslim community of Santabella, but since most of the Muslims lived in the southern part of the country, it had remained unused.

Haji and his people laid claim to it. They were Muslims; the land belonged to them. But powerful members of the Indian Muslim population protested, alarmed at what they perceived as a radical Black man laying false claim to their religion and their land.

What does this man, calling himself Haji, know about our religion, they wrote to the newspapers. What did Black people know about Islam? Who made him an imam?

Haji had answered them with the history of Islam in Africa; with the history of the Islamic Africans who had been brought to the islands, including Santabella, and forced into slavery by the British and the French, and prohibited from practising their religion. The television news featured him in a debate with Indian leaders over who had the right to call themselves Muslims.

Santabellans watched, some in fear, some in admiration, especially the young who admired his perspicacity. Crying out for a champion of their desires, the poorest, the voiceless, the desperate and the defiant rose up in support of the Haji's claim to the land, and to his right, and any other Black person's right, to call themselves Muslim.

They wrote letters to the newspapers, used their neighbours' phones to call in to the radio talk-shows, and defended him in arguments in the squares and parks of the city.

He had been to Mecca, he told them; he had made the Haj. He had connections way beyond Santabella's borders with powerful people who wanted to help their fellow Muslims. Never, in their born days, had Santabellans seen or heard anyone like him.

He travelled three or four times a year. To the Middle East, rumour said. And he always came back with money. What did the poor people of Santabella care where he got the money? So the Libyans wanted to help Santabellans? Let them. Santabella's government surely wasn't.

The main daily newspaper, *The Sentinel*, owned, Haji was quick to point out, by the brother of the Catholic bishop, denounced him and his foreign supporters, warning the populace that the Haji intended to overthrow the government.

They have guns, the newspaper claimed. They were storing guns in the old bunkers the Americans had left on the land.

Interviewed by another newspaper, *The Bomb*, Haji was pictured with a child in his arms and a big smile on his face.

"The only revolution we are planning," he was quoted as saying, "is a revolution of the minds of our people. We are about the decolonization of the people's minds. That is we revolution. What you talking 'bout guns? We have guns? You see me carrying gun? I am not a cowboy. I is police?"

His ability to segue from standard English to the native tongue, pungent with the parlance of *picong*, thrilled some people and made others, who could well recall the first prime minister's ability to do just that, and to win over the people, well, it made them very nervous.

Within three years of his return from America, the Haji had managed to build a mosque on the land near the sea. Behind the mosque he built a small school. Then he added a complex of buildings that housed key members of his group.

All this Beatrice had read in the newspapers and had heard over the radio and television. And of course, the Haji was the centre of much discussion by the men of Rosehill who prided themselves on keeping up with Santabella's politics.

She remembered the arguments between Uncle Willy, Sammy and Mr. Roberts when a story appeared in *The Bomb* about two of the Haji's wives.

"How he could get away with that?" Mr. Roberts had demanded to know. "That is against the law in this country."

"Not so," Willy had told him. "Government exempt Muslims from bigamy, man. Long before independence, the British give

Muslims the right to have more than one wife. They had to do that to get them Indians to cross the sea to come here to cut cane after slavery done."

"But that is for them Indian people," Mr. Roberts argued. "That wasn't for no black people."

"It was for Muslims, and the Haji is a Muslim," Willy laughed. "I admire that man too bad, man. Talk 'bout power? That is power father! To have three women as your wife, have two of them living in the same house, and they not trying to kill one another, and the law can't touch you. Beat that!"

Beatrice recalled the admiration she had heard in Willy's voice and marvelled, like him, Sammy and Mr. Roberts, at the Haji's audacity. But none of them had gone down to the mosque to join his group, as far as she knew.

"I too old for that bacchanal," Willy had declared in response to Sammy's tease that he should follow the leader.

Now here he was, interfering in her life. No, that was ungrateful. His men *had* helped her. But to send his wife to check up on her? And why had he looked at her like that in Ali's office? Why did he seem to be laughing at her? What kind of man was this? Did he really have the kind heart some people claimed, or was it all a plan for something else? Oh, she was so confused. But no way was she going down to that mosque. Mosque? The word was synonymous with trouble, as her mother would surely point out.

"You 'ent have enough trouble in your life all ready? Eh? You want to bring down the wrath of the police on your head again? Stay away from those Muslims, Beatrice, you hear me? Stay away from them."

Yes, she would stay clear of them, not because Reme had commanded her to, but because she had to start thinking about a new life for herself.

Here she was, twenty-one years old. Most of the people she had gone to school with were either working in the civil service or had gone away to England, America, or Canada. But she, fuelled by some passion she could not explain if her life depended on it, had stayed in Santabella, on Rosehill. Okay, okay, circumstances had forced her to stay, but all of that was over. Why, then, couldn't she summon up the desire to leave?

She turned on the radio. The news of the hour had already started. Two murders, the announcer was reporting. Two murders had taken place the night before. There was massive confusion surrounding one of them; bystanders were claiming that one of the victims, a police woman, was shot, not by the bandits the police were running down, but by the police themselves. With a deep, sad sigh, Beatrice turned off the radio.

EIGHT

In the early evening Miss Ann closed her parlour and began her slow climb up the hill to visit Beatrice.

Jestina, in her side yard hanging clothes on the line, saw Miss Ann passing by, shouted a friendly, "Aye girl. You looking good today," but muttered under her breath, "Miss Macometer on the prowl. Beatrice's business will be all over the hill before the sun set this evening."

The breeze might have carried the words to Miss Ann but she paid them no mind. Every few minutes she paused to kick a stone out of her alpagats or to chat with a neighbour: Sybil on the prettiness of her flower garden (and to receive a few roses in return); Mr. Roberts's on the bigness of the cashews and bread-fruits breaking down his trees – "Lordy Lord, what you give these trees to eat, man?" – (and to receive two of each in return).

Her arrival at Beatrice's was the coming of a market, and Beatrice laughed at the sight of the crocus bag of fruits breaking down one of Miss Ann's shoulders, and flowers in a basket on the next.

"It's a good thing I live just up the hill from you," Beatrice told her. "With everything you collect on the way you mighten be able to get back home if your house was further up."

"Say praise God I come to see you girl. Is you I collect these things for. Look. A nice hand of green fig, some cashews. Take two and leave me a few. Come, take this bag off my shoulders and let me rest my weary feet. Whew. How yuh doing, Beatrice meh dear? Is long time girl, me never see you. You making style or what?"

"So that wasn't you in the courthouse and in the rum shop,

eh?" Beatrice, laughing, joined in the picong. "Must be another fancy woman I see holding onto Uncle Willy for dear life with those barflies trying to light on him."

"Child," Miss Ann drew the word out as she sat down on the front steps and folded her dress between her knees, "you see them lowdown town women? They don't care that the man's wife right there in front they face. They up in Willy's nose-hole like snat. But I dig them out. Umm um. I don't play that game with my husband, nuh. No sharing with me. And speaking bout sharing, what those Muslim people want with you this morning?"

"You want some juice? I just squeeze some limes."

"Limes too acid for my stomach, girl. Doctor tell me to stay far away from limes. If you have a cream soda I will take that, but what those people want from you, eh?"

Beatrice brought her a glass of iced cream soda before she sat down on the steps to answer the question.

"They just come to say thanks."

"Beatrice, I look like a dentist? Why you want me to pull teeth?"

"The woman, she's Farouka or some name like that – that Muslim's man's wife. One of them anyway. She just stopped by to tell me thanks for helping out her daughter the other day."

"Helping her daughter out of what? What you have to do with those people, girl? Is more trouble you looking for?"

"Somebody was trying to interfere with the girl and I was passing by and I stop him. Look, I don't want to talk about this. I just help out the girl. She was good for herself too."

"Beatrice," Miss Ann said patiently, "I know you think because I does know what going on sometimes even before it happen, that I could read minds. But not today. The newspapers 'ent come yet. So try to be specific, okay? How, when, and why? You talking?"

So she made up a story – a story about how when she was crossing the Savannah the night before she see a man dragging a young girl toward the stables and how the girl was bawling, bawling, and how she, Beatrice, run up to them and start hitting the man in his head with her high heel shoes and how he start bleeding and how she help the girl to escape, and is only this morning she realize that the girl was the Haji's daughter, cutting across the Savannah on her way to their house when that man try to get her, and that is why the Haji send his wife to tell her thanks for helping his daughter, and please, Miss Ann, don't go telling anybody this story, okay?

"Well, Good Lord, Beatrice," Miss Ann said. "Your middle name must be Magnet. How come you always attracting trouble so?"

"I should learn to mind my own business, eh?" Beatrice laughed.

"I hope you jucked out that raperman's eyes. What this country coming to, tell me, eh? All these politicians talking bout law and order while crime running rampant in the Savannah."

"Crime doesn't live a life of its own, Miss Ann. Is people's sons doing it."

"A-A. You sounding like that Haji, girl. Next thing you know, you'll be down there joining them in that mosque mess."

"You tell me what's so wrong with what he's trying to do, eh? If he's taking the youths off drugs and crime and thing, what's so wrong?"

"I hear he has a lot of guns, girl. Guns to overthrow the government. Besides, what we black people want with that Muslim thing? That's for Indians."

Beatrice refilled Miss Ann's glass with lime juice. "I don't know about any guns," she said. "You believe everything the police say, eh? They raid his property twice already. They find any guns? Not one."

"He's too smart for them, girl. He used to be a police or regiment or something like that. Before he went away to America. Is over there he turn Muslim."

Beatrice laughed. "You say 'turn Muslim' as if the man turn green. Is just a religion, not a sickness."

"But is a religion for Indian people," Miss Ann argued. "What black people want with that?"

"If I tell you that long before they bring black people over here they used to follow Islam in Africa, you would believe me?"

"If you say so." Doubt dripped heavy from Miss Ann's lips. "You is the teacher. What I know? All I have is common sense. But I will tell you this: all them young boys who joining the

49

Muslims only doing it for one reason and one reason only. To get plenty woman."

"Hmmm..." Beatrice smiled. "So Clyde must be Muslim, right?"

"Clyde? My son? You mad or what? My son not in that." Miss Ann was incensed.

"Well," Beatrice said, "Let me ask you this. How many women Clyde has? Just the ones who have children for him, okay? You don't have to count the others."

"Wha... what you... you bringing my son into this for?" Miss Ann spluttered.

"I see," Beatrice smiled. "Well, at least Haji marries his women, and I hear he takes good care of his children. Unlike some people we know, right?"

"Look Beatrice," Miss Ann pushed herself up off the steps, "I just come up here to ask you what you going to do about the school. Holidays will be over soon and we have to put the children in school."

"Put them in the Muslim school." Beatrice waved a hand towards the building, its top jutting out from the trees.

"What's wrong with you, Beatrice? All the months Rosehill walking beside you when you in trouble, now you turning your back on we? Is so? I see. One day corbeau picking garbage; the next day he flying high, no talk to nobody. I see."

Beatrice put an arm round Miss Ann's waist. "I'll never forget my family," she told her. "But I don't want to promise to open the school and then I have to leave the children high and dry."

Miss Ann sat back down on the steps. "You mean you really leaving? You going New York?"

"I might," Beatrice said. "Then again... I don't know, Miss Ann. I might go to Canada, maybe even England."

"You hear from Sonny lately?" Miss Ann peered at Beatrice's face, trying to detect the truth.

Beatrice turned away from her. "Don't ask me about Sonny, okay? Last I hear, he marry a white woman up there. I have nothing to do with him and his life."

"But that was only so he could get permanent, girl." Miss Ann had always liked Sonny, had always hoped for him and Beatrice to get married – for her to make the wedding cake.

"Beatrice, the Virgin Mary self will have to come down here to convince me that Sonny don't love you, white woman or no."

"Love?" Beatrice sucked her teeth. "The only person Sonny ever love is Sonny. Anyway, I have to live my own life. I have to make my own way in this world. You know what Reme always say, right? When it come down to the wire, you alone dancing."

Miss Ann rose and set down the empty glass on the step. "Don't give up on him so easy, girl." She touched Beatrice's head. "You never could tell. One morning you could open your eyes and Sonny will be right on your doorstep. New York going to knock some sense in Sonny's head. He's coming back for you, white woman or no white woman. Mark my words."

Beatrice grabbed up the glass and held it so tightly Miss Ann thought she would break it.

"So you expect me to sit on my hands and wait for him? What I look like to you, Miss Ann? Eh? You think I have to wait for him to give me a life?"

"Noooo, no," Miss Ann, anxious that she had pushed too far, patted Beatrice's shoulders. "Don't get vexed with me. I promise your Tante Vivian I will look after you. You grow here on Rosehill like my own daughter, Beatrice. You know that. From the day Reme bring you into this world, I was there. If there is one thing I know about you, is that you have sense. You always do what is best, Beatrice, for Rosehill, for your family. Forget about Sonny. If he come back, he come back. You need to live your own life." She paused to take a deep breath, to look at Beatrice under lowered eyelids. Satisfied that Beatrice's face seemed calmer, she went on.

"Whatever little money you have, I know you'll spend it right."

"Oh-ho, so it come to that, eh?" Beatrice stepped out of her reach. "That is the real reason you come here? Well, let me tell you once and for all, Miss Ann, is not much money left. After I pay Ali is only a little bit I have. So you could put money right out of your mind."

She stomped into the kitchen, filled a pan with water, and began, furiously, to wash the glass.

Miss Ann calculated: if she left right then, hurt, because she'd been bawled at, Beatrice might feel guilty and come after her, might even agree to stay and be the schoolteacher. On the other hand, the way the girl behaving strange-strange, she might just say the hell with Rosehill. Then what?

She decided to make a last ditch plea.

"Lordy, Lord," she said loudly as she fanned herself with her skirt. "Is hot today in truth. Beatrice darlin, I know, I know how much trouble you see. That is we lot in this country, eh? That is why we have to enjoy we self when we can. Don't forget this Sunday is your goddaughter's birthday, eh. Simone is twelve already, oui. And she pass common entrance, you know. I know your head was so full of worries with the case you didn't remember to give her a lil' something. That's all right, come to the party still on Sunday, eh. Times so hard we not having anything big, but I making two pails of coconut ice cream."

When Beatrice didn't answer her, she added, "Lord, look at the time. Lemme hurry and open back meh parlour, girl. Some of we still poor, oui."

And leaving Beatrice gripping the glass to keep from pelting it after her, Miss Ann picked up half of the flowers and fruits before she went through the gate and back down the road.

She stopped by Mr. Roberts' house to complain, "I think that girl going to join up the Muslims, oui."

"Beatrice is a sensible young lady," Mr. Roberts dismissed her worry. "After all that police trouble she's been through, she has too much sense to get tangled up with those people. Is not Beatrice we have to worry about."

"What you mean?"

"Is only my suspicion, so I shouldn't say any more, but one or two of the men up here might be more involved with them people than we know."

Unable to get him to reveal names, or provide concrete evidence, Miss Ann continued on her way, more troubled than before. That night, long after Willy had rolled over her onto his back and was sawing a forest in his sleep, she stayed awake, staring at the moonlight through a small hole in the galvanize, wondering who could be tight with the Muslims, how she had missed seeing it, and planning what she would do to make sure Beatrice did the right thing.

NINE

Sonny. Trust Miss Ann to bring him up. In bed that night, Beatrice was unable to sleep. She kicked off the sheet she had just pulled over her legs. Deceitful Sonny. Selfish Sonny. Miss Ann, Uncle Willy, none of them would agree with her, but what did they know about the real Sonny?

Yes, he had come back from America when Tante had begged him for assistance with her case, but he had run back to America as if stinging bees were chasing him. Four weeks! Her life was in the hangman's noose and he could only stay for four weeks! As if he had come on holiday.

On top of all that, he hadn't even had the guts to tell her to her face that he was married. Left it up to Uncle Willy.

"The boy needs to get permanent in America, Beatrice. Try to understand, nuh. The only way was for him to marry the Yankee girl. I believe him when he say the onliest woman for him, ever, is you, and I know you don't believe me now, but wait and see. When Sonny come back, we having the biggest wedding this country ever see."

That's what all Rosehill believed, what they hoped for, and they fully expected her to hold strain with them. Well, all except Reme.

Reme had seen in Sonny the same selfishness she had found in Kelvin, and she had said so in no uncertain terms.

"They put theirselves, first, child. All men like that. I tell you: mind your own garden; don't expect no man to cut down the bush for you. Women must make their own way in this world, Beatrice. Even when you find a halfway good man, never forget that in the end, you dancing alone in this world."

Much as she hated to agree with her mother about anything, she had to admit that Reme was right. Maybe because men had failed her so miserably, Reme had learned to look behind the sweet promises they made when they were in heat, to weigh their actions against their words.

But to be fair, what had Sonny ever promised her? She reached back to the night before he had left for America the first time, when they had come together, both of them in pain, she because of what Doctor Chow had done to her, and he, because of his disappointment that the government was cancelling his scholarship. Pain. That was the laglie sticking them together?

It was more than that, even if she didn't want to think about it. Friendship. They had been like sister and brother since they could walk and talk, before her tut-tuts made the buttons on her school bodice burst, before Sonny put on his first long pants, and hair started to grow on his chest.

Then came the change. Oh, the talk that had floated up and down the Hill: Miss Reme had better have a serious talk with her daughter about Sonny. Eh-heh.

Miss Ann: "You see them last night down by the bridge? Hugging up and ting. Humm. If I was Reme, I would tell that Sonny to keep far from my one daughter, oui. That boy? That boy is a fast bowler."

Yes, Sonny did have an eye for any good-looking girl on the hill, and some of them claimed he had kissed them, touched them here and there, but all of that was old talk, he laughed, when she had told him about the rumours.

"I have one serious girlfriend, one woman on my mind, and you know who that is," he would hug her, squeezing the words into her.

She had believed him. Believed in him. Why? Maybe, she thought, it has to do with Reme, with her constant warnings about not trusting Sonny, not trusting any man, for that matter.

But Sonny was trustworthy. He might, if the rumours were correct, have touched other girls on the Hill and in school, but he had never given her more than a kiss on the forehead, and a tight hug. In the years they had known each other, as they grew into teenagers, he had not tried to go further with her.

It was as if he was saving her. There were times, she remembered, she used to get frustrated with him, wanting him to go a lot further than a kiss, vexed when he said, "Nah, girl. We can't do that." But later, after he had gone back to his father's house, and her desire had abated, she would be glad, grateful that he had stopped; pleased that he had shown more respect for her than she had shown for herself. That's the way it was, until that night, just before he was to leave for America.

That night, when he found out that the government intended to rescind his scholarship; that same night when she had the worst experience of her life with Dr. Chow, she and Sonny had finally come together.

Yet, she hadn't told him what Dr. Chow had done to her. Was it shame? Guilt, maybe, that knowing how much she had wanted him, Sonny might have thought that she had allowed Dr. Chow to do what he had done to her. She had believed then, as a part of her still did, that their coming together was the spirits' way of balancing out the ugliness of what Dr. Chow had done. But what had Sonny left her with? Had he really promised to send for her, or had she made it up, to console herself?

Stop dwelling on the past. She shook her head. Sonny has his life. Make one for yourself. Why was she even thinking about all those troubles? Miss Ann. Trust her to resurrect the dead.

The clock on her bureau said three a.m. but she got out of bed to search the boxes in her closet for her passport, glad that Tante Vivian had insisted that she should get one, just in case.

She found it, wrapped in a sheet of white tissue paper under Tante Vivian's crocheted pillowcases that she used to use only when special company visited. Tante, she laughed, untying the piece of string that her great aunt had wound around the book. Always so careful, always so wise.

Opening it to the page with her photograph, she shook her head. I look sad, she told herself. Poor me one. I look like the saddest person in the world.

Memories of the day the photo was taken flooded over her.

She and Tante Vivian had been to see Ali before Sonny had come back to save her. Walking up Saint Vincent Street, they had come to a door with bold yellow letters announcing PASSPORT PHOTOS. WAIT FOR THEM.

Ignoring her protests, Tante had pulled her into the office, paid the required ten dollars, then told the photographer that he had better make her grandniece look nice-nice or she would want back her money.

Despite the promise in the sign, the photos would not be ready until the following week. "The machine break down, nuh lady. I can't fix it before Friday. Is hard for people to make a living, oui."

Tante was undeterred. That was fine. It would give her time to locate Beatrice's birth certificate and have her fill out the long form the Immigration Department required. She spoke to the man as if Beatrice, her arms locked across her chest, her face unsmiling, wasn't in the room.

So much water had passed under the bridge since then. Who would have guessed that nearly three years later she would be holding that passport in her hand, planning to go away from Santabella?

Tante Vivian, the seer-woman, must have known they wouldn't find her guilty. She must have wanted her to leave, even if she had never said so, in words.

But where should she go? Canada? America? She had heard about the crowds lining the walls around the American Embassy; of people camped in cars overnight just to get a chance to apply for a visa, and she had not forgotten the rumours of trickster men, like that Valmond Jones who preyed on those poor people, promising to provide them with bank statements showing they had thousands of dollars in the bank so that the Embassy people would not think they were going to America to get on Welfare.

All for a fat fee, of course. Hundreds of people had been duped. Valmond Jones had disappeared with their money. Well, she was lucky. Nobody would "Valmond Jones" her. She had her own money.

Yet, on top of that thought, another had come. Was it her own money? She, Sonny, Tante Vivian, they knew Sonny hadn't given her that money. Tante was dead, but she and Sonny both knew that even if the court had found her innocent, she would still have her conscience to deal with.

So what if she had used much of it to buy the leases so that Rosehill people could own the land? Robin Hood, that man she had read about in her story books, might have been able to get away with it in Sherwood Forest, but she had little doubt that one day she would have to face a punishment for how she had gotten the money in the first place.

TEN

For two weeks I keep my eyes on Yusuf, and I don't see any progress. In fact, he was bringing weed into the compound and trying to get fellars who use to be like him, to buy it. That was the final straw. I had to take drastic steps.

I tell Yusuf that the Haji have an important assignment for him, but when I went by his house to pick him up, the man still sleeping. A bad sign. Eleven o'clock; broad daylight, and he still sleeping. All of we who belong to the movement learn long time to get up before cock crow. We have to prayer, we have to get our minds centre on what we have to do every day, with the help of Allah, all praises be unto Him.

Santabella is not a Muslim country where the sound of the muezzin making the call for morning prayer is as familiar as rain in August. Those Indian Muslims – I have to remember that we have Indian in the movement too – but I'm talking about the old-time ones, they lost they self, man. They forget how to conform to the religion, how to live inside the principles the Prophet Mohammed, all praises be upon Him, give to us in the Qur'an. The Haji set an example for us and for all of those other so-called Muslims.

Before the Haji start his movement, you never hear the call for prayer, but as soon as he start doing it, they follow-fashion. Now, all over the country, five times a day, you hear the call to prayer. If the Catholic could have their bells, why we can't hear the Imam's voice? But some people make a big row over that. The same ones who would go to the tent to hear dirty calypsos at Carnival time, complaining about a little thing like that.

But they couldn't stop us. What is good for the gander should be good for the goose, and with Haji, anything to bring the Santabellans closer to Allah was important, so he just dust off them complainers.

He teach us to get up early, clean ourselves, and make our prayers before the sun rise from behind the mountains. Discipline! That is a thing Yusuf and a lot of them young fellars who come to join the movement had to learn.

It wasn't easy teaching them. Haji alone couldn't do it. We all had to band together because a lot was at stake. If we couldn't make fellars like Yusuf into disciplined soldiers, the cause in trouble.

And failure wasn't no option for us. Not with the way the country going.

Seeing Yusuf come to his door rubbing his eyes and asking what time it was let me know that he wasn't following one of the essential practices of the faith. If I had had any qualms about what I had to do with him, that made me change my mind, right there.

By the time he got ready to go with me, the sun in the middle of the sky and it was time for midday prayers. I have to ask myself what kind of Muslim Yusuf calling himself because he don't even have a prayer mat.

I take mine from the jeep, wash myself at the standpipe in the road, and I kneel down in the yard facing east and say my prayers.

All the time, Yusuf watching me and yawning. I had was to say extra prayers for patience to handle him, and I see why it important for Haji to tell me to do what I going to do with him. Is like old people say: who can't hear mus' feel.

I pray a long time about the things I do for the Haji, and Allah, the Merciful, the Beneficent, all praises be upon him, offer me the guidance that it was my faith that was leading me, not Haji.

He's a man, a messenger; Allah is the one, as the Qur'an say, who will bring me to account for what I do.

Yusuf fall asleep as soon as he get in the jeep, and he still snoring when I pull into the shed down Carenage where we keep the boats. Then he jump up, rubbing his eyes and asking what, what, what we doing here?

I just tell him to get in the boat because we have to go out to collect something for Haji, and he had make us late already. I take

59

the small one with an engine because Yusuf don't know how to row, and besides, I coming back by myself.

So what we going for? He musta asked me that ten times but I didn't answer.

As the boat cut through the waters, I was disgusted by all the cans and plastic bags floating about. The sea like a *LaBas* where people just dump their garbage. The newspaper had a story a few weeks before about some foreign countries using the Caribbean Sea as a dump because all their landfills were overflowing. Haji had cut out the article and put it up on the bulletin board in the shed, and when he gave us his sermon that Friday, he ask everybody, especially the women, to go back to using the old-time baskets when they go to the market.

We pass three of the small islands and the big one that has the prison. Yusuf point out a man waving at us from on top of a hill on the prison island. I was thinking that if it hadn't been for Haji, Yusuf, and a lot of young men like him, might end up on that island.

"Abdul, you remember Boysie Singh?" he cut into my thoughts.

I nod my head. I was a little boy when the news break about Boysie Singh, but everybody in Santabella know the story.

"I wonder if he dead by now? They send he there, or he get hang?" Yusuf was pointing with his chin to the prison island.

I still didn't feel like talking to him, especially with what I had to do, so I just shrug my shoulders. But I start thinking about some of the things I hear about Boysie Singh.

Facts get mix up with fiction in Santabella, because people love to add on to stories. Everybody is a composer, so by the time you hear the story, you don't know what really happen, but what I remember was that Boysie put Thelma Haynes, a woman he was friending with, in a boat, and tell her he was going to take she down the Main, but he cut her up in small pieces and feed the fish – except for part of her intestines that he put in a glass jar in his bedroom, and that is how they get him.

Boysie was Indian and Thelma was Negro, and that cause a lot of people's parents to warn their girl children to stay away from Indian men.

Sudix was waiting on the dock for us when I pull in the boat to the small island on the far side of the one with the prison. He help me tie it up while Yusuf just lean on the rail as if he was a tourist. He don't even offer to help me with the two crocus bags I bring for Sudix who stay on the island four days a week.

The island just mainly rocks and shrubs, but on one side it have a wide sandy beach. Nobody live on the island permanently, but Haji have connections, and we were given the contract to keep watch on the place in case smugglers wanted to use it.

Haji had built two small houses high up between the trees. Sudix and Calu, the other guard, stay there during the week, and since there wasn't any electricity, all the food and fresh water have to come from Santabella.

Sudix is a big, hefty man. He use to box before his right hand get hurt to the point where he could hardly hold a pencil in it. But he had taught himself to use his left hand, even to write, and he learn to read the Qur'an in Arabic.

He was a man who live a hard-hard life, but joining the movement, reading the Qur'an, and living by its words had changed him. If there was one man Haji trust entirely, it was Sudix. Sometimes I would hear them talking in Arabic, a thing Haji couldn't do with a lot of other people.

He slung one of the bags over his shoulder, and I tell Yusuf to pick up the other one while I gather up the two cutlasses that Sudix had been sharpening when we arrived.

As we went up the trace to the houses, Sudix complaining to me about the garbage left on the beach side over the past weekend. The government allow some fellars to bring party boats to the island on the weekend and these people never took away their garbage, no matter how many signs we had put up about keeping the place clean. These party people had no pride in their own country. Tourists come from all over the world to see our islands, and some of the local people couldn't care less about where they live.

We step over hundreds of white foam plates and cups. Plastic forks, spoons and knives were all over the place. Garbage bags clung to low branches. It was disgusting.

When we got to the houses, with Yusuf complaining all the time we were climbing about his legs hurting him, Calu was waiting for us. He's a *dougla* from Arouca. People say he use to be in the police force for years, but when he became a Muslim, he leave the force. Talk about a man could swim? I bet he could swim back to Santabella without even breathing hard. Between him and Sudix, I couldn't say which one was more loyal to the Haji. Anything Haji give him to do, Calu do it without question, in half the time.

After we put the bags away in one of the houses, he lock the door, and we go to the other one. When I say house, it's just a big room with a few chairs, a gas stove, and a couple cots. And pictures of Calu's children. Not his wife, just his two children, a girl, seven, and a boy, five.

I could understand why he would cut out his wife from the photos. After all, is she who pour paraquat down those poor children's throats, and kill them before she kill herself. A spiteful woman, is how I see her. Indian, from Caroni. Bad minded. Kill your self if you want to, by why the children?

Bad as Sandra is, I can't see her doing that to our son, but then again, she's not Indian. Every year in Santabella, especially in the planting season, so many Indian drink that thing that people call it Indian tonic. I could imagine how Calu must feel, but I never asked him about it.

As a police man he must have come across plenty dead bodies, but when it is your family, how you going to get over that? Is soon after that he leave the Force and join up with Haji.

I tell Yusuf to stay inside the room and unpack the food while I went back outside to talk to Sudix and Calu. I explained to them what Haji wanted to do with Yusuf, and I give them the things I had brought in my backpack for them to use.

PART TWO

RAINY SEASON

ELEVEN

Around midday, a day after the radio announcer had predicted its coming, the first rain of the season began to fall. Just a light drizzle at first, to fool Santabellans into believing that it really wasn't coming, but by two o'clock, the dress rehearsal was over.

Showers poured down, shrouding Rosehill in a grey curtain, washing rubbish down the hill into clogged manholes, wetting down clothes still clinging, optimistically, on lines, and sending residents scampering for cover.

With its arrival came also the promise of three full months of rain every day, sweeping over the Northern Range, sometimes carrying wind so strong, many of the houses on the hills would teeter or fall.

Galvanize sheets would cut across the valleys; plywood would land in tree tops, as the cries of the unfortunate rose up to ask God why. The wind would carry their words away, leaving in its wake panicking insects seeking refuge from the damp.

Red ants crawled along window sills. Black ones, a new breed with wings, darted through crevices into kitchens. Flies flew around the floor boards, too low and too many to be killed in a hundred swipes from a folded newspaper.

Close the windows and the houses felt like the insides of steam factories; open them and the insects had their invitations to come in to play mas'.

The higher houses on Rosehill fared a little better than those lower down, but only in the daytime when the air seemed too thin for the invaders to breathe. At dusk, mosquitoes, a brand people said had *graduated* – no longer needing to sing for its supper – came out in full force.

They skipped through unscreened windows and doors, settled in skirt hems and pants pockets like an enemy army biding its time to attack. As dark fell, they would emerge to lay siege to bare arms, cheeks, necks and eyelids. The rain was a license for the mosquitoes to riot.

Rosehill, and the rest of Santabella, fought back with spray flitted from cans, filled with insecticides imported from China and sold over the counter in rum bottles at shops like Ling Chung's.

Gone were the days when, Beatrice recalled, so many others like her Tante Vivian had filled an aluminium bucket with special bush, then lit the green leaves to smoke out the invaders. Santabellans had become either too sophisticated for that, or the recipes for the old ways of doing things had died with the older generation.

Added to that, nearly all the wild bush around the villages had been cleared for houses as daughters and sons built rooms in the backyards of their parents' homes.

Even small-crop gardens had largely disappeared. Only Sammy and one of Mister Roberts' sons were still willing to suffer back pains to plant eddoes and tomatoes, dasheen and lettuce, and to fight the bugs that came to eat the crops before they were full grown.

But there was another side to the rain: mangoes ripened, green figs turned yellow, small tomatoes grew red skins, caterpillars bloomed into butterflies, and hummingbirds darted from one hibiscus to another, sucking nectar with their long beaks.

On Rosehill, roses unfolded their soft buds and the people grew quiet under their grace.

As she closed the windows and opened up the barrels to catch the rain, Beatrice was glad that she had followed her inclination not to go to town that day. She doubted the people who lived near the Embassy would allow those in the line to shelter in their galleries. Those people, she recalled, were the ones the Haji called *baccra-johnnies*, the ones who, having inherited the best of the country from the Europeans, thought of themselves as white first, Santabellans a far second – except at Carnival time or when the West Indies cricket team beat India, Pakistan, or the Sri Lankans.

Then they rejoiced, took out their yachts, and spread joy in their private fetes. They married within their group, keeping their wealth – made from rum, sugar, oil, and gas refining, and lately, massive housing structures along the coasts – circulating among themselves. They cared little for the rest of the largely poor Santabellan population.

Yes, Beatrice thought. It was a good thing she had stayed on Rosehill, otherwise she might have caught pleurisy in the rain.

Expecting a flood of mosquitoes once dark came, she strained her brain, trying to remember the names of the bush Tante Vivian had told her to burn to get rid of them. *Couzamahoe*? Was that one of them? And even if she could recall the name, where would she find it?

She didn't believe she could remember what the leaves looked like, so what was the use of trying to find it? How much she had taken for granted as she was growing up! Believing, first, that Tante Vivian would always be around, then focusing on her school books with their insistence on England's history and culture.

What did she really know about Santabella except that Columbus had discovered it, the Spanish had wiped out the native population, the French and British had colonized it, the Americans had taken their share, and what was left was being gobbled up by politicians whose only interest was in feathering their own nests before they flew away to Canada or Miami.

When a woman at the Red Cross office where she used to work had described to her the dramatic beauty of scarlet ibis flying into the sunset, she had been ashamed to admit that she had never been to the sanctuary where the birds nested. Oh, there was so much she didn't know about Santabella.

Was that why she was intrigued by the Haji – if she could call her interest by that name? He seemed to know everything about Santabella. She smiled as the thought flitted through her head that he probably knew the names of the bush to burn to kill mosquitoes as well, then quickly banished the idea.

She would just have to go to Miss Ann's shop for some cock-sets, imported from Asia, then rub soft-candle on her body to ward off the bites.

Watching from the kitchen window, she waited for the rain to abate. Children's voices floated up and she guessed that Jestina and Melda's girls were down near the bridge, dancing in the water in just their underwear.

That brought back the memory of herself, at their age, doing the same thing. Unashamed. Kicking up water in her grey chambray panties with the red rick-rack braid that Tante Vivian had sewn by hand, while the boys, ignoring her and her friends, even as Jestina's sons were doing at that moment, because they would be too busy making boats out of folded newspapers and racing them in the canals. Boys. Thinking about them carried her where she didn't want to go: memories of Sonny and herself in their young days on Rosehill.

He was her best friend, and as they grew older, he had become her only friend as they went off to town together, pupils at the best schools in the country, ones their families could not have afforded to send them to were it not for the grace of the first government after independence.

Rosehill had expected a lot from both of them, and she had tried to live up to their expectations, but that had only gotten her in trouble that Sonny had to help her escape. It always came back to Sonny, didn't it?

If she allowed them, the memories would flood her, just as the rain seemed intent on flooding Rosehill. But she had to stay afloat, to swim strongly through the water, if she were to get anywhere safe.

TWELVE

By the time they went to lime over the sea in the late afternoon, the rain and wind had caused trouble from one end of Santabella to the other.

Then all was still. Not a breeze blew, not a wind whistled, not a coconut palm swayed. The air was still and muggy.

Miss Ann, raising the sliding door of her parlour, regretted that she had not stocked her icebox with a larger supply of sweet drinks and ice because of the demand she expected, given that all up and down the Hill power-lines were down.

"Current gone," her neighbours groaned, as if she, herself, didn't know the news first-hand.

"Lemme have two sweet drinks, meh dear, and take them from the bottom of the icebox, okay? What you mean you can't put piece of ice in the cup for me. I'm not one of your best customers?"

Wise to the contrariness of storms and electricity, Miss Ann, unlike these neighbours, had not surrendered her icebox to the rubbish heap. Oh, she had a fridge, but it was mainly for decoration, with special use at Christmas time to cool home-made ginger beer and sorrel.

She would send visitors to open its door with instructions to "Get a cold drink, nuh," just so they could see how much more she had than they.

In her parlour, the small shop from which she sold quick-turnover items like newspapers, sweeties, soft candles, Vicks, matches and cigarettes, she kept her two ice boxes, one for butter, eggs, and the occasional piece of seasoned fish or chicken, and the other for the drinks her neighbours craved.

To Ling Chung's shop every morning, she sent Willy to pick up the two large blocks of ice the men from the ice factory would drop off for her.

On that Thursday, as she chipped a few pieces off one of the blocks for her complaining neighbour, she wished she'd had the foresight to have bought more. But she had spent the night, and too many before that, worrying about Beatrice.

Why wouldn't that girl listen to her? And Reme was as useless as a panty without string in the waist. But let them go. Let that Miss Beatrice get mixed up with those Muslims. When the mark burst, she will be in jail like the whole set of them, including that Haji, no matter how much power he thought he had.

The thought of Beatrice in jail gave her little comfort, she had to admit, and that was why she had to keep trying with her. Yes, she wanted her to go to America, in spite of what all the neighbours believed, but at the right time. If she told Beatrice that she had been having dreams of her trapped in ice, *black ice* – it have something like that in this world? – the girl would just think that she was making up stories to get her to stay in Santabella. But she had looked up the meaning of the dream in Tante Vivian's dream book, which, on the day of Tante's funeral, she had borrowed. Well, nobody knew she had borrowed it, but it wasn't as if she was going to going to keep it.

Right there in the book, she had seen the meaning of ice when a person was trapped in it, and if only Beatrice knew what was waiting for her up in them cold-arse countries, she would stay right there on Rosehill.

Beatrice herself was grateful that day that the refrigerator, left to her with the house in Tante Vivian's will, contained so little food to spoil. So absorbed had she been in the preceding weeks, even months, buying groceries had been the last thing on her mind.

The few limes, two eggs, and small piece of Fernleaf butter were not much for her to worry about in case current did not come back for days, as was often the case in Santabella's poorer districts.

"They have to fix the lights for the big shots in Cascade and Saint Clair first," Miss Ann would announce, as if she had gone to town herself and had seen the electricity men working around the grand houses with bougainvillea tumbling over their high fences.

"They need the light to see how much more they could thief."

She, the majority of Rosehill, and the other poor in Santabella, lived in a constant state of comparison. Whatever ugliness befell them, they were certain that the rich, the well-connected, those who ran the government from the Red House, or the Catholic Diocese, or the Anglican Cathedral, all of them were immune from that disease.

Those people were protected by fences constructed by the power of their skin colour, yes, even if now and then they let in a darkie whose parents had money.

When Beatrice would try to point out to Miss Ann that the country was changing, that its first Prime Minister had hardly been a light-skinned man, Miss Ann was quick to note that he had done his best to make sure his children were not like him.

"Didn't he marry a Chinese woman? What you talking? Prime minister or no prime minister, he know is only light-skinned people getting jobs in banks, and offices where they could help one another. The man wasn't blind, and while he could fix some things, he couldn't do it all."

That is why, she told Beatrice over and over, we have to educate we own children. Give them the edge. That is why we have to throw we su-su, save we money, send we children to England, Canada, America, even to Russia. I 'ent 'fraid no communist, and look how those communist children become scientist and thing. But when the children go away, they have to come back. We have to make sure of that. We have to see to it that they come back to Rosehill to help build up the community. Just like Sonny will do one day. Mark my words.

Beatrice would argue, on the days when Sonny's deception pulled on the strings holding up her heart, when she needed to be convinced again that he still had a scrap of good left in him to deserve her forgiveness, that Sonny had not done a blasted thing for Rosehill. What did he do, eh? Tell me that. What'd he do?

Miss Ann would recite a catechism of Sonny's blessings, although she had her own suspicions that she might be building a castle in a swamp.

"But how you could be so ungrateful, Beatrice? If it wasn't for Sonny, you would be fighting bed bugs in jail. A-A."

Sonny the saviour. Miss Ann's inscription. Rosehill's inspiration. Melda's children, Jestina's children, all the children on Rosehill pushed, prodded, to study their lessons, study hard. Become like Sonny.

When she lay awake, staring at the brown watermarks in the Celotex above her bed, Beatrice would imagine that one day, her name would be a benediction too:

Is Miss Beatrice who build this library, oui, and the pool. Now the children could learn to swim. Is she who send the money to put in this swimming pool behind the community centre. That girl never forget we. She is a blessing in truth.

Then she would laugh and remind herself that first she had to make something of herself. First, she had to line up in front of the American Embassy and beg the Yankee people to let her into their country.

THIRTEEN

After everything come to pass, I use to ask myself why I stay in Santabella. Haji wanted to send me away more than once, to go to school in Banghazi – that is in Libya, eh – or other places in the Middle East where he had friends, people who wanted to help us in Santabella. Some of the fellars and a few of the women in the movement went.

But I always back out. I didn't want my son to have to go and live with his mother, or with some of her people. It wasn't that they was bad people, but the area they live in was full up with crime.

I could have gone to places in the Middle East more than once, stay there and make a life for myself and my son, but I am a man does listen to my conscience, and when I see what Haji trying to accomplish, in spite of opposition from all quarters, how I, in good conscience, could leave my country?

I follow my faith, regardless of everything that happen, but my faith doesn't mean that I can't enjoy our culture. As a Caribbean man, I was a big follower of Bob Marley's music. I remember the words of many of his songs. He was a spiritual man, you know, and just as I go to the Qur'an, he went to the Bible.

One song in particular going through my head these days. Is about how they carry us away in captivity and still expect us to sing. Smile and be happy, no matter how much pressure they put on us. But you don't have to be a scientist to know time will come when that pressure cooker will explode.

Here, the calypsonians are the major singers, and a lot of them were friends with the Haji. They are the ones, aside from men like us, who really represent the people, and every year, they try to put to music the troubles Santabellans seeing.

When Friday come, calypsonians, doctors, lawyers, professional people, even some in government who have a conscience, would come to Juma. I can't swear that all of them convert to Islam, but they support what Haji was doing, and one of the ways they could express that support was to come, even one Friday a month, to hear him give his sermon. That was a lucky thing for all of us members, because they could testify, in the open, against what the government was claiming Haji's sermons were all about.

Inside the mosque, all males, including boys, would line up first, after they had cleaned themselves. Then the women and girls, barefooted too, line up a few feet behind us. All the faithful know the prayers in Arabic, so they could respond to Haji, and they know when to get down on their knees, and when to stand up. Haji always begin with:

In the name of Allah, the Entirely Merciful, the Especially Merciful.
All praise is due to Allah, Lord of the worlds –
The Entirely Merciful, The Especially Merciful,
Sovereign of the Day of Recompense.
It is You we worship and You we ask for help.
Guide us to the straight path.
The path of those upon whom You have bestowed favour,
not of those who have evoked Your Anger or of those who are astray.

Then he talk to us about how we should behave with our families; how we should take care of the old people and our children; how we should behave to our brothers and sisters in Santabella, for even if they were not of our faith, they were our people.

Yes, the Qur'an say a lot of things about unbelievers, and Haji was teaching us that there were some unbelievers in particular who were doomed to be consumed by fire. Hell was lying in wait for them.

All of them who transgressing against us, against our land, they would be thirsty in Hell, and all they would get would be scalding water to drink. All those hypocrites and liars, especially the ones who trying to expel us from our homes, from our place of worship, their day would come.

One day, one day congotay, as the old people say.

As for us, the believers, our day coming too, Haji warn us.

When the time come, according to the Surah 33, we the believers would be tested with a severe shaking.

"You have to stand firm," he tell us. "You can't run away. If you run from death or killing, you not going to get any enjoyment in life. Is like that fellar in the Bible. Remember how God tell him to sacrifice his son? And the man was ready to do that. His own son. But where you going to run, eh? Tell me where you could hide from Allah? Only Allah can protect you. To Allah belongs the dominion of the heavens and the earth. And the day the Hour come, that day, the falsifiers will lose, and you, all of you, who believe and act on Allah's behalf, will receive your rewards."

He tell us that, and I believe him. A lot of people believe him.

We were training the fellars for that Hour. The women didn't know what was going on. To this day, I wish at least one of them did know. It might have saved everybody a lot of grief. But what was to be, was to be.

We didn't do training at the compound. Haji too smart for that. And it wasn't just because we didn't want the women to know some of the things we have to do. Those women were loyal believers. It was mainly because we know, at least Haji know, that we couldn't trust every single man who was part of the inner circle. Every organization like ours has infiltrators, and sometimes, Haji teach me, it was necessary to keep them close, feed them information as if we trust them, but never turn our back on them in the dark. Just see what they do with that information.

I'm not talking about fellars like Yusuf. True, you had to be careful around them, until they went through the retraining, but a lot of those so-called bad-johns were like short matchsticks. One big, quick flame, and they done.

Haji put me in charge of them, and I do my job well, not just because I believe in the cause, but also because I am a faithful son of Allah, the Merciful, the Beneficent. I take full responsibilities for what I do, in his name. But I still wonder, every so often, how my life would have turned out if I had gone away.

FOURTEEN

After his night-shift with her, Jestina shook awake Charmers, one of her taxi-driver friends.

"Hurry up, man," she urged. "I promise Beatrice you'll pick her up at five. Come on, come on. You don't need no tea so early. Just wash up and go."

Reluctantly, Charmers – a name he had picked up because of his well-known ability to attract females – dragged himself to the shower, then hurried into his clothes and out the door.

Tiredness almost left him as Beatrice came out of the house, dressed in a black skirt that displayed ample portions of her thighs, a red sleeveless blouse, and lipstick to match it. She had parted her hair in the middle, and the strands bounced off her shoulders.

"Ummm-humm!" Charmers licked his lips. "A man don't have to eat all day after looking at you, Beatrice. You sitting up front, girl."

He dashed out to open the passenger door with a flourish that reminded Beatrice of the picture in her school book of Sir Walter Raleigh placing his cape on the muddy ground for the Queen.

She dismissed his *mamaguy* with a fling of her hand. "That flattery and a penny would get you a mauby in Miss Ann's parlour," she laughed. "The question is, what're you giving me for making your day so bright?"

She had learned years before that the best way to handle Charmers and his teasing, was to give some *picong* back in return. Men appreciated that not all women were offended by their sexual innuendo, which was built into the DNA of all male Santabellans.

"Anything you want, doux-doux." Charmers turned the car around and headed down the Hill. "What is mine is yours."

"After or before the rest of your ladies get their shares?"

He grinned in defeat. "You get me there, Beatrice. You get me there, girl. Is only so much ham a man could give away before he reach the bone, you know."

"Well, even the bone good for callaloo," Beatrice laughed, and Charmers laughed with her.

A scarf of haze was still tied around the head of the Hill as they made their way down through committees of dogs rushing to their fences to bark good morning, or at least to let the world know they were still alive. They had made it through one more night.

Mr. Roberts's goats, munching at the side of the road, barely glanced up at the taxi went by, but the donkey in Sammy's yard brayed three times, a sign, Beatrice hoped, of good luck.

Dew dripped from eddoe leaves, and half-ripe mangoes, picked at by hungry birds, fell from trees to hit the road.

Charmers switched on the car's radio and they listened to the highfalutin Englishy voice of the announcer offering the early version of the overnight news.

Miss Ann, brushing her teeth over the drain at the side of her house, saw them go. She didn't wave. A few minutes later, she was knocking on Jestina's back door, rousing her from the sleep she had curled back into after Charmers left.

"What you want," she growled at Miss Ann. "A person can't get no sleep in their own house? Somebody dead?"

She rubbed her eyes and grit from the mascara that she had not washed off before climbing into bed, slid under her eyelids to irritate her.

Her tangled hair looked, Miss Ann decided, like sea weed.

"Why you didn't tell me Charmers was coming for Beatrice?" Miss Ann tugged the sheet off Jestina. "Is Embassy they going, right?"

"Look, woman, I need some sleep. You need to ask Beatrice her business. Not me."

"You think I don't know is you prodding Beatrice to go away?

77

Eh? You working behind my back. You think that is right? Is me Tante Vivian asked to look after Beatrice, not you. Who put you in charge here, eh? Tell me that."

"I didn't know Reme dead." Jestina got up and pulled on a robe. "I didn't know you bring Beatrice into this world."

She yawned. She really didn't want to get into a row with Miss Ann, not so early in the morning.

"Look, you mind if we quarrel 'bout this later? I was just falling back asleep."

"Is after five in the morning," Miss Ann snapped. "You should a sleep last night. When we don't have a teacher to teach your own children in September, I hope you satisfy."

She was about to slam Jestina's bedroom door when she turned around for a last hit. "If you think when Beatrice go America, she sending for you, and you leaving your children by me, you better think again. You going to have to put them in the orphanage." Then she stomped out.

FIFTEEN

After their descent from Rosehill, Charmers took the route through the mountains to bypass the traffic congesting the main road into town. The steepness of the mountain road had been made manageable for the traffic coming from the airport to deposit tourists at the upside-down hotel overlooking the Savannah at the other end.

Already, men were at work on the fringes of the highway, their backs bent, their bare fingers pulling weeds which they then flung into piles for women with black garbage bags to collect.

"This is the only road the government maintain every day as God send." Charmers seemed to have read Beatrice's thoughts.

"Is the only one without potholes, you know. That wouldn't be good for the tourists and them. This road smooth-smooth. And don't talk 'bout flowers. You see how them fellars planting hibiscus all along the side there? Why they can't do that on all the major roads in this country? What you say, Beatrice?"

"Well, I agree that it look as if they make it nice for the tourists, but we driving on it too, so it's for everybody, really."

"That is not the point, Beatrice," Charmers insisted. "The point I'm making is this – and a bright woman like you must agree – that it have people all over this country who love flowers. It have Santabellans waiting years to get their roads pitched – and we have a pitch lake right in this country, remember that. They waiting to get lights connected, and proper running water, but they not getting it. The Yankee man come from America and build a hotel. Bam! He getting paved road from the airport to his hotel. He getting so much lights that when you pass there, you think the place on fire. And while boys watering the grass round the hotel three times a day, people like you and me, Jestina, and the rest of Rosehill, have to wait for a water truck to come once a week, if they feel like it. You think that is fair? Don't tell me that, man. That can't be fair at all, at all."

"But the government says the hotel providing jobs. You don't think that is a good thing?"

Beatrice could just have easily conceded Charmers' point, but that would have gone against the protocol of a taxi ride in Santabella. In fact, it was such an important ritual, that one wag – asked what was Santabella's most important export, after oil – declared it was "Old-talk".

"Providing jobs? Is how much pay you think people getting there? I know a woman working as a maid there since the hotel opened and she could hardly put one foot in front the other. And what about all the concessions government give them Americans to build the hotel? You don't read the papers or what. Is millions they get. And they don't have to pay taxes for fifty years. So you tell me who making out like bandits in this country. You tell me that."

Charmers suspected that Beatrice agreed with him, but the ritual required that she counter his points.

"I still say," Beatrice offered, "what is good for the tourists, is good for the people, unless they put a big gate to block us from driving on this highway."

"Look," Charmers conceded, "It's not that I don't want them to build hotels and ting, but these foreign business must put some of their profits back into the country. All them millions they making? Where it going, eh? Tell me that."

Before Beatrice could open her mouth, he provided his own answer.

"It going straight back to America, that's where. And we children still going to school half-day because the government crying they don't have enough revenue to build schools. And hear the next one: is Yankee who get the contract to build this road, you know. Is we tax dollars paying for all that."

"Well," Beatrice laughed, "maybe is a good thing I decide to go to America. I could get back some of that money. What you think?"

Charmers laughed and confessed that he too would like to go up there, but first he had to pay off the cost of his taxi.

"And meh children, eh girl. I have two boys here. I have to keep meh eyes on them. The mother tries she best but they hard-ears sometimes."

Beatrice complimented him on his willingness to take such interest in his children, even though he and "the mother" were not living together, and for a while they talked about the sins of this father or that mother known to all on Rosehill for turning their backs on their children.

Less than an hour later he was forced to brake suddenly as he turned his taxi into Harley Street.

"Christ!" he exclaimed. "Is people like peas here. Look at the long line, nuh. Girl, I'm telling you, this ship sinking faster than the *Titanic*. Look at people."

Beatrice, too, was amazed at the length and depth of the line. People were standing three-deep in an L around the embassy's walls.

"Maybe I should come back another time," she said. "I hear they give out only so many admission tickets in one day."

"Well, you're here already. Might as well join the line," Charmers advised. Then he added, laughingly, "By the time the sun come up, half these people might have fainted away because I bet they ent even drink a cup of bush tea before they leave home. You could get your chance to move up. Get out quick before somebody else join the line."

He pocketed his fare without counting it as Beatrice scrambled for her purse and umbrella.

Weaving his taxi through more and more people getting out of vans and cars, some with paper bags of food in hand, Charmers shook his head in sorrow for Beatrice and the long wait he knew she would have – with the possibility that she might not even get the visa. After all, he told himself, she had that criminal charge, and them Americans pay attention to that.

Beatrice smiled hesitantly at an elderly Indian woman, dressed in a red sari, standing in front of her in the line.

"Morning," she whispered, and for a while could say no more

because she suddenly felt ashamed to be in the line. I bet they don't have to beg our embassy in America for a visa to come here, she thought.

"Furst time yuh here?" the Indian lady asked.

Beatrice answered with a nod, then shook her head to signal the regret she felt at having to be there at all.

"I going to *Michigan* to meh son and he children, nuh," the lady continued proudly. "I hear it cold fuh so up dere. Where you going?"

"That's a good question," Beatrice laughed softly. "According to some of my neighbours, I going mad. But seriously, I have a friend in New York."

"A man friend," the old lady smiled knowingly.

"Is my boyfriend." Beatrice swallowed the lump that always rose in her throat when she told a lie. "He's a lawyer up there. He send for me."

"Ah!' the lady beamed. "So is big time wedding in New York, eh? Yuh lucky, girl. When these boys and them go America is not easy for them to stay away from temptation, yuh know."

Then she dropped her voice to add, "The white ladies and them, nuh. They tie up the boys, yuh know?"

Beatrice nodded in agreement, amused that the lady was whispering. Here they were, in their own country, in the open air, and this mother was nervous about speaking. Did she think the Americans, if they heard her, wouldn't let her into their country?

One of the embassy guards had come abreast to order them to "Make two lines, please. Make two lines."

She was a tall, strapping woman in a green uniform, carrying a baton in one hand that she kept slapping against the other palm to emphasize her words.

"If you were here yesterday, and you were given a number to come back today, join the short line. Hear me, people! If you have a number from yesterday, join the short line round the corner, and take out that number to show the guard at the gate. If you do not, I repeat, do not have a number, stay where you are, and if you are lucky, you will be given one today."

A few people quickly left the queue and Beatrice and the old lady moved forward.

"I hear people line up since last night." The old lady looked back down the line. "Look how long the line still is."

Then she surprised Beatrice by tugging on the guard's arm to ask, "Yuh tink we getting to see the counsel today, Miss?"

The guard nodded reassuringly. "Good thing you come early. We'll start giving out new numbers in a little while. You should get in today."

Beatrice stepped off the pavement to look down the two rows. "I coming back just now," she told the man behind, then touched the Indian lady on her shoulder. "I just want to see how far back we are from the gate. Hold my place, okay?"

Walking down the line, she felt herself straightening her back, raising her head in opposition to the nervousness she felt was riding the heavy silence of the people. No, it was more than nervousness, she thought. It feels more like fear.

Fear of being rejected; fear of having to remain in Santabella with no future, no hope to see their way through. She couldn't look at them, but she knew they were staring at her, staring and wondering where she was heading. Did she think she could break into the queue ahead of them? Was somebody up ahead holding a spot for her? Did she have a special appointment? Wonder who *she* knows in the embassy to curry favour for her?

Reaching the end of the street, she saw that she need not go any further as she could see that the line stretched halfway up the block, well beyond the high walls surrounding the embassy's compound. She turned around, then stopped.

Guessing the thoughts that had been floating around her, for a moment she felt a little embarrassed as she moved to turn around and go back to her place. It might have been that, or something else she couldn't explain. Whatever it was, it moved her legs across the street, it raised her hands to push open the unlocked gate and it moved her body into the church of All Saints, where, the thought came to her, Tante Vivian and Uncle Reginald had been married so many years ago.

A service was in progress: five or six women and three men were kneeling as a priest – a young Indian priest, Beatrice noted with surprise – intoned a litany. She slid into a pew off to the side, in the back, well away from the others, knelt down, and began to whisper the 23rd Psalm: "The Lord is my Shepherd, I shall not want…"

The prayer over, she stood up just as the others were doing so. She shook her head. *What I doing here? What make me come in here? I need to get back to the line. They're probably giving out the tickets.*

But she couldn't move. Her feet were rooted.

Confused, embarrassed, even though only the priest had looked up at her, she reached for a hymn book and turned to the page the priest had just announced. The congregation had already started the first line – *Just a closer walk with Thee* – as she joined them with:

"Grant it Jesus, if you please,
Daily walking close to Thee,
Let it be, dear Lord, let it be…"

This was one of Tante Vivian's favourite hymns.

In the glow of the words, the priest descended the altar, and followed by his acolyte, came slowly down the aisle.

"May the peace of the Lord be always with you," he called out.

"And always with you," the people answered.

Hoping to escape before the priest could take up his position at the entrance to greet the congregation, Beatrice tried to move swiftly to the door, but he was waiting for her, his right hand stretched out, and she could do nothing else but place her hand in his.

"Come again," he said, eyes twinkling.

And for some reason that to this day she could not explain, she asked him, "Father, could I borrow one of the hymn books for a little while? I promise I'll bring it back before the day is over."

The priest gazed at her, question marks in his eyes. Then he said, "All right. But be sure to return it. We don't have many."

He signalled to the acolyte to hand her one.

With a combination of assurance and anxiety bubbling inside of her, Beatrice went quickly back to the line. She smiled at the quizzical look on the face of the man behind her, then squeezed the Indian lady's hand.

"Yuh gone so long I thought yuh give up," the woman whispered. "Lucky ting they didn't give out the numbers yet."

"I went in the church," Beatrice smiled. "I don't even know

what made me do that. Look, I even borrowed their hymn book."

She flipped it open to the hymn she had sung, and a hum escaped her as the old woman's face broke out in a smile.

"I know that one," she said. "I is a Methodist, yuh know. We sing that all the time. I know it by heart, since I small," and she added her voice to Beatrice's, softly, hesitantly at first, as if they didn't want to disturb the other people in line or cause the guards to shut them up.

But then, a strange thing happened: ahead and in back of them, voices joined theirs, some humming, some singing the words, some off key, some a little shamefaced, heads hanging, while their song sprinkled the earth, but that was all right, that was all right, because others had raised their faces up, stretched their necks and straightened their shoulders so the sound could come out lustier, and they sang and they sang, not just the one hymn, but hymn after hymn, Beatrice or another voice giving out the first line to the raggedy choir, not stopping as the guards came along to see what all that commotion was, but even they, smiling slightly, not telling the choir to stop, just handing out tickets and getting a smile in song in return.

At the end of that day, when the Consul asked his staff for a tally of the number of visas granted, no one could explain how it was, on that day, as never before, more than half of the visa applications – "Even these who had no bank statements?" – had been approved.

SIXTEEN

At the end of July, a loudspeaker van drove up and down the curving tracks on Rosehill to announce that Haji was coming. He would hold a meeting across from Ling Chung's shop to talk about the new school he planned to open on the site of the old government elementary school.

For several weeks before, truckloads of sand and concrete, bricks, lumber, cement, paint and men, had been arriving each morning to work on rebuilding the school that had mysteriously burned down some years before. Its black carcass had been a sore to the eyes of Rosehill's people, whose delegation after delegation to the Ministry of Education had failed to yield the promised new school.

Instead, the government had built one ten miles away from the Hill, to serve the children of families in the brand new development of Diamond Vale. Frustrated, Rosehill had opened its own school for the small children; Beatrice had been its teacher.

The Haji's foreman had made sure to hire several of the Rosehill men to work on the new school, and Clyde, Miss Ann's son, had given up running his taxi during the day to work for what he claimed was a lot more money than he could make running taxi in a week.

Clyde and the other Rosehill men brought news up the Hill of the scraping and painting going on inside the new school; of dividers being installed to separate classrooms; of the piles of boxes containing blackboards and pencil sharpeners and shelves for books and glass cases for exhibits ranging around the walls.

Most of Rosehill looked on in wonder at this activity, curious and anxious at the same time, pleased that somebody cared to bring them a new school, but frightened over the questions they had about where Haji was getting all that money to do what he was doing, because, according to the newspapers, he was building other schools in other neglected areas.

Willy had said to Sammy, "The man ent working nowhere. So tell me where he getting the money from?"

As usual with Sammy, when he couldn't, or didn't want to answer a question, he resorted to a joke. "Is one thing for sure, we know he's not getting it from Russia like Castro. I ent see no red dollars floating round Santabella. As far as I'm concerned, if the man want to build schools, more power to him, regardless of where the money coming from. It doing good."

But there were rumours in some quarters that Haji had indeed been to Cuba; that he was trying to turn Santabella into another Grenada, another Soviet satellite. What people didn't know, they made up, so rumour became truth.

Miss Ann pressed Clyde for nightly reports on the advancing work. One evening, shaking with excitement, he told her about the hundred – he had counted them – a *hundred* gallons of paint he had helped to off-load.

"Is the best paint. *Lead-free*, you know. The best paint money could buy. Expensive for so. The old kind the government use has this lead thing in it that could make children sick-sick. I hear Haji say nothing like that going on this school, no sirree. Is *lead-free* all the way, Ma."

A new word entered Rosehill's vocabulary, rolling off tongues as the highest compliment they could pay each other about a new dress, new shoes, new pants, new anything: "Hummm. That is *leadfree*, Pappy."

More was to come. Where before, as Clyde reminded Miss Ann, teachers and pupils all had to go outside to use the latrines, they would now be able to use indoor *facilities*. The word *facilities* had, for him, a delicious taste, like the juice of a mango Julie on his tongue, so he used it at every opportunity, appropriately or not, until the fellars began to refer to him as Mr. Facilities.

Haji instructed the men to cement over the holes of the old latrines and, shortly after, they installed playground equipment, imported, according to the marks on the bins, directly from Germany.

The red, blue and green steel, twisted and stretched in odd and lovely geometric shapes, invited even more curiosity. Never had Rosehill seen such things. It was a play zoo inviting children, even before the school building was completed, to climb on rocking horses or wiggle through marble fish, swoosh down smooth slides into sand pits, or swing on chains that would send them flying higher in the air than any rope on an old tyre tied to a mango tree could do.

Not everyone was pleased. *The Sentinel* carried a front page story claiming that Haji had taken over the old school property without permission from the proper Government authorities, that wiring and plumbing were being installed without proper permits or inspections.

"Proper my arse!" Incensed at these claims, Jestina had brought the newspaper to show Beatrice. "As soon as we black people start doing something constructive for we self, Government start criticizing."

"But the government is black too," Beatrice laughed.

"Only on the outside. Outside they brown and black like old coconuts, but see inside them and what you have, eh? What you have? Is white meat all the way. That is their mentality."

Miss Ann, arriving just then, nodded in agreement. "Much as I don't like this Muslim business," she said as she sat down on the steps, "I see what you saying. When this Government take over we thought things would be different. They make all kind of promises about water, lights, roads. What we get, eh?"

"Lies, lies, and more lies!" Jestina exploded. "I fed up listening to that Prime Minister. Look how long he and Robbley, we so-called representative, promising to fix the bridge so we could get over to the ravine. If it wasn't for Haji, we would still have to go down in that mud to cross. And what about the lights they promise? Two years now we waiting on a light pole. People have to walk home in the dark with all these bandits around."

"Down where Reme working," Beatrice told them, "you think anything ever spoil in their fridge? Current gone up here three-four times a week but it's always on down there. They never have to wait for no water truck. Water flowing like the river in rainy season down there."

"Is so, oui," Miss Ann shook her head in resignation. "Is same old khaki pants from one government to a next. Poor people have to struggle. And on top of everything, I hear they going to put a tax on the children's school books. What happened to all the promises about free books? We going to have to buy them and pay a VAT on them as well."

"So you should be glad the Muslims come," Beatrice teased her. "New school, new bridge. Rosehill's more for higher, girl."

"Hmmm..." Miss Ann's face squinted in worry. "Laugh all you want, but what I'm wondering is what the children will wear to that school. Long dress and head tie?"

"Wear to school? You talking about what they will wear to school?" Jestina was flipping through the newspaper. She stopped and pointed to a story. "You don't see here where the editorial calling for the Minister of Education to stop the school from opening?" She pushed the newspaper into Miss Ann's hands.

"But I don't understand that at all." Miss Ann glanced at the article, then passed back the paper to Jestina, before turning to Beatrice. "How come they didn't stop us when we opened up the school here after the fire, Beatrice? Answer me that. How come?"

"Is not the same thing," Beatrice told her. "This is a different scale entirely. We used the downstairs part of your house for the school, not any government building. And it wasn't a big show place to make them shame."

"And we not Muslim. That is the *real* difference." Jestina slapped her thigh to emphasize her point. "This government 'fraid them Muslims for so. You think it want them educating the children?"

"It's a strange thing," Beatrice mused. "On the one hand, it seems like the government's against the Muslims. They constantly raiding their compound, and the Prime Minister come out and accuse them of having guns and thing. Yet somebody in the government must be on the Muslims' side."

"Why you say that?" Miss Ann demanded.

"See for yourself," Beatrice said. "For all the talk in the newspapers and for all their announcements about his weapons, they're still letting him put up the school, no matter what the newspaper advocate. He must have people *inside* the government on his side, otherwise bulldozers woulda been up here long time to knock down that school. And I don't believe he's so foolish as to invest all that money in something without having the right permissions. Uh, uh. Is more in the mortar than the pestle. I could put my head on a block for that."

"Well, I tell you this," Miss Ann's voice was grave. "I have a bad-bad feeling all this ending up in violence. We just pass through one misery with the hurricane, and I could see another one coming. What I tell you, Beatrice? If you did follow what I tell you and agree to open back up the school, none of this would a happened."

Beatrice shook her head in disbelief. "So is *my* fault the Muslims come to Rosehill? Is *my* fault they take over the burn down school and build up a new one? A-A. But what I hearing at all?" She stared off angrily, her gaze fixed on a rosebush at the side of the yard.

Vexed on Beatrice's behalf, Jestina tapped Miss Ann on her head with the rolled up newspaper and told her, in a low voice, that if she didn't leave Beatrice's yard that minute, she, Jestina, could not be held responsible for what would happen next.

Miss Ann sucked her teeth, lifted her skirt, and rose up from the steps. Without glancing at Beatrice, she walked slowly, deliberately toward the gate.

Her hand on the latch, she turned back to shout, "Is you, yes! Is you self. Who the hell tell you to help that Haji's daughter? Eh? Is you causing these people to come up here. You self! But you will live to regret it, watch what I tell you." She flounced down the road without looking back.

Beatrice tightened her shoulders and swallowed the cuss words she wanted to fling at Miss Ann.

"Don't take she on." Jestina touched Beatrice's arm. "She just vexed because you're going to America. As soon as she find somebody else to order around, she'll be back to her old self. You going to the Muslim meeting?"

"What meeting?" Stung by Miss Ann's words, Beatrice had forgotten that Haji was coming to Rosehill that evening. She shook her head.

"We could at least go and hear what the man has to say,"

Jestina nudged her. "Is Rosehill children will benefit from the school."

But Beatrice couldn't let go of Miss Ann's accusations. "Haji started to build that school long before I even meet his daughter. Miss Ann knows that full well. Yet she's going around telling everybody that I'm abandoning the children to the Muslims. Long before these people come up here I tell her I wasn't going to teach the school any more. But she wouldn't give up. She had ample time to try to find somebody else, but no, she's still harassing me."

"Well, in a sense you can't really blame her, you know." Jestina knew she was treading in hot water with Beatrice, but she had always been able to talk the truth to her, and Beatrice would listen.

"As far as the school is concerned, is not only her grandchildren involved. All the little children on Rosehill who can't go to that school the government build in the Vale need education too. My two included. All of us parents should have band together to find another teacher, but like everything else, we leave it up to Miss Ann. We get so used to her being in charge. So when you add the fact that she can't persuade you to stay to the fear she has of the Muslims, you could understand how she's feeling. Don't be too hard on her, Beatrice. She feel as if she fail all of us. So when she shout at you, is for us she's doing it. I and all the Rosehill parents really need to beg your pardon."

Beatrice looked at her. "So *you* apologizing for the hurtful thing she say to me?"

"Yes," Jestina nodded. "You know she didn't mean it. Mark my words, before it gets dark, she will be sending up one of those children with a piece of that sponge cake and some sour-sop ice cream for you."

She grinned. "Keep a lil' piece of the cake for me, okay? I smell when it was baking, but I didn't want to beg her for a piece. I'll get it from you when we meet up to go to the meeting."

"I tell you I going down there?" Beatrice sucked her teeth and looked away, but she couldn't fool Jestina.

"I hear he putting a whole room in the school for books, girl," Jestina pinched Beatrice's arm to emphasize the wonder. "A library. Imagine that. The children not going to have to wait until that bus come once in a blue moon with books for them to read.

If nothing else, I want to go and say ah salaam to the man for that. And for the bridge too."

"So is Arabic you talking now?" Beatrice's face relaxed; she smiled. "No wonder the government getting worried. Haji changing Santabellan's language and all."

Jestina knew, by the sound in Beatrice's voice, that she would need no more persuading to attend the meeting, so announcing that she had to go home to burn some bush to get rid of the mosquitoes, she went down the road to her house.

Before she got to her gate she saw Miss Ann's granddaughter, Veneta, hurrying up the Hill with a basket.

Jestina smiled as she went in search of matches to light the bush.

Beatrice accepted the gifts with some reluctance as she didn't want Miss Ann to believe that she could so easily be forgiven for her insults. It would be rude, though, to refuse the cake and ice cream, and doing so would involve the child in a quarrel that was between adults, so she told Veneta to tell her grandmother thanks very much, her mouth was really watering for some ice cream.

After the child left, she wrapped the piece of cake in a napkin for Jestina. The soursop ice cream she stored in the freezer for a day when she wasn't so vexed with Miss Ann.

Gathering several newspapers she had not had time to read over the past few days, she settled into a chair to read what they had to say about the Haji, and there was plenty.

In one issue, there he was with wife number three. In response to the reporter's suggestion that he was committing bigamy, Haji had said playfully – a trait for which he was famous – "Big-a-my? Who bigger dan me, boy?" And even Beatrice had to laugh at his audacity.

She studied his face, his bold, clear eyes, his mocking smile. He looked much younger than the forty-six the newspaper gave as his age. His new wife, her head and body shrouded, came up only to his chest. The newspaper reported that she was the daughter of the most important Chinese dentist in the country; that she had been married before, was childless, had been a member of Haji's mosque for over a year before becoming his wife, with permission granted by wife number one. Beatrice wondered why wife number two was not mentioned.

The more she read, the more fascinated she became – and the more uncomfortable she was becoming with that fascination, so she put away the papers and turned on the television.

But she couldn't avoid him. There he was, sitting behind his desk in what the running cut-line below the picture called a file photo.

A reporter, mike in hand, was standing in front of the compound telling viewers that at that very moment, police were again raiding the Haji's compound [*Camera pans over the compound pick up only canvas sheets draped over the fence*]. Back to the reporter who explains that the police had put up the canvas sheets and posted officers with guns to keep reporters away.

Back to file footage of a previous interview with the Haji in his office, during a previous raid.

Reporter: You have said you will defend yourself. You said you have guns.

Haji: A lot of people own guns in this country. We living in an armed camp. You yourself tell us every day about the amount of guns in this country. Since when is a crime to own guns in Santabella?

Reporter: Not everybody who owns a gun has threatened the government.

Haji: I could threaten government? I? I am a lowly citizen, but I will tell you what we have said. We have said – and I will repeat it for those of you who may not have heard it correctly, including you – we have said that we, the people, have a right to defend our homes, our places of worship, our businesses, from invasion by any source. We stand by that statement.

[*The camera swerves suddenly to pick up a blue jeep pulling up to the gate of the compound*.] The reporter dashes forward, his mike raised to catch any words above the heads of his colleagues and police, as cameras are thrust into the face of Haji as he emerges.

Three grimfaced men clad in army fatigues, their heads turbaned in what was being called, locally, Yassah wraps, triangular shaped pieces of white cotton with black dots, push their way toward the closed gates of the compound. But they are blocked by several policemen in riot gear, heads covered in steel, guns pointed.

The reporter shouts: Is this an invasion, Haji?

The Haji turns toward the cameras. He is dressed in lily white tunic, white pants. His head is covered with a fez made from Ghanaian Kente cloth. He raises his hands as if in surrender and keeps them aloft as he speaks:

Haji: Members of the press. As you can see, the government has sent its forces, again, for the third time this month, to search for arms they say I have. But if they want to find arms, all they have to do is ask me. But is like they have *yampee* in their eyes, because as all of you could see, here are my arms. [*He waves at the cameras.*] These are the only arms I have, and if the government wants to find them, all they have to do is look right here. [*He grins.*] But they blind, and they want you to be blind too, blind to what they are doing inside our compound. Ask yourself, because you can't ask them, right? Ask yourselves why, if it is in the interest of the people, in the interest of public safety, they searching down this sacred place, why they hiding what they doing behind canvas. After all, if they find guns here, they should be glad to show the press the guns. You don't agree? But what they have to hide? They push all the women and children out. Little children who only learning to read and write, who have a right to an education. They crash the place, push out the women and children.

[*Cameras pan to pick up several women and children, all shrouded from head to toe, huddled at the side of the road across from the compound.*]

A reporter: Do you intend to retaliate? Do you consider this an invasion?

Haji: Invasions are for UFOs, and as you can see, or maybe you can't, the ones wrecking our compound have official status. But what you have to ask yourselves is who they are representing? You think the people of Santabella, I mean the poor, suffering people who eating the bread the devil knead every single day, you think is on their behalf all this [*a sweep of the raised arms*] going on?

Horns blare. The police guarding the gates step to the side, and three grey vans, back flaps open to reveal other grey and black clad police officers inside, sweep through the gates. A fourth van stops; the policemen at the gate hand in their long guns before leaping in, and the whole convoy sweeps up the highway, away from the compound.

94

The reporters, camera people, all seem unsure about what to do – follow the convoy or stay with the Haji. A camera follows the Haji as he moves toward the women and children. Two white maxi-taxis pull up; the women and children are loaded into one. The Haji and a group of men who had come from behind the compound enter the other. Guards close the gates of the compound.

Beatrice, with a deep sigh, turned off the television.

Maybe he would be so caught up with what had happened that there wouldn't be a rally, she thought, and that, for a reason she did not want to accept, made her sad.

SEVENTEEN

The air around Rosehill was punctuated with the sound of drums just as dusk began to cover the galvanized roofs. Not steel drums from the pan yard; not bongo drums from Jestina's backyard where Clyde taught a group of boys to dance on their heels and their fingertips, too.

No. This was a different drumming: a hot, peppery rhythm, urgent, so demanding that women on the Hill stopped stirring rice, dropped clothes-pins they were holding between their teeth as they took down clothes from their lines, left hot irons lying dangerously near the edge of iron tables, to go to their front yards, to look down the road to find where all that drumming was coming from.

Miss Ann shouted to Willy to shut the parlour for her as she was going down the Hill to see what the bacchanal was all about.

Melda abandoned the basket of clothes she had just taken off the line to join Miss Ann and some neighbours.

The road was still wet from the mid-afternoon shower but no one paid attention to the mud or slippery moss: not the women, not their children, not the men who had just taken up the evening *News* to read, or a beer to sip, but had to put them aside to answer the call of the drums.

What they saw as they crossed the road was a flame of fire in the elementary school yard.

What they heard as they drew nearer the fire was the staccato intensity of fingers and palms drawing the beat from drums held between the thighs of four young men sitting on stools around the flame.

Sweat dripped from the men's foreheads, poured from their

chests and armpits to wet down their shirts, but they didn't stop drumming. They seemed mesmerized, tranced by the rhythmic creation that drew from the souls of unsettled waters flowing in the Ganges and the Niger.

The drums insisted that the people come close and listen without fear; told them that they could shuffle their toes in the sand if they wanted, lift their skirts round their knees without shame, dip their shoulders in praise to Dangbwe if they felt like doing so.

They could dance "Indian", letting their fingers play with the air above their heads, as one arm akimbo, they circled the drummers on one foot. Or – and some did – they could wine their *bomsies, dingolay*, or do a little *boatay*. They could do whatever they wanted. Nobody would stop them.

An old man, shouting "Ajohu! Ajohu! Ajohu" between cackles of joy, dragged his bad left foot into the circle of light and began to spin as if he were young again.

Miss Ann, hearing his shout, muttered to Melda, "But what the hell going on here? I used to hear my grandmother shouting that very word. This is African thing."

And Melda, shuffling to the drums, told her, "African Muslim! Is African Muslim we hearing."

Back up the Hill, Jestina, ready and impatient, shouted from the gate to Beatrice to hurry up, hurry up, but Beatrice was not yet finished turning the coo-coo she was making for Reme.

Yes, she told Jestina, she had heard the drums, but she couldn't let the coo-coo burn. In a fit of remorse over how she had been treating her mother, she'd decided to make some coo-coo and curried shark for Reme, who'd said she was coming home later. Coo-coo required constant turning, and she'd been doing that when the drums had begun.

She removed the pot from the burner, then made a spoon-sized indent in the middle of the mound for the pat of butter that would continue to season the cornmeal and ochre until Reme arrived.

The fish was ready. She had stewed it earlier in a curry gravy thick with thyme and chives, tomatoes, onion, ginger and garlic, but not too much because Reme hated the taste of garlic.

From the tree in the back yard she had picked three full limes to make the juice that would set off the meal. Everything ready, she made sure, for the last time, that the food was safe from marauding insects flying into the kitchen from the unscreened windows. Then she joined Jestina, impatiently tapping her feet to the drums.

"That sound like tassa drumming," Jestina said, as they went down the Hill. "Is Indian talent on parade?"

Beatrice laughed at the wonder and consternation coming from Jestina – who was hardly ever surprised – and said, "Wasn't it you who remind me the other day that all of we is one? If Indian boys can beat steel pan, and Indian women could sing calypso, what's so wrong with Creole men beating tassa drums?"

"This life is a *pelau*, girl." Jestina threw up her hands in despair. "I give up. Everything so mixed up. Black people calling their self Muslim. What else coming?"

"But why they beating drums anyway?" Beatrice asked.

"Is all part of the Haji thing, girl. The blending of Santabella's cultures," she added importantly. "Charmers tell me a whole lot of them come up in maxi-taxis from town. It was like a caravan. Indian people, Negro people, Dougla people, about a hundred of them. They build a fire, then the fellas start beating drums to call the people out to hear Haji give his talk. Watch out for that jeep."

The jeep bathed them in its headlights, swept past them, then turned around, stopped, backed up, and stopped besides them. Beatrice recognized it as the same one that had brought the Haji's wife to her a few weeks earlier.

The window on the front passenger side slid down and a voice called, "Good evening, Ladies. Going to the meeting?"

Beatrice continued to walk.

Jestina tugged her skirt and Beatrice turned around, reluctantly, her head down. Why, she wondered, was she overcome with this odd feeling each time she saw the man?

Jestina tugged on her arm again. "We riding in style, girl," she said.

Haji alighted, opened the door to the back seat, and ushered them in.

Beatrice crouched near the door, refusing to look at Jestina.

The tinted glass began to slide up and she said, "Can you leave the window down please?"

"It's air-conditioned," Haji said, and the window slid up.

Disappointed that the people they were passing would not get to see her riding in style, Jestina slumped in her seat, but Beatrice was glad that they could stay hidden, at least until they reached the corner.

She hit Jestina with her elbow, disgusted that she had accepted the drop.

Haji had not looked back since they had gotten in. Beatrice stared at the sharp mark of his hair against his fair neck, the fez with its alternating rows of green, red, and black braid covering his head, his broad shoulders covered in a white tunic.

As if he could feel her eyes on him, he said, "My name is Haji. This is Bolo." A nod from the driver who had also not glanced at them, but Beatrice could tell by his stiff shoulders that he was listening intently. "You all live up here long?"

"We're Rosehill people. Born and bred," Jestina said proudly.

"Children?" He still had not turned around, which irritated Beatrice. She wanted to see his eyes.

"I have two," Jestina said. "My friend here had…" She winced at the knock on her elbow from Beatrice, then whispered, "Sorry, sorry," before repeating, "I have two. The older one is ten."

"Where're they going to school?"

"Well, the older ones used to go to the school we opened up on the Hill, but we don't know what will happen when the year opens. Miss Lady here was the teacher, but looks like she's headed for New York."

Then he turned his face to them. One wreathed in a smile, brown eyes dancing. "New York, eh? Newoo Yuk. Flatbush Avenue, Labor Day in the Brook. Going to seek your fortune?"

He's laughing at me, Beatrice thought. Just like that time in Ali's office. And why is he behaving as if I don't know who he is? She tapped the driver's shoulder. "Will you put me down here please?"

"Where you going, Beatrice?" Jestina held her arm. "We're almost to the corner."

The driver cast a swift look back at her, then at Haji, but he did not stop.

"Miss Salandy is embarrassed to have her friends see her with those bad Muslims," Haji said, as if he was explaining a universal truth.

His speech, Beatrice, noticed, was crisp, formal. No more laughter.

He shook his head slightly at the driver, who pulled the jeep over to the side and stopped. "I'm sorry to have offended you." His eyes were on Beatrice, steady, unsmiling.

Her cheeks, she thought, must be looking like rookoo, as a feeling that she was being stupid, childish, swept over her.

Haji got out and held the back door open on Beatrice's side, and she, muttering a thanks she hoped he heard, without looking up at him – for she suddenly realized how much taller than she he was – hurried across the road with a stupesing Jestina bringing up the rear.

Why? Why had she behaved like that? Just because the man had laughed? No. It wasn't that. It was something else about him. A feeling she had but couldn't, wouldn't name. It was his neck. Admit it. She'd wanted to press her palm against his skin. No. No.

Jestina was shouting her name, demanding that she wait, so Beatrice stood in the doorway of the bakery that Ling Chung had recently added to his shop, away from the crowd gathering in the school yard, her face tight, her arms folded across her chest to show Jestina that she wasn't pleased at all, at all.

"The man called your name, Bee. The man know you." Jestina sounded as if she'd had a revelation.

"So? You want me to make a kaiso about that?"

"You know damn well what I mean. He's *interested* in you. You couldn't see that?"

"I don't know what you talking 'bout. I come down here to hear the man talk, not to ride around in his car. Okay?"

"So you lose your manners all of a sudden? The man was just giving us a little drop. Why you have to get so vexed?"

Beatrice turned her face away and was saved from the struggle of a lie by a blast of calypso music.

The drums had stopped, and from the amplifiers mounted at the side of the stage, the voice of one of Santabella's most famous calypsonians, The Mighty Shadow, began to belt out his hit song, "Poverty is Hell".

For a minute, Beatrice was stunned. Calypso? Kaiso? At a Muslim rally? And drums? African drums? What kind of Muslim was this? Then, remembering her earlier complaint about everything in Santabella being mixed up, like a *pelau*, as Jestina had said, she smiled and followed Jestina closer to the sound of Shadow's sweet voice explaining how hell and poverty in Santabella had become synonymous.

Just ahead of them, they could see Miss Ann and Melda moving nearer to the front.

"What Sammy doing up there?" Miss Ann asked Melda.

"You asking me?" She and Miss Ann had managed to place themselves immediately in front of the stage. "You don't know Sammy turn Muslim long time?"

"What you mean, 'turn Muslim'? Sammy ent no damn Muslim. Sammy working Shango since I was a little child."

"Umm hum..." Melda was shaking her waist in time with the music, "but that ent stop him from joining up with Haji. I hear that all people who do Shango in Africa are Muslims too, so why not here?"

Miss Ann was incensed. "Who telling you all that foolishness? Muslim is Indian. What Muslim have to do with Africa? You talking chupidness."

Melda paused in her wining to grin at Miss Ann. "You don't know everything, you know. Other people read book; other people have sense."

"What books and sense have to do with it? In Santabella, all my life, is only Indian people practice Muslim religion. In America, yes, they have some people calling theirself Black Muslims, but I never hear about them mixing Shango and Islam."

"Ah," Melda grinned, "but Haji say all over Africa, people practice their own African religion and Islam at the same time. So why not here?"

"You talk to him? He tell you that? When this happen?"

"He didn't tell *me*. I never meet the man. But my sister's son is tight with him, and is he who explain it to me. And Sammy tell me that too."

Now, Miss Ann was truly vexed. That Sammy could be a Muslim without her knowing was one thing, but that Melda knew and had not told her was the height of treachery.

Before she could open her mouth to voice her anger, Sammy had risen and had begun to speak.

"Neighbours, oye! I glad to see all yuh here because tonight, tonight you will hear some truth which is a foreign word in this country these days. All yuh know me. I born and raised here in Rosehill. I am your neighbour. We live as one, and yuh know I never lie to you. Tonight, we have a man who will soon be one of our neighbours. No, he's not coming to live here, although I wouldn't mind it if he do that, but he's our neighbour because he cares about Rosehill people.

"He care so much that when he hear that the government, after a multitude of promises, still leave us without a school for our children to get education, he say, 'I will do it. I will build a school; I will put books in it, and desks and blackboards, and any child age five to twelve on Rosehill can come to it free of charge' (*Applause from the crowd, except Miss Ann*).

"Is my grandchildren, your children and grandchildren will benefit, but you must be asking why. Why he doing this for we? So I have to tell yuh: A good neighbour is not just somebody who living next to you, somebody who come from Rosehill. A good neighbour is somebody who care about your – our – wellbeing; who want to see we and we families make good in this world; who know about pressure, and how it could press us down and who want to lift the evil of ignorance from our people.

"A good neighbour is somebody who know, like we, that poverty is hell, and he want to deliver us from that hell, because neighbours, we don't deserve hell, and we don't deserve poverty, not after what we, what we fathers and mothers and grand and great grand parents contribute to this country. No!

"So my friend, my neighbour, a man I went to and ask, 'You could help Rosehill? You could help we get a school going for the children?'

"He shake my hand and he say, 'Yes, brother. I will help, because all of we are one, no matter where we live on this island, all of we are one.'

"So tonight, is my pleasure, by the grace of God, the Merciful, to introduce you to a man who really needs no introduction because he is our neighbour, the Haji!"

Jestina had pulled Beatrice until they were just behind Melda and Miss Ann, who, as Jestina said later, was standing so still, with her mouth open in wonder, that she, Jestina, had to pinch her to make sure she hadn't had a stroke.

To shouts of "Neighbour! Neighbour!" Haji took the microphone from Sammy, and raised his arms in a gesture similar to the one Beatrice recalled from the television scene earlier that day. The shouts ebbed.

"Ah Salaam Allah kum! May peace be upon you all, my neighbours, and may the strength of Allah, the Holy, the Merciful, the Beneficent, may peace be upon him, and may his peace extend itself to my lips this evening so that my words may be a delight to your ears, as truth should always be to the people."

(*A voice shouted, TRUTH, Haji! and the call was picked up and carried through the crowd for a minute*).

"Brother Sammy has told you that I am your neighbour, and let me echo his words (*and here he sang*), I am your neighbour, neighbour, neighbour!

"In a few weeks, the school will open and, as Brother Sammy tell you, it will have books, a library, desks, everything a school these days should have. Everything the schools in certain parts of Santabella favoured by this government have. But this school, your school, will have even more (*Applause*). Wait, wait. Let me tell you. Your school will have computers! (*Drums! Screams!*)

"Yes! Neighbours, your school, Rosehill, will have computers I buy with money from friends overseas. Your friends – even though they may never have met any of you – they like yuh!

(*And here he went seamlessly from the voice of standard English, to the jokey picong voice of a man of the people.*)

"All yuh don't get frighten. We having teachers, computer teachers too."

(*Applause, loud.*)

"But that ent all, neighbours. Is not just machines we having free. Every morning as Allah send, every child in this school goin get free breakfast; lunch time they having free lunch, and if I had

103

my way, they would have free dinner too, but they have to come home sometime (*laughter*), so all yuh have to feed them in the evening (*laughter, applause*).

"But neighbours, all yuh must be asking yuhself, what he expect for all this freeness, eh? He expect we to turn Muslim too? As if turning Muslim is like turning a bake on the fire. No, neighbour. No.

"What we give, we give from the heart; what you give, you give from the heart. I not goin lie to yuh. I come here to speak the truth. There will be prayer time in the school. And all yuh know that prayer time is tradition in Santabella. If there is one person here, man or woman, who went to school and didn't have to pray in the morning before school start, whether that was a Government school or a private school, raise yuh hand. I say raise yuh hand if yuh never pray in school.

(*Not a hand raised*.)

"So we keeping with the tradition of this country, and we going to say some prayers a few times a day. But I nearly forget one of the most important things we doing at your new school. Leh me tell you.

"Yuh know how close Santabella is to Venezuela, right?

(*A chorus of Right!*)

"And yuh know how just up the road, we have sister islands where the people, people who look just like you and me, speak French, and in Haiti, Kreyol. Well, neighbours, in this new age of computers, we have to be able to communicate with our sisters and brothers in Venezuela and up the islands, and for that matter, round the world. So we giving the children languages! We giving them Spanish!

(*Loud applause, shouts*.)

"We giving them French!

(*Even louder applause*)

"We giving them Haitian Kreyol!

(*The applause so loud, his last words are nearly drowned out*)

"And we giving them Arabic too!

"Neighbours! Neighbours! Poverty is Hell. And poverty means more than empty belly, we know that. Poverty of the mind can lead to all kinda crime. Why you think this country seeing so much crime, eh? People suffering and they don't know which way to turn. They turn to the government and they get blanked!

"Let me tell yuh a story. Is a true story. Some of you might a read bout it in the newspapers, but what you might not know is how it's connected to me.

"Is a story bout a woman who went to the General Hospital, the so-called People's Hospital, in town. She was feeling bad for three days; her medicine had run out; but she was fraid to go to the General Hospital. I ent have to tell yuh why.

(*Hoots of laughter.*)

"But this lady, I will tell yuh now that she was my oldest sister. She wasn't ready to die. Sadly, I was out of the country at the time, so I couldn't do nothing, and all her children living in New York.

"My wife take her to the People's Hospital, and they put my sister on a stretcher and tell my wife that they would take care of her, don't worry. Well, my wife had things to do and she leave the hospital. That was about seven o'clock in the morning. Six o'clock that evening my wife get back to the hospital, and what she see? She see my sister still lying on a stretcher, right there in the corridor.

"Nobody, all day, had stopped to give my sister a cup of water. Not a nurse, not a doctor. By nine o'clock my sister was dead.

"Later, a friend of mine who is a doctor at that hospital, but wasn't on duty that day, tell me my sister didn't have to die. What killed her was dehydration.

(*Groans from the crowd.*)

"Now. Now I'm not saying the hospital, run by this government, kill my sister. Maybe nothing could have saved her. Some people believe when yuh time up, it's up.

"But what hurt me is that my sister die without getting a last drop of water to drink. Why? Because all around her, in that hospital, nobody cared. She didn't have a single neighbour in that hospital that day.

"So when a man like Brother Sammy here reach out his hand and ask me to help Rosehill, how I could say no?

"I can't say no because I am your neighbour, and you have touched me!"

(*The people on the stage – Sammy and five men dressed in tunics and wide pants with covered heads – rise up to join in song with the Haji*)

"I am your neighbour, touch me. Touch me."

A hand grabbed Beatrice, pulled her forward, and she found herself on the stage, standing beside Farouka, next to the Haji, clapping and singing with the crowd.

Miss Ann shook her head. "What this man talking bout?" she asked Melda. "We can't even get a light pole up here. Current gone half the time. What he talking bout computers? He powering them with flambeaux or candle?" She let out a long stupes.

Melda didn't answer her. She wasn't listening. She was too busy staring up at the stage, at the way Beatrice was looking at the Haji, and the smile on the Haji's face.

Food and drinks – no alcohol, Jestina noticed – appeared on trays carried by young women dressed in white, and Miss Ann, for a minute, was reminded of Mother Dinah and her feasts and the young women who used to serve them, all dressed in white with their heads tied, just like these girls.

Refusing to take a cup of juice, she looked about for Willy. Unable to find him, she turned away, pushed herself through the crowd, and walked up the Hill, alone, her thoughts ablaze. That Haji was a smart one, she told herself. He swift too bad. He had Santabellans eating out of his hands, and there was nothing she could do about it.

Why, why couldn't they see that there was something wrong with all this Muslim business? She wished she could find the proper word, any words, to describe the feeling of doom that was coming over her. But if she couldn't explain it to herself, how could she convince her Rosehill neighbours that all this freeness would have a price? At times like these, she wished Tante Vivian was still there. Rosehill would listen to her. They always did. Maybe, she thought, she should go to see Mother Dinah in Moruga, where she was now living with her granddaughter.

The light breeze tickling her face convinced her this was the right decision. Mother Dinah might even be able to reach Tante Vivian. She looked up at the stars and whispered a prayer as a small contentment came over her.

It was hours before Melda, Jestina, Beatrice, Sammy, and the people of Rosehill left the school yard, exhausted, plump with shrimp roti, shark and bake, and all the juice they could swallow.

As they went up the hill, they formed lines as if they were in a carnival band, their arms linked, their waists shaking, their bodies moving from one side of the road to the other, their voices loud in ragged unison, singing over and over "I am your neighbour. Touch me. Touch me."

Willy, forced to walk a little slower with Mr. Roberts, wished he had a bottle or a piece of iron and a nail so he could hit them together to make music too. But all he could do was shout, in between *neighbour*, and *touch me*, the words, *Poverty is Hell*.

EIGHTEEN

I didn't know that Haji try to give Beatrice a ride down from the Hill until much later because I was too busy getting things organized for the rally.

I am one of the few fellars that the Haji trust to do things right. Never mind that we have hundreds, maybe thousands of followers. Is only a few of us know what is what, and don't have to have everything spell out for them when Haji say do this or do that. So I was down at the school early getting things ready. I organize the drummers from Morvant.

Them guys – two Indian and two Creole – could drum too bad, and they never take any pay. They realize that what Haji doing is for people like them, poor people in this country catching their *nenen* day in and day out under this government.

Just a few weeks before the rally, they raise prices on rice, sugar, and flour, and put a value added tax on school books. Imagine that! Staples. Things people need every day of their lives. And think about it. We growing sugar right in Santabella, you know. But hear what our government doing. It giving Guyana the sugar in exchange for rice, so they say. But guess what? Guyana send one shipload of rice to Santabella, and then claim the crop having trouble. But they lie! Haji have friends all over the Caribbean, South America, all over, friends in high-high places, and he find out that Guyana was exchanging the rice they should have sent to us for guns from Columbia.

And listen. It was really guns, not rice, that we government was getting from Guyana. Haji know all that. His main interest is in helping the people, so he set up his own network, and we going to take care of Santabellans. That is what he wanted to announce at the rally.

So I went up early to make sure everything in place. I couldn't stay for the speech, but I know what he was going to say. Rosehill was not the only place in Santabella we have plans for.

Haji has a habit of not arriving until after the rally start, after the crowd warm up, nuh. So he would drive about the village until the drums die down, and right at the end of the kaiso – and he always picked them carefully to signify the troubles in Santabella – right after the song stop, he would come on stage, and a local leader would introduce him.

That night, Sammy, a man who lost everything a few years back in the hurricane, and who the Haji was helping, was to introduce him. Before I leave, I give him the mike as Shadow's voice belt out the last line to his kaiso, which the crowd was chanting as well, "Poverty is Hell".

I had something important, as I say, to do that night that involved Bilal, Calu, and Sudix. Bilal went with me down the islands.

Talk about rough! The sea that night was so rough, even Calu, who could swim in any kind a water, had a hard time. But with the help of Allah, the Merciful, we get the job done. By the time them Coast Guard boats went out on their patrol, we had finished.

It was foreday morning by the time me and Bilal get back to the compound, and the rally was over. I was dead tired, so I stay at the compound until some of the people who went to the rally come back.

I hear that the police was at the rally in plain clothes, pretending to like what Haji was saying, clapping and all that. They could fool we? We know all their tricks. You have to remember that Haji use to be one of them, and he has a lot more intelligence than half that force. They even have some fellars from the Regiment in plain clothes, too. But we mark them long time.

Is common knowledge now, but then, most people didn't know that a lot of fellars in the Regiment was on our side. I not talking bout fellars low down the line. I mean near the top. Haji was a smart man, never forget that, and what he do, he didn't do for himself. He never wanted to be prime minister. But other people in Santabella could see their self in that position, and he just make use of their ambition.

I remember learning in school that ambition could kill you, you know. If what you want is mainly for yourself, with no regard for the people, then what you trying to do is exploit them.

Haji could see that kind of ambition in some of them army men, and he wasn't always easy with that. But we had was to use them for certain kind of things. So, like I say, when they send fellars from the Regiment to monitor what the Haji was saying at the rallies, or to listen in the mosque, them pretending they were believers, we already scoped them out. Long time.

NINETEEN

The morning after the Muslim rally in Rosehill, Miss Ann decided that before she went all the way down to Moruga where the roads, in this rainy season, were often flooded out, she would try one more thing, even if it went against her will.

She would go down to Ling's grocery to call Reme at work. She and Reme had never really been friends, not just because each suspected the other of having too much control over Beatrice, but more so because Kelvin, the man Reme claimed was Beatrice's father, had taken up with Miss Ann's sister.

According to Reme, the sister had met Kelvin at her house, and Reme had never forgiven her for what she believed was her encouragement of the affair. She had proclaimed her innocence of all such knowledge but she could not convince Reme, who had heard about gifts of clothes and shoes Kelvin had brought back for her from Florida where he went, as a temporary worker, to pick oranges in a place called Dundee.

All this Miss Ann had wrestled with during the early morning as Willy snored next to her, but she couldn't put a partition around that uneasiness. She would just have to accept that she and Reme would never be friends, but when it came to Beatrice, maybe Reme would be able to put aside her feelings. So she gathered up her coins and made her way to the phone booth outside Ling's grocery.

A child answered the phone, told her to wait, then Reme came on the line. Miss Ann identified herself.

Reme gasped, "Oh God, something happen to Beatrice?"

"No," Miss Ann tried to sound reassuring, "But I calling about herself."

Before Reme could interrupt, she hurried on. "Is about this Muslim thing, nuh. You know they had a rally up here last night?"

"What that has to do with Beatrice?" Reme demanded.

"Well that's what I come to tell you. I think she's planning to join up with them."

And over Reme's astonished "What?" she continued: "That Haji call her up in front of everybody to say how proud Rosehill should be bout her because of all the things she do for us, and how she was a hero and how school children should be reading bout her instead bout some Englishman named Walter Raleigh. He announced that he want her to be the Headmistress of the school they opening up here."

Into the quiet, Miss Ann asked, "You hearing me?"

"What Beatrice say?" Reme asked softly.

"She ent say yes or no, but I have a feeling she's going to do it. That man has a lot of charm, you know. You should a see how Rosehill people clapping for him. Beatrice too. Is a feeling I have that she's going to join them."

"So you calling to bother me about *your* feelings?" Reme's scorn reeked across the telephone line.

"I just think you should have a serious talk with her about those people. They always having trouble with the police. Beatrice don't need no more trouble. If Tante Vivian was still alive..."

But Reme had had enough.

"Why you don't mind your own damn business and leave my daughter to me?" And she slammed the receiver down so hard, Miss Ann jumped.

The noise echoed in her eardrum all the way back up the Hill, adding injury to her sense of dissatisfaction in her failure to turn Reme into an ally.

The woman too stupid for her own good, she decided. She can't see I just want what is best for Beatrice? Stupes. I shoulda just gone down Moruga.

This wasn't just about the school. Them Muslim could open all the school they want; she wasn't going to send her grandchildren there and she would see to it that none of Melda's children went either. But they were taking over the whole place. In no

112

time, Rosehill women would be walking round with their heads covered and long-long dresses dragging in the mud.

And that Sammy! Sammy! Who tell him to go and beg that man for help? She would fix him good. Just wait. He was bound to come to ask her to sell his crop of tomatoes and lettuce. She would turn her back on him. Let him take it down to those Muslims for them to sell. She was finished doing business with him, and she would stop Willy from playing All Fours with him on a Saturday. The gall of the man.

As for that Jestina, you couldn't put your head on a block for her. That woman was just like a damn windmill, turning this away and that, and besides, she was the one who had taken Beatrice to the rally. She was the one who was encouraging her to go away at a time when the children needed her.

Yes, Beatrice should go away. She wasn't trying to begrudge the girl a future. Her own daughter was in England. But not rightaway. But if she stayed, she would get involved with these Muslims...

Oh, she was so confused, she felt her head bursting with pain.

Concluding that it was all Jestina's fault, Miss Ann decided that when Jestina came to her parlour to collect her five loaves of hops bread, she would tell her that she'd sold out. Let she go and get bread by them Muslims for her children.

TWENTY

Unable to concentrate on her work after Miss Ann's phone call, Reme asked her Madam if she could have the afternoon off to take care of some family business concerning her daughter.

She wished she'd taken the previous night off, as she'd planned, but she'd kept hoping and hoping for the postman to come, and by the time he arrived, it was much too late for her to go to Rosehill. Besides, he hadn't brought what she was hoping for. But if only she'd gone, she would've been able to prevent Beatrice from making the biggest mistake of her life.

As she hurried through the laundry, then the cooking, making a custard for Mr. Ames and almost slicing off a finger as she made fruit salad for the children, she thought about the state of her relationship with Beatrice since the end of the case.

She could sum it up in one word. Tension.

Every time she had tried to talk to Beatrice about the future, Beatrice had gotten vexed. She had never been rude to the point of saying Reme should mind her own business, but the message was clear in her eyes.

But if it wasn't her business, whose was it? She wouldn't give up. She had to keep trying to get Beatrice to see the light; to see that in Santabella there was no hope for a good future. Even if a part of her felt that cocks would get teeth before she would be able to convince Beatrice of that, she had to keep on trying.

She knew that God was on her side when, just before she left, the postman handed her a letter from Sonny. The airmail envelope felt thick and she prayed, as she slit open the flap, that it contained the invitation letter she had begged Sonny to send.

Inside she found a handwritten page folded over a sealed

114

envelope addressed, in typed letters, to the Counsellor for Visas, American Embassy, Santabella. Pinned to the letter with a paper-clip was an international post office money-order for two hundred dollars.

With trembling fingers and a racing pulse, she read Sonny's letter to her, handwritten under an official letterhead she assumed was that of the law firm where he worked:

> *Dear Miss Reme,*
>
> *I can't tell you how glad I was to get your letter. I've been thinking about Beatrice, wondering what she was going to do now that the case was finished. I called Ali and he told me what happened. I wanted to write to Beatrice but she's still so vexed with me that she probably wouldn't have answered. I hope Uncle Willy gave you my message about why I had to do what I did. Sometimes, though, life doesn't turn out quite the way we planned it and now I have a son to think about. That doesn't mean that I don't have feelings for Beatrice, although I don't think she has anything but hard feeling for me. I will still help her all I can because no matter where I am, you all are my family. I'm enclosing a letter to the American Embassy. Have Beatrice read it first, and if it's okay, she can seal it and take it with her when she has her appointment. I've also enclosed a little something for you. I can never repay you for taking care of Moko after I left Rosehill, and for all the nice things you did for me when I was growing up.*
>
> *Please give my regards to Miss Jestina, Miss Melda, Uncle Willy and all the rest of them. At the top of this letter you'll see my office telephone number. Please be sure to give it to Beatrice so she can call me, if she wants to, when she gets to New York. I promise to do everything I can to help her get settled.*
>
> *Your loving godson,*
> *Sonny*

Reme slumped to her knees as tears of relief rolled down her cheeks.

Thank you Lord, thank you Lord, she cried, over and over again, until drained, she rose up, took off her uniform, slipped into her blue pique dress without stopping to iron it, passed a powder puff over her shiny forehead, grabbed her purse, and left for Rosehill.

She was halfway down the road, her hand raised to hail a taxi when she realized that she had left the other envelope with the letter to the Embassy, and the attached money order on her bed.

She wanted to dash back to her room for it but a taxi had stopped in front of her to let out a passenger, and with rain starting to drizzle, she decided she would give Beatrice the letter later. The important thing was that Sonny had said yes, he would help. He was still on their side. She would go to the embassy with Beatrice and they would have no trouble getting her the visa with Sonny's letter in their hands.

Getting to Rosehill took her longer than she'd hoped. In her haste she had neglected to take her umbrella and the midday rain trapped her under the Salvatore Building, opposite the taxi stand in town, for nearly two hours.

It poured down, warm and hard, causing the humidity to rise so that her bodice stuck to her arms and her chest. Pressed against other damp bodies under the narrow overhang, waiting for a lull so that she could cross the square to the taxi-stand, Reme thought of how much she hated the rainy season with its biting mosquitoes, insects crawling through every crevice, streets and roads with cargoes of rubbish, and the miserable stickiness of perspiration.

Knowing that thousands of poor people in Santabella desperately needed the free rain to fill their empty water tanks and barrels in the face of escalating costs of pipe-borne water did little to mitigate her despair. She could focus only on the negatives – clothes that wouldn't dry; roads you couldn't cross; and the sickly smell of overflowing sewers that made you want to throw up.

Where was the beauty in this country, she asked herself, as a large man, his mouth open to display two front teeth on either side of his upper gums, like football goalposts, pressed into her with a smile.

"Good evening Miss Experience," he said sweetly.

Caught between the insanity of his appearance and the intelligence of his greeting, all she could do was bend her head to stare down into her damp shoes, while her insides rocked with sudden laughter.

Miss Experience.

The lines on her forehead that she had only recently begun to notice, the black sacks under her eyes that she feared were a sign of high blood pressure, the forward bent of her shoulders as if, as Tante Vivian would have said, she had TB. All of it and some that she wasn't even aware of – but the man could clearly see – told of her miserable experience in this world.

Miss Experience indeed. For nothing, nothing had ever gone right for her. Not Kelvin, not all her hopes for Beatrice, all the money she had spent on her schooling wasted. Life, Reme decided, was like eating bitter cassava everyday until they put you in the grave.

And if Beatrice joined up with those Muslims, she'd better buy a spot alongside Tante Vivian's in the cemetery because she would rather be dead than see her only daughter covered up with a black hood and a long black dress dragging in the dirt and talking bout Allah this and Allah that.

As suddenly as the downpour had begun, it ended, and Reme slipped past the still leering man, leapt over several puddles, and made for the taxi stand, shoes soaking wet.

Beatrice, surprised to see her mother, left the iron on the board and went into her room for a towel so Reme could dry her damp hair. Coming back into the living room she paused to lower the volume on the American soap opera, *The Young and the Restless* that she had been watching as she ironed.

"I didn't know you was coming up today," she said. "I ent cook yet."

"I eat aw-ready," Reme said, which was untrue. She had been so vexed after Miss Ann's telephone call, and so excited after she received Sonny's letter, that she had clean forgotten to eat lunch.

But she was more thirsty than hungry so she asked Beatrice to bring her a Solo from the fridge.

Beatrice, certain that something important must have happened to cause her mother to leave her job in the middle of the day to come to Rosehill, but afraid to ask what it was, even as she suspected that it had something to do with her, took a little time in the kitchen to prepare her mood.

Because she had promised herself she would try to be patient with Reme, she forced down the anger that had begun to build inside her chest with the growing suspicion that Reme had come to harass her again to leave Santabella.

With more care than was necessary, she poured the red liquid into a glass she held tilted so that the foam would not overflow, then she opened the freezer for a tray of ice cubes, tapped three cubes out of the tray before returning it to the fridge, dropped the cubes into the glass, before searching for a paper napkin to wrap around its base to keep the condensation from leaving a mark on the centre table.

On the way in the taxi, Reme had discarded several approaches before she had settled on a strategy of how to tell Beatrice about the invitation letter from Sonny. She knew Beatrice would get vexed if she told her that she had written to him to beg for the letter. The girl had too much false pride. She would just have to leave out that part.

She'd tell her that Sonny had written to say that he had heard from Mr. Ali that the case was finished, and that because he knew Beatrice had always wanted to come up to America, he was sending the invitation letter for her to take to the embassy.

Beatrice handed her mother the drink and went back to the ironing board.

Reme said, "I hear from Sonny."

Beatrice turned the knob on the iron to its highest heat level, and turned up the volume of *The Young and The Restless*.

Reme said, "I talking to you, Beatrice. Have some manners and turn off the TV, nuh."

Beatrice set the iron on its base, went back over to the television and turned it off. She studiously avoided looking at Reme as she returned to the ironing board.

Reme said, "You hear what I say? Sonny write me."

Beatrice really wanted to say, "What that have to do with me?" Instead, she said, "About Uncle Moko?" knowing full well that Sonny usually wrote directly to the nursing home where his father was living.

"No, Beatrice. He write me bout you."

Beatrice blew air from her nostril and a humm sound escaped her closed lips.

"Apparently he was keeping in touch with Ali all during the case," Reme said, ignoring Beatrice's sign of disgust, "and Ali tell him how it end up."

"That's good." Beatrice had decided she would keep her tone as neutral as possible and ask no more questions.

"You remember how, before he went away the first time, Sonny say he was going to send for you, Beatrice?"

Beatrice took up a bottle and began to squirt water from it on to a white blouse. Squish, squish. She knew where her mother was headed.

"You know I never believe Sonny, Beatrice, but the boy prove me wrong. He come back to help you out with the case. Is true he had to go back to America before it call, but I have to give him his due because he keep in touch with Ali all the while and once he hear that the case done, he send down the letter for you. He keep his promise, Beatrice. As God is love, he send down the invitation letter for you to take to the embassy to get the visa."

Reme had said all this is a rush, her eyes on her daughter, while her thoughts raced along a parallel line of prayer, that Oh God the girl would see sense, please Father.

Beatrice ran the iron over the blouse a few times, not looking at her mother.

Reme said, "You hear what I tell you, Beatrice? You listening to me?"

Beatrice turned the blouse over to the back side before she answered. "I don't need no letter from Sonny." Her voice was calm, even.

Reme flung the towel onto the floor and rose up, arms akimbo, ready to do battle.

"What you mean you don't need no letter from Sonny," she mocked Beatrice's tone.

"How you going to get a visa without one, eh, tell me that. Is hard enough with your name in the papers with the case and all that, you think the Americans just giving way visas to any and everybody? You know damn well you must have a letter from somebody in America to say they will be responsible for you. A-A. Look my crosses, nuh. The boy so kind to send you the letter and you want to spit on it. You going mad with all this Muslim

119

business I hear you getting involved with?" There, it had slipped out and she couldn't get it back. She had told herself and told herself that she was not going to mention anything about the Muslims but there, it was out and she knew it was only going to make the girl more vexed on top of all this talk about Sonny and going to America. Oh Lord, put a hand. She slumped back into the chair.

Beatrice rested the iron on its base, slipped the blouse onto a wooden hanger, hung it on a peg behind the door to her bedroom, all the while biting her lips and swallowing hard.

Reme, in a sad, pleading voice, "It's bad manners not to answer people when they talking to you, Beatrice."

Beatrice drew up Tante's rocking chair in front of Reme. She reached for her mother's hands, and clasped them in hers, still warm from the heat of the iron.

"I don't need the letter from Sonny, Ma, " she said gently. "I don't need it because I get the visa already."

Reme's mouth opened and closed without a word as Beatrice continued, "I was going to tell you this weekend. I went down a few days ago and I didn't have any trouble at all. They give me an extended visa for ten years."

She rubbed the blue veins on Reme's rough hands. "I could go anytime I want."

Reme withdrew her hands to brush away the tears rolling down her cheeks. "Praise God. Praise God," she murmured, as Beatrice reached for the towel to wipe her mother's face.

TWENTY-ONE

A few days after the rally, Haji send me up Rosehill to see how the work on the new school going. I was in town when he call, so instead of going down to the compound to get one of the cars, I decide to take a taxi.

I am not a man for reading horoscopes and all that kind of hocus-pocus thing, but I just happen to jump in a Rosehill taxi with this lady who was making jokes with the driver about her horoscope.

She said she was an Aries – my sign – and she had read the prediction in the newspaper that morning, and it say this was her lucky day.

The driver ask her, "So you win plenty money?" and all of us other passengers expect her to laugh and say no, but we get a shock when she answer yes. A piece of land she was trying to sell for over a year and couldn't because of all kind of confusion with another family member whose name was on the deed, well, the family member drop down dead, didn't leave no will, so now she could get the land sell. It was like winning a lottery because the land was near the sea, and it could sell for plenty money.

It make me a little uncomfortable that she should profit from a dead man, and if it was me, when I sell that land, I would give some of the proceeds to the man's wife and children if he had any, but this wasn't my business so I keep my mouth shut before the lady cuss me out.

I was hoping though, that since I was Aries too, something good was going to happen to me that day.

After I see everything was going okay at the school, I stop by my Tante Melda's house. It just so happen that Beatrice was there. As soon as she see me come into the yard, she try to get up and leave, but Tante Melda tell her since she didn't have any fowls to feed, she might as well stay.

She introduce us, and although is not the correct thing for Muslim men to touch women like that, I stick out my hand to shake hers.

You know how people does say that they meet a person and, just like that, thunderbolt strike them and they know, this is the one? Well, Pappy, I touch that girl's hand and something hit me, wham! Like some kind of chemical reaction vibrating through my body.

I don't even remember how long I was just standing there, holding her hand, staring at her – I don't even remember saying anything – before I hear Tante Melda asking me if I was laglie, why I sticking to the girl's hand so.

I was staring at her, not saying anything. Cat got my tongue, man. Is not correct to talk about how a woman look before marrying her, but after that one day, Beatrice face engraved in my mind.

I had to say something, so she could see that I wasn't no tie-tongue stupidy, so I ask her how she liked what Haji had to say.

Before she could answer, Tante Melda tell her, "He's Haji's right hand man, you know, so be careful what you say about his speech. I don't want no Muslim trouble in my yard, cause with this one, religion thicker than blood."

"I'm not afraid of any Muslim." Beatrice look me straight in the face.

I tell her, "Why people in this country always put the word fear and Muslim in the same sentence? What we do so in this country? We ever do anything to hurt you or anybody you know? Muslim or no Muslim, we treat everybody like family."

"What you all doing is none of my business." And Beatrice shrug her shoulders. "Anyhow, you asked about the speech, but it wasn't really a speech. It was more like a talk, and it was mainly about the new school he's putting up here."

Then, as if to emphasize a point, she add, "I don't have any problem with what he had to say or with what he's doing, except that he expects me to get involve. I don't know where he get the idea that I want to have anything to do with his school. He has a lot of brass, I could tell you that."

"Haji can be a little hard, sometimes," I tell her. "I hear that he make the announcement that you would be the headmistress. That's because he knows you're a good teacher and that you used to run the school. I hope you didn't mind him too much."

She didn't answer anything negative, so I decide to press my luck.

"So if I invite you to come down to the mosque you could talk to him about it. Maybe this Friday?"

Tante Melda was sitting across from me. I could see her rolling her eyes, shaking her head, skinning up her face and Beatrice must have sensed something because she turned to Tante and ask her, "You think if I go a certain person will pelt me down with big stones?"

I thought she was talking about her mother. A lot of parents, when their daughters first join up the Muslims, they feel betrayed, especially if they're Catholic. Some of them throw out their children from the house, all kinds of things like that. We had to find places for a lot of the young ladies to live.

Is a funny thing. Those girls could dress up in all kind of shorty-short clothes, walk half-naked in the street with their belly pomp out, and the parents ent saying nothing. Let them join the Muslims, put on a long dress or cover their heads, and is as if they commit a felony. Is that kind of backwardness we having to deal with in Santabella.

Anyhow, back to Beatrice. She and Tante Melda start laughing about this Miss Ann who I find out is the lady who own the parlour down the Hill. She was worried that Beatrice going to join we. So I ask them if Miss Ann was the boss lady of Rosehill, how she get to the point where she could control what Rosehill people do.

Beatrice was looking at me. I know she could tell that I was just prouging her but she's a woman like a challenge, so she asked me, "What time Friday?"

Tante Melda groaned, "Oh God, now I dead! Why all-you want to bring Miss Ann's wrath down on my head? Abdul, when you gone back down in that compound with Haji, is I have to contend with Miss Ann, you know. The woman not easy."

Beatrice was laughing at the way Tante was holding her head and groaning. "That's what you get for making me stay here when I should be back in my yard hanging out clothes," she said, before asking me what time they should come to the mosque.

So she was serious.

"We?" Tante Melda flare up. "Who you talking bout? I say I going down there? Police raiding that place morning, noon and night. You think I want to end up in jail?"

"Listen to yourself," Beatrice tell her. "Since when we have to be 'fraid to go in a place where people worship? You see what this country's coming to? You can't walk in the Botanic Gardens; you can't walk down Frederick Street with a gold chain round your neck; you can't do this; you can't do that. This is why we get independence? This is why we have Black people in power? If this is the case, is best I leave this country in truth."

"You don't have to leave." I could see she was getting vex, her eyes opened wide, her face serious-serious. "These are the very things Haji trying to change. Wait. You will see. This is we country. We have to make it better, even if we pass through hell to do it. None of us can enter Paradise without catching some hell."

"Paradise?" Tante Melda was getting really upset. This Miss Ann must have some serious power in Rosehill. "Paradise? Ent that where they have a whole lot of snakes tempting people to turn bad?"

I try to laugh it off, just to lighten her spirits, even though there was some truth in what she saying. "But it have apples, and nice fruits in Paradise, and for the men, a whole lot of virgins."

"Ummm-humm, I know that's why all-yuh young fellars following Haji. Just like Miss Ann say. Is only women all-yuh want."

"Well if that is what you think following Allah in this island mean," I tell her, as I get up to leave, "is best you don't come to the mosque. But what about you, Miss Beatrice? You believe the same thing? You among the disbelievers?"

She shake her head; eyes on Tante. Hard.

Tante Melda take up a hammer and bring it down on a dry coconut, brakat! Brown shell scatter all over the yard.

"Okay! Okay!" I laugh. "I know I have a coconut head, but why you have to treat your one nephew so bad, eh? You don't want me to fix your kitchen cupboards any more?"

That got her. "I guess is a price we have to pay for everything," she grumble as she start chewing on a piece of the coconut meat. "Even with your own flesh and blood. What time we should come? I'm not spending no whole day down there."

I tell her to come about quarter to one so I could show them the compound before prayers start at one, then, without looking at Beatrice, I went through the gate, but I could feel her staring at me, and I was wondering what she thinking. I know what was on my mind.

Up till then, love was only something I use to see in theatre shows, but something happen to me that day that I had never in my life feel before. It was excitement, fear, all mix up together. I could feel my back straightening up, my chest thumping. I didn't know how I was going to wait until that Friday to see her again.

TWENTY-TWO

The following Friday morning Beatrice woke up praying for a day full of rain. What had she gotten herself into? Why had she promised she would go to the mosque? She knew Abdul was trying to get under her skin, just like that Haji when he had made a big announcement, without even consulting her, that he wanted her to run the Muslim school.

These men were too boldface. They took for granted that she would do what they expected. But knowing that, why hadn't she told him to go to hell?

The voice that answered gave her the reason she didn't want to accept. Haji. You know you want to see him again. Admit it, Beatrice. You like the man.

Oh, God, she prayed, let the rain come, please.

God wasn't listening.

The sun, defying its duty to the rainy season to stay behind heavy clouds, came out in all its glory to style its big bold self over Rosehill, giving the people morning glory under which they could dry their damp clothes or walk down the road to the corner without mud sticking to their shoes.

Listless and disappointed, Beatrice wandered about the house after breakfast, with nothing much to do. She had cleaned, washed, and ironed with a vengeance all week. Tante Vivian's mahogany flooring – she still thought of the house as Tante Vivian's even though her great aunt had left it to her in her will two years before – was shining, and a new brassiere and two pair of panties with frills on the edge were neatly folded into her new suitcase.

Her passport with the stamped American visa, and six hundred

American dollars, for which she had cleaned out her account at Barclays Bank, were tied into a white linen handkerchief and tucked into her pillow.

She had opted to take the last hand in the susu Jestina ran. With that money, she could buy her airplane ticket to go away. As Jestina would say, matters fix. So why, why was she holding back?

She should be excited to be leaving, to go to America, a country any Santabellan would give their right arm to reach. Not only Santabellans. She'd heard on the radio about Haitians risking their lives to cross the sea on rafts to get to Miami. One report said that some evil men had taken the Haitians' money, and then dumped them overboard in the middle of the sea.

Cubans were riding on pieces of wood strung together to get to America. Yet here she was, dilly-dallying.

The situation was so dread calypsonians had begun to sing about it, calling Santabella and all the islands people were trying to escape, sinking ships.

> *To see how we country suffering*
> *Pass by the embassy any morning*
> *Is people like peas you goin' to see*
> *Massa leh me go to your country*
> *Help me escape this misery.*
> *So much people trying to run*
> *From these islands in the sun*
> *Is only the dead and the sick staying*
> *From Puerto Rico to Port of Spain*
> *Only corbeaux will get to feed*
> *The only food left is the bread the devil knead.*

In spite of its dismal story, Santabellans, and people all up and down the islands, had made the calypso a road march hit, dancing to it on Carnival day as if the dance itself was a cleansing ritual for the dread they lived every day.

People, the ship is sinking, Even the rats leaving, they had sung in chorus.

That's what I would be, Beatrice thought, one of those rats, if I leave Santabella, because in spite of all the hardships, she loved her country. Loved it even more as she thought of Haji and his people and what they could do if they had a chance. So maybe she should go down to the mosque, not to join up or anything like that, but just to hear what the man had to say.

"Beatrice! You there!" Melda shouted as she came through the gate.

Beatrice opened the front door to let her in, drenched in perspiration, fanning her wet face with a piece of newspaper.

"Lordy, Lord, girl," she slumped her wide body into a Morris chair. "I must be getting old. Meh two knees hurting me too bad, girl, just walking up the hill."

Beatrice handed her a fresh towel. "Why you have on that long-long dress on this hot day?"

Melda pulled the dress over her knees, began to fan her thighs, as she spoke between deep intakes of breath. "Girl, I get up this morning, and I say the best thing for me to do is to go to the mosque. I need some prayers mehself. Lemme go get a blessing from the Haji."

"So you not frightened Miss Ann will ban you from her parlour?"

"Stop talking foolishness and get ready, Beatrice. Why you not dressed? Is after eleven. And you know you have to cover your legs, right? So put on some long pants. What you have in the fridge to drink?"

Beatrice started toward the kitchen but Melda said, "Girl, go and put on your clothes. I could get the drink mehself," and she lumbered into the kitchen, took a glass from the cupboard, filled it with ice, and opened a red sweet drink.

She had to wait several minutes while the fizz evaporated so she looked around the kitchen, pleased that Beatrice was doing such a good job keeping the place in tack. Maybe, she thought, she'll rent it out when she goes away. That way, her daughter, Princetta, could leave that nasty man who was always beating her up, and come and live in Rosehill.

She called out to Beatrice, "I tell Clyde to come and pick us up by twelve. Is hard like hell to get a taxi in town to go down by the mosque since that big highway build near the sea. You ready?"

Still dressed in the shift she had been wearing all morning, but holding a pair of white slacks and a blue blouse, Beatrice came into the kitchen.

"I really don't think I should go down there," she shook her head. "I just don't feel right about it."

"A-A. But what the rass-arse I hearing? Is you self stand there looking vexed at me when I was telling Abdul I didn't want to go. After all that, I say okay, you seem to want to go, so I will go with you. After all that you come saying you not going? Girl, put your clothes on. What you fraid? We just going to hear the man preach. And I need to make sure Abdul coming to do the cupboards, next week. Woodlice eating out them old things in my kitchen. He's a good carpenter, you know."

"I never tell you I was going, and I didn't tell him so either."

Melda's eyes opened wide, her lips pulled back in disbelief. "But you shake your head when he asked you. Come on, Beatrice. You tell him you going to come." She cocked her ears. "Listen, that's not Clyde's old car chugging up the road? Put your clothes on. Come on, Bee."

Beatrice let out a puff of air, shrugged her shoulders in defeat, and went back to her bedroom to change into the long pants and a blouse that came nearly to her knees. She grabbed a scarf to cover her head as Clyde pumped his horn.

Miss Ann was leaning over her gate, chatting with Mr. Roberts, as Clyde's taxi went past. If she saw the top of Melda's head – for Melda had slid her body low down in the seat – she said nothing, but she certainly saw Beatrice sitting up front in the passenger seat, staring straight ahead.

TWENTY-THREE

As Clyde's taxi approached the compound, Beatrice peered at the white painted fence, and just beyond it, mounds of dirt on which children – girls with their heads covered, and boys in black pants and cream shirts – were playing. That's where the police must have been digging for guns, she thought, but said nothing.

Behind the dirt hills she could see a cream and green building that she knew, from television photographs, to be the elementary school the Haji had erected, and for which the government was refusing to donate any funds on the claim that it was a private enterprise. A claim, Haji had been quick to note, that applied to at least ten schools in the country run by the Catholic Church, which were the recipients of millions of dollars each year from that same government.

Clyde drove his taxi through the opened gates of the compound, and having deposited Beatrice and Melda at steps leading up to an open shed, drove off with a wave to Melda who was shouting to him to come back for them at three.

A man, dressed in black, his head tied with the Yassah scarf, led them through the shed toward Abdul who, he said, was busy in the back. In spite of the slight breeze, the air was thick with humidity. Beatrice could feel sweat dripping down her forehead, sliding down her eyelids, but she'd forgotten to bring a handkerchief, and had to use the back of her hand to wipe her face.

On one side of the shed, the entrance to the mosque, she noticed a concrete drain over which were two standpipes where, Melda whispered, the faithful had to cleanse themselves before talking to Allah.

She wanted, badly, to wash her face at the taps, but had to

follow Melda and the man toward the far end of the shed. Three old women, one barefooted, her busted sandals on the ground below her feet, were sitting on a bench. One was writing furiously with a pencil on a scrap of paper. Just beyond her was a notice board with various announcements.

The old woman called to the man: "Brother man, he come yet?"

The man answered, "No, Mammy. I promise I will come and get you as soon as he reach."

One hand braced on the bench, the old woman tried to stand up on thin, rickety legs, to pass the note to the man.

The man reached out to grab her from falling. "Let me get you a sweet drink, Mammy." He sat her carefully onto the bench, then motioned to Beatrice and Melda to wait. Melda strolled off to peek into the mosque as Beatrice read the notice board.

> **Say No to Alcohol and Gambling,**
> **The Qur'an 2-219.**
> WE the willing
> led by the unknowing
> are doing the impossible
> for the ungrateful.
> We have done so much
> for so long
> With so little, we are
> now qualified to do
> anything with nothing.

The man returned with a glass bottle of orange liquid and a small white paper bag stained with oil. Beatrice could smell curry.

He handed the bag, the drink and two paper napkins to the old women. Their faces broke out in crinkly smiles.

"I know all-yuh waiting long," he told them. "But you know how things is with the Haji. Is plenty people he has to take care of, you know. But he's coming just now, and I promise all-you up first."

Then he led Melda and Beatrice round the back of the shed to where Abdul was coming out of a white painted brick building.

Abdul greeted his aunt with a slight bow and Melda giggled at his formality.

Beatrice noted the crispness of his long white tunic, his polished black boots, the head scarf with one end hanging slightly over the right side of his forehead. Face clean-shaven, eyes alight. She thought he was pretty good-looking.

"Ah salaam Allah kum," he smiled at her, bowing deeply. "Haji ask to bring you to the office about two-thirty. You could stay?"

"I tell Clyde to come for us round three," Melda said. "We have a lil' time, eh Bee?"

"You have more changes than a lizard," Beatrice told her. "Is not you who say we not staying here long?"

"Well we here already," Melda grinned. "Might as well see what the Haji could do for me."

"You and a whole lot more." Beatrice pointed with her chin to women, many of them elderly, sitting on stools and benches near the mosque, anxiety riding the ridges along their foreheads.

Abdul said, "Is like this every day as God send. People have no where else to turn. Is 'Haji do this'; 'Haji help me, please. Haji, help meh son, meh daughter'. If is not one thing, is a next. And he can't say no to any of them."

"Well, he must have a big account at Barclays," Melda said.

"Is by the grace of Allah we do these things," Abdul said solemnly, then waved his hand towards several women who were busy taking food and fruits out of baskets to place on tables before them. "Sister Joyce has some nice roti. Let me buy you all one, nuh?"

"One roti? For two grown women?" Melda's voice held laughing astonishment.

"You miss a key word in the sentence, Tante." Abdul smiled. "*All*. Come on."

By the time he had led them to Sister Joyce's table, he had pleated his tunic, and reached into the pockets of his black pants to retrieve several dollar bills.

He offered the woman the Arabic greeting and she responded, "Salaam Allah kum, brother," with a nod to Melda and Beatrice.

He told her Melda was his aunt. Before he could introduce Beatrice, Sister Joyce said, "I know who you is," and she rested the knife she had been using to slice a sponge cake into thin wedges, to shake Beatrice's hand.

"Put way your money, brother. What you'd like?" she asked Beatrice.

"Girl," Melda grinned. "You famous as Amos. I travelling everywhere with you from now on."

But Abdul, holding out the bills to the woman, was protesting. "I can't let you do that, Sister Joyce. Flour too expensive these days." In spite of her protests, he slipped the bills into a coffee can that contained a few coins.

With chicken rotis in their hands – Beatrice's with extra pepper sauce and Melda's with a big spoon of mango chutney – they moved over to another woman selling soft drinks. Something about her seemed familiar to Beatrice, but only her hands and eyes were visible as she was covered from head to ankles in a flowered garment.

Abdul greeted her, "Salaam Allah kum, Sister Fareeda. What you have cold today?"

Beatrice thought, Sister Fareeda? No. The woman she knew was named Clare Barrow. They had been to Bishop's together. Clare always took first in maths. Bound for Oxford University she was, with a scholarship to boot.

Abdul was saying, "You should get to know these ladies, sister. They from Rosehill. They could probably tell you something about the children who'll be going to the school."

"I already know Beatrice." The woman nodded. "We went to school together."

Beatrice could see the fabric covering her mouth expand as she laughed. "Yes, Beatrice."

Her eyes wide in astonishment, Beatrice said "Clare? Clare Barrow?" Her thoughts were asking, *What the hell I seeing at all? Clare?*

"Yes, Beatrice, it's me," Clare voice almost sang in confirmation.

"You have any juice?" Melda interrupted them. "All that sweet drink does give me gas."

As she handed a plastic bottle of orange juice to Melda, Abdul said, "Sister Fareeda squeezed that with her own hands this morning, you know. Is only fresh-fresh juice she sells. And mauby, ginger beer, peanut punch. I'll take a peanut punch. Miss Beatrice, what you taking?"

Why did he insist on calling her Miss Beatrice. Was it some Muslim rule?

Melda was saying in a mocking voice, "Miss Beatrice, my roti's getting cold. Cold curry gives me gas, you know. Get your juice and let we go and sit down under that tree in the shade."

Still wondering what could have led Clare not only to abandon her scholarship to Oxford, but become involved with these Muslims, Beatrice indicated that she would like orange juice.

Abdul took the food from her hands and from Melda's, then nestled two plastic bottles of Fareeda's juice in the crook of his right arm, before leading them to the bench under the guava tree.

Watching him go back to Fareeda's table for his peanut punch, Beatrice decided she liked him. He had good manners. He carried himself well.

Melda took in her gaze. "He went to the Royal College, you know. One good head on his shoulders, I can verify that. I don't know what he doing taking up carpentry and all that kind a thing. Waste of brains if you ask me."

"But you still want him to come and fix your cupboards, right?" Beatrice asked her.

"You know what I mean, Bee."

"Not really." Beatrice didn't quite understand why she was being argumentative since she knew Melda was right. Anyone lucky enough to have gotten to go to one of the best secondary schools in the country was supposed to be more than a carpenter, but she couldn't help herself.

"Just because he want to the RC he can't be a carpenter? He should go to America and become a lawyer? Everybody is not like Sonny you know. Thank god for that."

Melda slowly wiped her greasy fingers on a tissue as she looked at Beatrice under hooded lids, questions swirling though her mind. What was up with Beatrice? Why did she have to argue about a little comment like that? Was she still vexed about Sonny? Was she getting interested in Abdul?

He was back with his drink. "Haji should be here soon. The office full of people waiting for him since early morning. But I know he want to see you, Miss Beatrice."

Vehicles rumbled into the yard.

"He's here," Abdul announced, and there was such happiness in his voice his declaration was a song.

Beatrice stared at him in surprise as he stood up, fidgeting with his clothing, barely able to stand still, as three jeeps and a blue car in between swept into the compound. Men in army-style clothes leaped out to surround Haji as he strolled toward his office. Two women, one Beatrice recognized as Farouka, followed him.

"I have to go." Abdul threw the bottle, still nearly full, into a bin, and rose.

As she watched him hurry away to join the group, Beatrice could still hear echoes of his eagerness, the joy in his voice, and wondered, again, what it was in Haji that made men, and women, so devoted to him.

What was he giving these people? What would make Clare give up her promising future to become a member of this group?

As if to compound her questions, hundreds of men, women and children began to enter the compound from maxi-taxis and private cars, to join others emerging from building in the rear of the shed, all headed toward the standpipes to wash faces and feet, the women to pull coverings over their heads, before entering the mosque.

Fareeda came over to lead her and Melda through the ritual of washing.

Beatrice pulled her scarf from her handbag and tied her head. She noticed that Melda had brought a scarf with lions and tigers on it, which she wound about her head like a pad, as if she was getting ready to carry a basket of food, or water from the river.

About half-an-hour later, they joined the women and girls lined against the back wall to wait yet another fifteen minutes before Haji entered, again with his retinue of soldiers.

He ascended what Beatrice would have called a dais to look over the heads of what must have been three or four hundred men arranged in an arch in front of him.

As he took a microphone from a man dressed as a soldier, Fareeda whispered to Beatrice, "The prayers are called *namaaz*. Just follow what I do."

Beatrice found herself going down on her knees, her face touching the floor, rising back up with palms raised, then down

135

again, as the Haji called out prayers in what Fareeda said was Arabic, to which the people responded in Arabic.

In a glance to her right, she saw Melda sitting with her feet folded beneath her, her head bowed as if in prayer.

Haji began to speak again in English in what Beatrice assumed was his sermon. First, he welcomed all those who were new to the mosque, and those who were visiting, "enemies working for the government, and friends as well, because this is a house of prayer, a house of peace, where all hearts are clean."

In a voice that rose and dipped as it moved from standard English to native Santabellan, he went on to exhort the young men and women to live clean lives, to obey the Qur'an, to listen to the voices of their elders so that they would receive the gifts that came to the faithful.

"Is a lot of ugly things happening in this country. Look at what the government decide to do. The government announce, just this morning, that it intends to spend half a million dollars, let meh repeat that for you, half a million dollars, to put up a statue in the middle of the Savannah. And who is this statue of? Is it of one of the leaders of this country who brought us out of coloni-alism? No!

"But maybe the government can't honour that man – and I don't have to call his name because you all know his name – maybe the government knows full well that this country is only a quarter-mile away from colonialism – that we are in a state of neo-colonialism, so they can't be brass-face as to celebrate the end to colonialism with a statute to that man, hard as he worked for this country.

"Okay, not him. What about the great Stokeley – all yuh know he changed his name to Kwame Toure, right – a born Caribbean man who went to America to fight for civil rights for Black people. And not just Civil Rights, for the right to live like anybody else, with the hopes and dreams of all that is possible like any white man or woman in America.

"You think we could erect a statue to him? No! The man can't even set foot in this country! They ban him from coming home. If his family dead, they wouldn't even allow him to come to the funeral. Statue? They'll put a bullet in his head first.

"So if not a political leader, who? How about a statue of a great leader of the poor workers in this country. A man who represents the thousands of men and women who, since the time of their great-grandparents, have slaved away in the sugarcane fields of this country. No, that would make too much sense, and besides, as the government sees it, poor workers don't need no statue.

"Well, you know, I agree with them to a certain extent. What poor people, the vast majority of ordinary people in Santabella need – and you tell me if this is a lie – is good health care, nurses and doctors and medicine in hospitals.

"What the poor in Santabella need is good schools, and what they need is good jobs. Ah, but they have good jobs, right? A ten-days here, cutting bush at the side of the road – and this is not to insult you brothers and sister here who do that work. It putting bake and margarine on the table, but when you all going to get jobs that last for more than ten days a month so you could eat bread and butter?

"Well, looks like you all have to wait a little bit longer because this government has decided it is more important to build a statue of a woman who has never done a thing for this country.

"If one of you here knows of a single act of generosity from this woman – and I don't have to call her name because all of you know who I'm talking about, her name has been in the papers day in and day out because she's involved with certain government ministers, who as we all know, have taken a lot of money out of this country to build mansions in Miami – but if anybody here can name one good thing this woman has done for poor people in this country, I want you to come forward and take this mike from me, and tell us what that is… I waiting…"

Nobody, not even the children near Beatrice, stirred.

Haji continued: "I don't have to lie to any of you about the state of this country. You see it yourselves; you feel it in yuh bellies. Look how many hundreds of people we feed in this compound every day? People coming from south, from the east, from the farthest reaches of this island to this compound every day to ask me to help them.

"They bypassing the government offices and coming here.

Why? Because they know that the only people who getting help in those offices are the friends and family of people working there, or the ones who take bribes.

"What I want to know is who bribe who to get a statue costing, by government figures, half a million dollars, put up in the heart of the city to insult poor people as they make their way to this compound for help.

"I tell you this: A lot of things this government do make me vexed. They ransacked this compound. I vexed; you vexed, but Allah gives us patience to deal with the wicked.

"They shoot down our people, yes, that young woman who they killed recently, as some of you know, she was a police officer they shoot. They claimed they do it by accident when they went to catch some criminals. Killed by the crossfire, they say, but we know better. Well, she was one of our people. One of us. A good Muslim woman. I know her since she was a small girl. Now they killed her, and force her parents to let them give her a state funeral. She was a Muslim. We should have buried her.

"I get vexed, but Allah give me patience to deal with these people. Sometimes, patience could run out. Sometimes, you have to look at it as a sign from Allah to act. This beat all. This take the cake.

"I want you all to think about these things as you make your way back to work, school, to your homes.

"Think about who this government really represents in this country.

"Think about the value added tax they impose on school books for your children.

"Think about the last time you were able to go a dentist and get a tooth filled or a doctor and get a plaster to put on a cut without having to pay your last dollar.

"Think about these things.

"But don't just think about it. I don't want your brains to burst.

"Talk to your neighbours about it. Talk to people in the taxis about it. And tell them, when the time come, they have to stand up with us. Because they all benefiting.

"A ship, loaded with medical supplies, coming soon. We have books for your children – free books, and any mother who can't afford to buy school uniforms, come to me. No matter where your children in school, we will help you get their uniforms.

"Help is on its way for those who believe.

"Remember the story of David and Goliath? Allah does not like corruption. In the name of Allah, the Merciful, the Beneficent, from whom flows all blessings in this life and in Paradise, help is on the way."

Then he added words in Arabic.

The people rose, responded in Arabic, and began to greet each other as Haji and a group of stern-faced men moved swiftly out of the mosque toward his office.

Out in the shed, as she joined Melda to put back on their shoes, Beatrice could still hear Haji's voice resounding in her head.

"You see Sammy?" Melda nudged her.

Beatrice shook her head.

"He was with the men up front near the Haji. A-A. I didn't realize that Sammy was so serious about this Muslim thing. I thought he just went to the Haji for help with the school. But look my crosses, nuh. Just wait till Miss Ann hear this. But if Sammy could join, then we better think of joining up too, eh Bee? Maybe the Haji could get we a work."

"I have a job already, remember?" Beatrice answered, but she did so distractedly, her head down, her thoughts still on Haji's words.

She could feel anger beginning to rise up in her as she thought of the money the government was willing to spend on the statue when even the main road through Rosehill still needed to be paved, not to mention the school that was still to be rebuilt.

She knew he was right about government ministers stealing money from the Treasury to build mansions in Miami. She had worked at the Treasury after the hurricane.

She had seen what was happening to the money from oil and gas explorations even as Santabellans tried to piece back their devastated lives. He was right. The man was telling the truth, and Santabellans, if only they would open their ears, should join up with him to make things better for themselves.

Yes, she could see why Clare, who, when they were at school, was always writing essays about what independence for the West

Indies should really mean, and winning prizes for them, she could see how Clare would be a part of this movement.

Out of the corner of her eye, she saw Abdul beckoning her. She looked around for Melda, but she was off talking to a woman, so Beatrice straightened her blouse, pulled the scarf a little lower over her forehead, and went to meet Abdul at the door of the Haji's office, its waiting area crammed with women and children, some dressed in *abayas* and *hijabs*, all waiting quietly.

Abdul led her past them to the guard at the inner door.

TWENTY-FOUR

What had she expected? Not to be left alone with him, that's for sure, after Abdul led her gently into the spacious office. She'd thought that one of his wives, maybe Farouka, the one who had come to see her in Rosehill, would be there. Or one of the others. She was curious about those women. In the mosque, she had looked around her but had not recognized any of them from pictures she had seen in the newspapers. So many of the women had their faces covered that she wouldn't have been able to make them out anyway.

Haji was alone, and when he rose from behind a large mahogany desk, for a second she didn't quite know if she should be looking up at him, down at the papers on his desk, or the far wall. Her eyes strayed to the plant hanging at the window behind him. It was one she'd seen in Mother Dinah's yard. Tante Vivian had said it brought good luck.

He must have indicated something to Abdul, for the door closed softly behind her. Haji pointed to one of two chairs near her.

"Sit, please, Miss Salandy," and waited until she had done so before he resumed his seat.

Panic zinged through her. What was she there for? What did he want to say to her? What did she want to say to him?

Nothing! She had nothing to say to him. It was Melda who'd wanted to talk to the man, not her! But even as she thought it, she knew it was a lie. She did want to see him. The man was like a magnet. No wonder all these…

He cut into her thoughts.

"So you've made up your mind about the school?" He said it

as a question, and she relaxed a little. Maybe he wasn't as presumptuous as she had thought.

She shrugged her shoulders in what she hoped was a noncommittal response.

A half-smile played on his face. He shook his head as if he knew this was a game she was playing and he would play along.

"So. You don't think it will be best for Roseshill's children to have a headmistress from the area? Somebody who used to teach them. Somebody who have their best interest at heart?"

So that's it, she thought. The man thinks he can guilt-trip me. He was no better than Miss Ann.

"It have a lot of people on Rosehill who has the children's interests at heart. And, they could teach." All this came out more rudely than she had intended.

"Name one," he challenged her.

"Miss Melda. Miss Jestina. Even Miss Ann could do it." But even as she rattled off the names, she knew she was standing on hollow ground.

"I'm not talking about nursery school here, Miss Salandy. And I'm surprised to hear you mention those names. We want teachers qualified so that these children could pass the Common Entrance Examinations with flying colours. These women you mention. They went to secondary school? That Miss Ann. She finished elementary? I'm not casting aspersions on her, but how's she going to teach children mathematics? It's not one and one make eleven we're talking about here."

He was right. She knew that, and the awareness made her feel foolish. And vexed. She snapped, "What about my interest? Eh? You obviously don't think I could have interest other than staying on Rosehill."

He laughed softly, and she noticed that his eyes were twinkling with that same mocking expression she had seen in Ali's office.

Leave. Get up, girl. Get out before you say or do something else stupid.

"So you want to leave. Surprise, surprise. You and half the country. Everybody wants to go to New York. Paradise. You think it's easy up in New York? People who go there never tell the truth about the place, believe you me."

142

"How I would know? I ever went?" Hearing the churlishness in her voice, she thought, *I sound like a spoiled child.*

"Okay." He opened his palms in a gesture of resignation. "You want to go to America. Supposing I make you an offer, eh? Supposing I get you a visa, and a plane ticket? You go up New York for what, three months. If you like it so bad, you stay. You don't even have to send me back the money. We'll call that George. Good luck to you. Good luck to you. But if you see what I say is true, that West Indians catching their *nenen* up there, then you use the return ticket, and I pick you up at the airport. What you say?"

What I say? What I say? But look my crosses, nuh. The audacity of this man! Who the hell he thinks he is? Okay. Okay. He wants to make deals. I'll fix him.

She smiled at him. Nodded as if in contemplation. "Ummhum. So you going to get me a visa – you must have family in the embassy – and buy me a ticket. What about clothes and shoes? I can't go up there with empty suitcase. And money. I'll have to have some money to live off for three months, right? You giving me some Yankee dollars too, right? I'm sure I'll need at least five hundred."

He studied her as she talked, and she could see his facial muscles tightening, but he let her finish, then he shook his head as if to rid it of a nuisance.

"Whatever you want," he shrugged. "You could have the visa next week. Just bring me your passport. Or give it to Abdul if you don't want to come back here. I don't make jokes." His voice, she noticed, had lost its humour.

Someone knocked lightly on the door. He ignored it.

Beatrice got up. "Thanks," she snapped, "but I could get my own visa. And I don't need your money."

"You can't have that much left from…" then he stopped himself, shook his head again as if to clear it, stood up, and with a laugh that sounded hollow to Beatrice's ears, said, "So you know people in the visa business too, eh?"

He came round his desk on the side away from her, went to the door, placed his hand on the knob, then pivoted to look at her.

The suddenness of it stopped her movement towards the

143

door and something ran through her that she couldn't identify. Fear?

But his voice, when he spoke, was soft. Yet it had a hard quality to it that she felt was a warning.

"I'm a serious man. I had you for a serious woman, too. I know you have courage. Not many women in Santabella would do what you do. You have any idea how many women get abused in this country every day? Children too. Look out there in the office when you leave. Half them women suffering. They need women like you to show them a way out."

"So now you want me to be nursemaid too? I thought you wanted me to teach?" *Why am I arguing with this man?*

"The women in this movement do a lot of things."

Yeah, and they probably all sleeping with you.

"Those women learned from small not to resist. Just lie down and take it," he was saying. "You could teach them different. They need good examples. We're in for some massive changes in this country, you know. You don't want to be in America, fighting that racism. Put your energy to use where you born."

Someone knocked on the door again, this time a bit louder, more insistent, and Haji, still looking down at her, called. "Two minutes."

She stepped toward the door but had to stop as he stepped away from the door, came and rested one hand lightly on her shoulder, while with the other, he tipped back her chin, forcing her to look up into his eyes.

"I admire you," he said softly. "I admire you a lot, Beatrice." His fingers moved past her chin to caress her lips and her cheek, and she closed her eyes as her lips parted at the touch of his finger rubbing against her teeth, her lips, her cheeks and she could feel heat flowing down through her body. She wanted him to hold her, hold her tight-tight, but the telephone on his desk rang, and her eyes flew open. She covered them with her palms in embarrassment as he left her to pick up the receiver.

Stupefied, her head dropped. What should she do? Was he finished with her?

His back to her, he was saying ""Yes?" into the receiver. "Tell them one more minute."

144

She waited another couple seconds, wanting him to turn around, to acknowledge her with a smile, a lifted hand, any kind of gesture at all, that… that what? But he did not turn around.

She went out through the waiting women, past the guards, the children, the old women, her head bent, not seeing them, not listening to one of the guards tell her that Brother Abdul had said for her to wait there until he come back, not hearing him over the rapid beating of her heart, not feeling anything but the warm touch of Haji's fingers against her cheek, and wanting, suddenly, to cry.

TWENTY-FIVE

The Friday that Miss Beatrice and Tante Melda come to the mosque, I was excited, nervous, like a little country boy just get his first khaki pants. A kind of giddiness had come over me which even a blind man could see, because some of the fellars started giving me picong, asking if I meet a girl or something, how my face so fresh.

They know me as a serious man, not like some of them who start making moves on every new woman who come to the mosque. Me? I keep myself straight. With all these diseases going round, I preferred to keep myself to myself. I not in all that, but that Friday, seeing Beatrice there, seeing how she fit in with everybody, how she had the decency to cover her head; how she listened to Haji, and the respect she show him when I take her to his office, well all the feelings that had stirred up in me from the first time I see her just well up in me again and I find myself thinking she would make a good Muslim woman, and in time, maybe, I could ask her to get married. Married? I get a little frightened even thinking the word. The last time I do that, it only end up in trouble.

Yes, I had a wife already. I met her right after I leave secondary school, before I join the movement. I use to play football in the Savannah on Saturday, and Sandra was always turning up with some other girls at the football games, screaming my name.

Finally we start talking, and before you know it, I was spending a lot of time with her, but I didn't have any intention to get married. I wanted to save my little money to go away to further my education, but Sandra would wrap her legs round me and before long, I get myself tied up with her. I know she wasn't with

146

me alone, so I wasn't too worried, but then, things happen. She come and tell me she was making a baby. By that time, I had joined up with Haji.

I wasn't even sure the child was mine, but I married her because Haji tell me it was the right thing to do. He was always preaching about taking responsibility for our actions. That's why you have to think before you act, I tell these young fellars. Watch where you putting your thing because you never know how big that one little minute will cost you.

Sandra join the religion with me, but she couldn't stand the rules. All she want to do was party-party. Every Friday and Saturday that woman gone to a fete. And when she come home, foreday morning, she would be so drunk, she had to stay in the bed the rest of the day.

I stay with her as long as I could, but after a while, I get fed-up. I had was to give up, not just for me, but for my son.

She didn't object even when I take Shaquille – he was only a year old – and went to live by myself. Every now and then she used to come and see him, but for all intents and purposes, she was living her own life.

Still, when I tell the Haji that I was thinking seriously about Miss Beatrice, he instruct me to get permission from my wife, or divorce her. Divorce in Santabella could take seven years, so I make up my mind to find Sandra and get her permission, just in case things develop between me and Beatrice.

I know Beatrice didn't have anybody in her life because I had asked around. I heard about her and a fellar named Sonny, but he had gone America long time, and she wasn't involved with anybody else. She looked like a serious, stable young lady. Somebody I could make a life with; build up a future. I didn't think I would ever get like Haji with three wives. One good woman would satisfy me. Besides, you have to have plenty money for that.

While Beatrice was in with Haji, I wanted to go and ask Sister Fareeda about her, but I had to meet with some of the other men close to Haji. Word come down that we had a three-day fast coming up. Not everybody, mind you. Members were only required to fast during Ramadan, but for some of us, the ones closest to Haji, fasting was a requirement before we do anything important.

When I think about that day, maybe knowing that the time was near make me even more nervous.

It wasn't that we hadn't gone on special fasts before, but this time, this time something feel different. Might have been the phone calls from overseas, Haji running here and there, a lot of fellars coming in from the hills. I can't put my finger on it, but my bones start to feel funny.

The government had stepped up their harassment, not just of the compound, but of the women. They'd killed a sister. And who was going to call them to accounts for that crime?

Day after day, week after week, they putting pressure on poor people. Who would think that your own Black people could make you suffer so much? But you just have to look at some of them countries in Africa. People chopping up one another and all of them have black skin. In Santabella is like they hate poor people. Poor people is a tribe all their own. A tribe called strugglers. Who out there to defend them? Was only Haji and people like us who come from the dirt, the hills, the LaBas, the swamp. The rich ones couldn't care less if we suffer. What that government was doing to us, trying to run us off the land, well, multiply that by the thousands and that was what they doing to strugglers in this country. Well, eh-eh. Somebody had was to take a stand. Some people might say that two wrongs don't make a right, but the Qur'an teach us that if we believe and act for justice and right-eousness, then Allah will forgive us and give us great rewards.

So I was meeting with the others down in the back while Beatrice went in to see Haji. I figured he wanted to talk to her about the school, and I was hoping she would say yes. But I couldn't concentrate on that because things were heating up and I had to pay attention to my own responsibilities. It was hard because my mind kept going to Beatrice as I listened to the plans getting outlined.

We had to discuss the special cleansing we would do, and who would lead, what and where. Two of the ones at the meeting had special training overseas, after they'd gone to Mecca. Haji had promised me that next year would be my turn to go. If Beatrice could go with me, that would be the icing on the cake for me. That would really be Allah's blessings. But before that, I had to concentrate on what Mahmoud and some of the other men saying about the preparations.

"You have to be extra careful. More than any other time," he warn us. "They watching us like hawks. They know something's up but we have to keep the element of surprise in our hands. That means full commitment from everybody. Haji's expecting that. When you leave here today, go home, think about matters. Pray. If you have the slightest doubt about what you have to do, you could still step away. Nobody forcing you. Nobody tying any-body foot in this."

I know he had was to say that, but it was a waste because all of us in that room, except one, had made a full commitment long time. We just waiting for the signal, and Mahmoud say it could come any day. "So pray. Fast. Pray. Fast. And watch your back."

I was glad that Clyde didn't come back to get Beatrice and Tante Melda because it give me the opportunity to take them home. Haji has a whole fleet of cars, some we run as taxis, so I take one of them. Then I went to the general office and picked up a new Qur'an. I wanted to give it to Beatrice but I started feeling nervous all over again. What if she refuse to take it? Well, I tried to console myself. If she didn't take it, that was a sign. If she accept, matters fixed.

As she was coming toward the car, she looked so serious, I decided not to hand her the Qur'an there and then. I was wondering what happened between her and Haji to make her look like that, but Tante Melda started bugging me to go and get her some food to take home so I had was to leave them in the car.

When I get back, Tante was in the front passenger seat, and Beatrice was in the back of her, staring out the window, her face serious-serious.

Tante Melda took the roti and the bottle of sorrel. She pointed with her chin to Beatrice.

"I asked Miss Lady three times if she want something but like her tongue tie up."

I leaned over to the back seat and placed a paper bag with a chicken roti and a bottle of sorrel on the seat next to Beatrice. Her eyes didn't move from the window.

I put my bag with the Qur'an I had for her on the back seat, and started the engine. All through town Tante Melda's mouth couldn't stop talking and chewing. I was only half-listening to her because my mind was on Beatrice. What had got her so uptight?

Tante Melda was saying, "They don't care about Black people. They black too, yes, but some of them hate their own colour, so they discolour their minds. Haji's right. All this government care about is people in their own class, them who went to Saint Mary's and Saint Joseph's. The first thing they want to know when they meet you somewhere is where you went to school, and if you didn't go to one of them top schools, they look on you as if you is a dog. I know them well. It need a real revolution in this country to change things. As long as them kind of people stay in power, poor people suffering pressure and misery until the day they dead. And even when they dead, them corbeaux will pick their bones. You hear bout that one who own all the funeral agencies? He was paying fellars to go in the cemetery at night and steal back the coffins? All that money people pay to bury their dead and that thief robbing the graves. How much money the man want so? He have three big house, four cars, who knows how much millions in the bank, and he still thiefing from poor dead people. You going to tell me he not going to burn in hell? Eh Beatrice? Why you so quiet back there? You see jumbie or what? All you have jumbies at the mosque, Abdul? Eh? All you frighten Beatrice with one?"

She leaned back to poke Beatrice.

"You daydreaming or you sleeping?"

"I hearing you," Beatrice answer quiet-quiet. "I listening to everything you say."

"Well, what you think, then? You don't think I right in what I say? Them Holy Name convent people all for themselves. Bunch of criminals."

Beatrice breathed a deep sigh. "Maybe you're right about some of them, but you can't just generalize. Remember I went to that kind of school. Clare – Sister Fareeda – too. And we don't behave like them."

150

"Same thing but different," Tante said. "I can't talk for Sister what's her name, but I know you, Beatrice. You never set yourself higher than Rosehill's people. With you, is always one for all and all for one. Tante Vivian grow you up like that. In a way, you and Haji would make a good team."

"What you mean by that?" Beatrice snapped, and I thought, Oh God, now she sounding really vexed. Why Tante couldn't keep her big mouth shut?

"What you getting so hot up for, Beatrice? All I mean to say is that no matter how much education you get, you have to remain grounded with the people, and seems to me you and Haji similar in that way, right Abdul? You agree?"

"That's why I admire Haji," I nodded. "He went away to university and get all his degrees, but he come right back home. He coulda stay in America and make big money but he had a higher calling. He set a good example for a lot of us to follow. You know how I first come to know him? I was working in a store in town, trying to put aside some money to go away to further my studies after I get my GCEs.

"Haji used to come in to buy flour. Big-big bags of flour. The clerk used to always joke with him about how he was trying to run the Chinese bakeries out of business. Then I read in the newspaper that he feeding the vagrants in the square, and his bread was so good, people start lining up down by the mosque twice a week just to get some of his hot bread. I remember when I was small how Ma used to go up to Mount Saint Benedict and every time she come back, she had bread from the priests."

"I remember that too," Tante Melda chimed in. "That was good bread, man. Every Friday as God send your mother and me used to…"

"Let the man tell his story, nuh," Beatrice interrupted Tante.

"Well," I went on, glad that she at least wanted to hear me talk, which mean she wasn't vexed with me, "I read where they say he was kneading the flour with his own hands. According to the newspaper, he would stay up all night twice a week to make bread. I say to myself, what kind of man is this? That must be ole talk, so one Tuesday night I stop off by the mosque, and in truth and in fact, Haji was there with flour up to his elbows."

"So why the women and them wasn't helping?" Tante Melda jumped in again. "The man have a dozen wives and none of them could kneed flour? A-A."

"The point I'm trying to make," I tell her, "is that Haji was happy making the bread. He wanted to do that for the people. Yes, it have plenty women in the mosque who could do it, but he like doing it. We have machines these days that come from overseas, but back then, I see that man with my own eyes making that bread."

I take a quick glance in the mirror. Beatrice had turned away from the window. Her head was still down, but I could tell she was listening.

"That touched me. Here was a man with three university degree. He coulda come back home and get some big government position and live up in Saint Clair or Saint Anns with them rich people, but he choose to teach people to live a different way. By making the bread himself, I feel he was sending a message to a lot of macho men in this country. I went back that Friday to hear him preach, and soon after that, I decide to get involve. He was the only man who was doing anything constructive for ordinary people. That was more than five years ago."

"So you doing all this because of *him*?" Beatrice ask me.

"Because of what he's doing for Santabellans," I tell her. "But is not only that. When I became a Muslim and I start to read the Qur'an, I begin to understand how I have to live a life consistent with my faith."

"But you born Catholic," Tante Melda announced, as if I didn't know that.

"Yes. I could recite long prayers in Latin, but what I realize, working alongside Haji, was that you can't just be a person of faith one day of the week and forget about the teachings the rest of the time. Them same people who will stand up in church and sing with you on Sunday, then kneel down and take communion with you, will spit in your face if you ask them for a penny or a job on Monday morning. We Muslims don't live like that. Friday to Friday, we live the teachings in the Qur'an."

"But what I don't get is this..." Tante Melda like to argue, which was why Ma keep away from her, but I figure Beatrice probably had some of the same doubts, so Tante was actually helping me out, even if she didn't know it.

"Why the women and them have to dress up as if they playing Midnight Robber, covered in black from head to foot?" she ask. "I thought all you Muslims don't believe in Carnival?"

"That is exactly what I mean by people not living their faith. Women should present theirselves modestly in public. The Bible says that too, you know, but the so-called Christians want you to believe that only the Qur'an says that. That is not true. It's in the Bible. If you are a good woman, you do not present your body in public to encourage men to look at you, to be tempted by you. You save yourself, the way you look, for your husband. But there's more to it than that. When you become so wrapped up in how you look, you spend your money on clothes and shoes, and all that sort of thing. Who is the real you? In Islam, women concern theirselves with their soul, not only their bodies."

"You sure right about that," Tante mumbled. "All them shapeless long-long dress. Well, if I have to give up my powder and lipstick, then I staying Anglican. What about you, Beatrice?"

She turn to look back at Beatrice and I try hard to keep my eyes on the road.

"You ready to give up your tight pants? To get down with the people, as Clyde would say? Eh?"

"I saw women with lipstick and powder," Beatrice said quietly. "Even black eye-shadow. But you know very well it's not about make-up or sexy clothes. Is about carrying yourself decent in the world, and if you want to do that, then you dress decent."

When I hear her say that, my heart start beating harder. I know that she was the right wife for me. She had qualities. All those things I hear about her? That she was a thief, a murderer even? That stuff had to be lies, and if they weren't, if she really do them, then she musta had good cause. Besides, I was thinking that when she become a Muslim, Allah would forgive her anything she'd done.

I racked my brain trying to figure out how I was going to make a serious approach to her. I would have to tell her about Sandra, because you can't expect to start out a good relationship with lies. I wondered how she would feel about my son. According to

Tante Melda, she never talked about her little boy who get killed by the bees.

So much to figure out. Then I realize that I was assuming she was interested in me. Maybe the girl wouldn't even want to go out with me. That just make me start worrying even more.

Tante Melda was prattling away, and every now and then Beatrice would say something, but my mind was full up thinking about how to approach her, then I would remember that in the days to come I had other things to concentrate on, things bigger than me or Beatrice, but that make me worry even more.

When we reached Rosehill, I dropped Beatrice off first because I couldn't be alone with her in the car, not feeling the way I was starting to feel about her. Old habits don't just go away the first time you say Insh'Allah. I was breaking out in a sweat thinking about holding her, and all that sort of thing, so I decide to take in front before in front take me, and drop the girl off home first. I was careful not to touch her with my sweaty palms when she try to say thank you and shake my hand. I just hold on to the car door and smiled.

On the way back down, Tante Melda say, "You have it bad, man. I see it all over your face. Whew! Is a long time since I see a man turn *totolbay* like that." She start laughing at me, shaking her head in pity, but I didn't mind.

"I so transparent?" I had to laugh at myself too.

"Like plastic wrap, man. You could hardly look at the girl. And you a married man to boot. What's going on with Sandra? That girl's scarce like rain in dry season. When last you see her?"

She had to bring up Sandra, right?

"I can't talk about Sandra, Tante. You know she's living her own life. But you could see I like Beatrice a lot, eh?" I was a little embarrass, but I figure I had to get some help, so I had was to admit that I didn't know quite how to approach Beatrice.

"What you think? You know her from small. You think she would go with me? You could try to find out in a subtle kinda way, you know what I mean?"

Tante laughed. "Boy, is time this family have a wedding. That's not against the religion, I hope, because if that is the case, you could count me out."

154

"Muslims have big wedding in this country," I remind her. "You don't see their pictures in the papers?"

"That's true. But you know. Haji and all-yuh is a different brand. I don't know if all-yuh have different rules and ting."

I parked the car by her gate. "Most of them Indian Muslims don't trust us," I tell her, "but we live by the rules of the Qur'an. They don't own the religion and we don't own it either. Look how you and Ma grow up. You Anglican. She's Catholic. All-yuh read from the same Bible, right?"

"Is true," she admitted, but I know that wouldn't be the last I was going to hear from her about Islam.

"So what you want me to tell Beatrice for you?"

"Is not so much that I want you to tell her something for me. Just feel her out, you know? See if she's interested in me. She doesn't have anybody right now, true?"

"I could put my head on a block and say no. She keeps to herself. I think since Sonny leave her high and dry, then the little boy die, she just keep away from men. But is time, boy." And she slapped my arm. "Time for Beatrice to come out from the desert. But what you going to do about Sandra? She might not want you but she's like a lot of women who as soon as the man start looking around, even if they ignore him for years, they all of a sudden on him like curry on dhal."

"Don't worry about Sandra," I tell her. "And besides, you know we Muslims can have more than one wife, right?" I said it in a jokey way, just to tease her because I was so happy she was going to help me with Beatrice.

She laughed. "But women could only have one husband. You see the unfairness of it all? That's why I can't join that religion." She got out of the car and I went to open the gate for her.

"When you coming to do my cupboards?" she ask. "One hand can't clap, you know."

I shoulda known that she would make a bargain, and I wanted to fix her cupboards, but with what was going to happen any time soon, I didn't want to promise a specific day, so I tell her I would try my best, God willing, to do it the following week. Man could make all the plans he want, but sometimes God have his own plans for you. I was to find that out the next week, but right then and there, I had was to make the promise because I want her to talk to Beatrice for me so bad, I could feel my insides hurting.

When you read books about love, the writer usually concentrate on how the women characters feel. Anything about a man usually has to do with him having sex. But I have to tell you, just the thought of being with Beatrice, not having sex or anything like that, mind you, just holding her hand, talking with her, watching her eyes – she has small, slanted eyes that look a lot like they Chinese, I tell you, just imagining us starting a life together was sending my whole body into spasms. I find myself looking right and left to see if people could see me shaking.

That last for a while, then I would get worried that she wouldn't want me, and my body would hurt in a different way, like a coconut tree swaying hard in a hurricane. In my bed, I could hear myself groaning, my body rocking back and forth as if I was autistic or something. This love business was mashing me up bad-bad. If them fellars see me, they bound to start calling me *dotish*, *totolbay*.

"Yuh have *tabanka*, boy," they would laugh. All my life I hear those words. I even used them myself, laughing with my friends at some poor fellar suffering pain from some woman. Now I was in the same position. Beatrice was in me so bad, I had to pray to Allah to quiet my nerves. I had was to squeeze a pillow over my head just to get some sleep.

I was glad I had important things to do at the mosque that weekend, just to keep from thinking about her. Plus, I had was to go back down the islands to make sure everything about Yusuf was under control, and to bring back some equipment that come in from Grenada.

PART THREE

FIRE AND WATER

TWENTY-SIX
Beatrice

All weekend, after I'd gone down to the mosque, I stay in the house. I just couldn't leave. My whole body feel paralysed, as if somebody had hit it with a big stick, and keep on hitting it. I wanted to cry; then I would feel foolish and start laughing at myself. I'm surprised I can even relate what happened because the way I remember, I was totally confused. When something hit you hard like that was hitting me, you can't think straight. How you going to marshal the words to put them in sentences with commas and full stops, eh? Especially if you don't have anybody to talk to about it.

When I was growing up, any time I was confused about anything, Tante was there.

Yes, Reme is my mother, but I never feel comfortable telling her the kind of things I could tell Tante Vivian. But she was gone, and that weekend it really hit me, for the first time, that I didn't even have a close girl friend. Not one. Jestina. She was there, but she was about ten years older than me, and Melda was the last person in the world I was going to tell my business. Because of how I grow up, my head in books all the time, Sonny was my only real friend.

When Clare – Sister Fareeda – and the other girls in my class go to football games in the Oval, when they play mas' together in the same band on Carnival Tuesday, I never used to join them.

At first they would ask me, but time after time I had to tell them I couldn't, so then they spread a rumour that I was a Seventh Day Adventist. I just let them believe what they want to believe.

I couldn't very well tell them that Reme couldn't afford to

159

buy me the kind of clothes their parents bought for them, and I wouldn't even ask Tante to spend her money like that. Clare and the rest of them had two parents working, a lot of them in the Civil Service. I couldn't match them, so I just stayed with Sonny.

Poor Moko couldn't afford to buy nice clothes for him either. We never talk about that kind of thing, but maybe deep down the two of us know that it was money that make the difference between us and Clare's family, or the boys Sonny went to school with. That's why Sonny want to leave Santabella so bad, to make money in America. And I had the chance to leave too, so what was I doing getting involved with the Muslims?

I wanted to join them. I can't lie. I wanted to join them. But I had to ask myself if it was really the movement or the man I was interested in. This far away from that time, I like to believe I had doubts, but what is closer to the truth is that I was consumed with thoughts about Haji, about how my stomach start turning over and heat start rising in me when he touch me in his office.

Why? Why'd he do that? He knew well what he was doing. But he had three wives already, and lord knows how many other women. Three wives. A week had only seven days. How did this man partition himself? How many nights did he spend with each one? And what about the children? One of the wives had six or seven children. Did he have to spend more time with her because of that?

Add all those people lined up at the mosque to see him day in and day out. Where'd the man get the strength? The way he'd touched me. He wanted me. And God knows I wanted him. He'd set off some feeling in me I never thought I would experience after Sonny… Oh God. He had three wives. But why was I even thinking he wanted to marry. How many times had I seen him? I wasn't somebody to rush pell-mell into anything with a man but the way I was feeling about him, I couldn't explain it even to myself. Even if, even if he and I got together, what about the other wives?

I remembered reading somewhere that Muslim men had to get permission from their previous wives before they could take on more, but why those women would give their permission?

Besides, Haji didn't strike me as a man who would ask any woman's permission to do anything. What I really know about the man? At times he was arrogant. The next minute he was soft and kind. Who was the real Haji? Those wives loved him, according to Melda and what the newspapers said. Not one of them ever said anything bad about him so he must treat them good. But why would they agree for him to take another wife when that would mean less time for them? That would be abnormal. What planet them from? But everything about that man was different.

Hour after hour, Saturday into Sunday, my head was pounding with questions. Melda stopped by the house but I told her I had a huge headache.

"I know what you need, girl," she laughed. "You want me to call up a certain person?"

I was so embarrassed to know that she could read me like that, but then she said. "Abdul is a nice-nice man, Bee. You could trust him. I'm not saying that only because I'm his auntie."

Abdul? I liked Abdul, but where did she get the idea that I was even remotely interested in him? Still, I didn't say anything. Maybe I was too ashamed about how I was feeling about Haji.

After she went home, I closed my eyes so I could take myself back into his office to feel his fingers on my face and to remember how my whole body shook as if it had a fever and the more I think about it, the more my body feeling good but I start to cry because my chest was hurting and I could hardly breathe.

I don't know how I made it through that night without trying to get in touch with him, but even then, I didn't know how I would do that. Maybe Abdul. I could ask Melda to tell Abdul I wanted to see him. That wasn't fair, though. If he was interested in me, I didn't want to give him any false hopes, but the way I was feeling, I would have walked to Toco and back if I knew I would get to see Haji.

Monday come and I decide to get a grip on myself. It wouldn't be easy, but I was not doing myself any good wallowing in desire for that man. But no matter how hard I tried, my mind stayed on him, on how he look when he was preaching. I tried to concentrate on his words.

He was right. Poor people had it hard-hard in Santabella. Their ancestors build the country from the ground up, then when the British abolish slavery, it leave them high and dry while it give the Indians and them land for the same work that black people spend all their lives doing for free. How that was fair?

The Bible say the poor will inherit the earth, but the only thing poor people in Santabella inherit was dirt.

The British were long gone. Black people take over the government. In fact, Black people running the government for over thirty years and except for the first Prime Minister, all of them who run things turn out to be the same old khaki pants. Nothing ent change for we people.

Oh God. I was getting myself riled up. I tell myself to stop. Stop thinking like that. I could hear Reme warning me. I know she was frightened for me. We never really talk much to one another but that didn't mean I didn't know she want the best for me. That she was frightened I would get myself in trouble again. Maybe she regretted leaving me with Tante Vivian to grow up because Tante had given me a free hand. With her, I would have turned out different.

Tante Vivian had spent her whole life helping people, and she set a good example. It wasn't that Reme didn't care about Rosehill, but she wanted me to have more than she had gotten from her hard life. She wouldn't say it, but I know she would be thinking, What about me? What about all the work I do to send you to school? All the prayers I make to keep you from going to prison. What about me, Beatrice?

She would be right. I owe her a lot, and the only way for me to give back something to her, to show her that she didn't waste her life for me, was to leave Santabella, but I didn't know how I was going to do that with the way I was feeling.

Oh God. Haji. I couldn't tell anybody how in the night, all I could think of was him in bed next to me. No! The man had three wives. I must be mad. I must be mad. I must be going mad in truth. I had to leave Santabella.

But he was so good-looking. And smart too. I was counting the days until Friday when I would go back down to the mosque, not with Melda. Just by myself.

When Ali stop by that Tuesday with a message from Haji, I was so happy, I couldn't barely talk.

"You don't have to open it in front of me,' he laugh as I held the letter. "That man have some kind of magic, oui. I don't know why I wasting my time with the law. I should just bottle Haji and sell him. You remember how some guy in America bottle Florida sunshine and people line up to buy it? Haji is like Florida sunshine, you don't think so, Beatrice?"

As he drove away I was thinking how he and Haji seemed so close. Fate? Was it fate that the man who'd had my life in his hands for two years was in with the one I couldn't get out of my mind; the one who could cause me to change my life with one touch?

Just as I was going back into the house, the postman ring his bell and called out that he have a package for me.

"Is from my man Sonny, Beatrice," he announce. "My man Sonny. How that boy doing? Look, is not even Christmas and he sending you a package. Special delivery too. Sonny is a good man, Beatrice. Good man like him too hard to find these days, your present company excepted, of course."

But I wasn't paying any attention to him and his jokes. What the hell? Special delivery from Sonny? Sonny who hadn't written a word to me in months, sending me special mail?

In the kitchen I ripped open the package with a knife and a cassette dropped out. Sonny sending me music? The only writing on the cover was *For Beatrice, Side A*, and on the other side, *Side B, From Sonny*.

I wanted to open Haji's letter, but a part of me was afraid, so I put it on the sideboard, then went to get a cloth to dust off the cassette player. What kind of music was Sonny sending me, and why didn't he write a letter? My hand was shaking as I put in the tape and pressed the button marked to *Play*.

TWENTY-SEVEN
Sonny's Story

Dear Beatrice, You're surprised to hear from me, eh? It take me a long time to get to this point, but I have to talk. What I going to tell you is not always going to be nice. You mighten want to hear it, but I owe it to you, to us, to tell the truth. You know whatever happen in the dark must come to light, right? So bear with me, Beatrice. Don't get vex and shut off the tape, okay? Where to begin? Sometimes I think that is the crux of the problem: not knowing where to begin, not knowing where this story start being mine. Maybe I should start with that night when I come up to see you, the night of my farewell party. That was my night all right, the whole of Rosehill turn out just for me. All except you.

You were supposed to be there, supposed to give a speech, according to Miss Ann, but you never come and I couldn't wait to escape, to get away from them, Miss Ann, Jestina, Uncle Willy, Moko, all of them. I remember running all the way up the hill to your Tante's house to find out why. At first I thought it was because you were jealous, jealous that I had gotten the scholarship and not you. Yes, I know you had applied for it – you didn't tell me but I knew. I could read it in your eyes when I came to tell you that I had won it. I could always read you through your eyes. So I thought that was it, you couldn't take the pressure of hearing the whole of Rosehill congratulate me for something you deserved just as much as I did. But when I got to the house I found you curled up on the sofa, trembling.

You wouldn't look me in the eye, Bee. You wouldn't let me see your face when you told me that cock and bull story about getting wet down in the rain that afternoon. I knew it had to be more than that but I never guess, I never guess. But I don't want to get into that. Better leave that alone. Let it die.

You were trembling with ague and I was frighten, frighten for the first time, because I had gotten that letter from the government rescinding the scholarship and I hadn't told anybody. I told you. I put aside your sickness and concerned myself with me that night. Yeah, I could hear you saying 'So what's new,' and in spite of the way you were feeling, you was the one to come up with the plan. You were always better than I was in a crisis, Bee. You would have made a good lawyer. You could think fast on your feet. I did what you advise me. I left the next day for New York, pretending that I hadn't gotten that letter, pretending the scholarship was still intact. But I'm jumping ahead with that part of the story. I wonder why. Maybe I don't want to dwell on what happened between us that night, because then I'll have to remember that you had a child for me, a son. You had that child and you never sent to tell me. I will never understand how you could do a thing like that. But whatever your reasoning, you didn't write me about him. Not when he was born. Not when he died.

Three years that child lived. A walking, talking, laughing part of me and I didn't even know he was mine. After, after I find out, I used to wonder if he was like me when I was a little boy. I know he liked to play with pigeons, like me, but I wondered if he liked to eat dirt like I used to do, or if he had bandy legs, or sucked his thumb, or if he look like me or more like Moko, or like Angelina. Angelina was half Chinese, you know that? People use to say I take after her, that I had her eyes. That's why they used to call me Small-eyes in school, remember? He had my eyes, Bee?

If I could feel so mashed up, if I could feel like this and I never touch the child's flesh, I could imagine how losing him had to break you down. Uncle Willy say you nearly went mad. Like Miss Lezama after her children died in the fire, only quiet-quiet. Not talking to anybody. Walking the road with your head down as if you looking to find something you lost, as if the ground could give you some answers. I hear you went down to the sea a lot, and Miss Ann say she used to send one of her children to follow you. You didn't know that, eh? That was to make sure you didn't walk into the sea with all your clothes on.

I had to hear all this from other people, Bee. There I was, back in Santabella to help you after Tante Vivian write me, begging me to come back and get you of jail. I put my life on hold and rush back home to help you out, all that time not knowing about the child. Imagine how I feel when I get to Rosehill and everybody start telling me how sorry they were that the child died. My God! All those bees stinging the poor little boy! Every time I think about it I want to cry.

I was vexed with you. That's why I had to leave before they called your case. But at least I did what Tante Vivian ask me to do. I'm satisfied that when she closed her eyes she knew that I had come back, that I had given a signed statement about the money.

I had to run from you. You looked so hard. Like a batchac. Your hair all tangled up. And your eyes, Bee. Red-red. Like a jumbie. I had to run from you before you sucked me into all your madness.

I don't know why I ask Uncle Willy to tell you I was married. Maybe it was spite. Maybe a part of me wanted to cuff you down for all them blows you land on me. If it's any consolation, I was sorry the minute the words come out of my mouth.

When I was small and the children would harass me about how my mother run off and leave me with my broken-foot father, and I would come home crying, Moko would try to console me. He would say words are wind, that was all. Words are wind. They can't hurt you. He was wrong. You and I know that, Bee. Even the words that didn't pass between us hurt, so you could imagine how the ones we used mash us up. Hard-hard words all around. I pelting you, you pelting me. That could only result in bruises.

Yes, I married an American woman. I should have told you that to your face, but it probably wouldn't have made any difference. It wasn't what you wanted to hear. I wish I could have explained why I had to do it, Bee. I wish I'd had the chance to tell you the one night with you, that night before I left for America for the first time, that wasn't a thing I could forget. That was putting a seal on a bargain. I wouldn't forget you. I would send for you. We used to talk about all that. You think I didn't mean it? I wanted you to have faith in me. But you could be so hard. You have a hard time trusting anybody. You never believe they would live up to their promises. But I meant to live up to mine.

I had just passed the bar exam when you got in your trouble back home and Tante send for me. So I come down. Dropped everything and came to help you. If I hadn't been married to an American, if she hadn't helped me get my permanent visa, you think I would have been able to come down to help you? It was because of her that I could help you. I loved you. Then I find out Sonya was going to have a baby.

I'd met her while I was in law school. She used to work in the drugstore right around the corner from the university, and I was always going in there for cold medicine. That's how we meet. She was kind. Is a long time since a woman was kind to me.

She's white. I can hear you now, yeah, that's just like Sonny, but it wasn't like that at all. She like me a lot more than I liked her. She couldn't believe I didn't know how to swim, coming from an island and all. So she volunteer to teach me how. I was living in Harlem then, not far from the YMCA where they had a pool, and we used to go there. At first, people used to stare us down, but water don't care what colour you are, and anyway, her skin was more the colour of cashew nut than milk. I used to tease her that she must have some black in her because she liked black things. Books, music. One time she invite me to go to hear some poetry and you know me, you know how I used to laugh at you with all your poetry writing, but I went and you would have liked those guys. All the time I was wishing you could be there. But what am I telling you all this for, eh? I guess I'm trying to get you to understand why all this happen, Bee. I'm trying to tell it the best way I know how. That is one of the reasons why I'm taping it. You used to say you could always tell when I was lying. You could hear something in my voice. You hear it yet? Eh? No. No. You can't answer yes because I'm telling you the truth, as God is my witness. I know you're saying you don't want to know anything about that woman. But if I don't tell you about her you wouldn't understand how it happen.

I never ask you for anything. You know that. Now I'm asking this one small thing. Don't turn off the tape recorder. Just listen to all I have to say. After that, well, at least I would be satisfied that you hear the whole story from my own mouth. I love you Beatrice. I love you today stronger than I loved you in Santabella in spite...

TWENTY-EIGHT
Beatrice

But I had to stop it. I couldn't bear to hear any more. Why now? Tante Vivian used to tell me that nothing happen by chance, so was I supposed to see Sonny's tapes as some kind of message? I was supposed to believe Sonny when he said he love me, just when I had my mind on… I couldn't even say his name to myself.

The envelope Ali had brought me from him was on the table, next to the tape recorder, staring me in my face. Three times I pick it up, but my fingers would not open the flap. I was frightened and nervous at the same time. A part of me wanted to cry and I didn't know why. I guess when your mind is confused, your emotions spin in all directions. Okay. Okay. I tell myself, think if Tante Vivian was here, what she would say, eh? And as I start concentrating on Tante, my mind began to cool down, and the voice tell me:

Sit down quiet. Fix your thoughts on what Sonny is telling you. Nothing happens by chance.

TWENTY-NINE
Sonny's story, side B

You hear me, Bee. I love you. I know you're saying, 'Love me? The only person Sonny loves is himself.' That was true for a long time, and honestly, maybe it's still true now. Maybe I'm saying I love you because I need you, and you'll see that as selfish. But I do need you. I know this beyond a shadow of a doubt. So what about Sonya and my son? I was honest with her. I told her I would take care of him but that I wanted you, that I was going to ask you to come up, and that I wanted a divorce. And you know what, Bee? She said if all the love she had for me, and I had for my son – his name is Malcolm; we named him after Malcolm X – if that wasn't strong enough to keep us together, then is best that we live our own lives. She's a good woman, Bee, and I'm lucky to have her as the mother of my son. So it's up to you. I don't know how to say it any different. I want to take care of you. I want us to be together. I know how much you want to help Rosehill, and I do too. We're not going to abandon our country, Bee, but we need a chance to make our lives better if we're going to help anybody. I gave Reme my telephone number to give you, but here it is again. 718-965-1324. I can't wait to see you, girl, to laugh and talk the way we used to. I'll send you the ticket. This tape coming to an end soon so I better hurry up. So what more I could say to convince you, eh? I wish I could remember some of those poems they used to make us read in school. Lord Byron and guys like that. I always like his poetry, and you did too. I use to imagine him kissing girls behind the shelves in a library, but now I can't recall a single line of his poems. Funny, right? Because today I feel so full of love for you, it's like I'm under the waterfall on a hot-hot day. Now I'm getting embarrassed, but you know what I mean. The day I see you walking through that airport will be the happiest in my life. Okay, so no Lord Byron. How about something from one of we own lords. Lord Kitchener. You remember "Ting tang, darlin', The Queen and the Duke comin'"? Well, let me put it in my own way: Ting tang, darlin, Soon Beatrice will be comin'…

THIRTY
Beatrice

Sonny singing. I couldn't believe my ears. And all that talk about love. Sonny? Lightning must have struck him in his head. He have me so confused, I didn't know where to turn. For over two years I'd tried my best to put him out of my mind and just when I start to think about somebody else, he makes an appearance. Whoever was running this universe was really jokey in truth. So what I was supposed to do? Which road was I supposed to walk down? Knowing Sonny, he wouldn't take the time to bare his soul, especially on a tape, if he didn't mean it.

From the time I was small, everybody, except Reme for a time, thought we would end up together. All that history we had together should count for something, but the feelings I had for him were different from what I was feeling for Haji. Lord, I didn't even know the man's real name. And what was in that letter he had sent me?

An airplane ticket to America to show me how serious he was? I picked it up; hefted it to see if I could guess the insides. Then I put it down again, thinking I should make up my mind what I was going to do before opening it. I don't know how long I sat there, in a daze. When I looked out the window, it had started to make dark.

THIRTY-ONE
Abdul

The fishermen from Grenada have a little trouble dodging the Coast Guard, but Sudix show them the way so by Tuesday night they land on the island with the boxes. When I reach there on Wednesday, Calu come to help me tie up the boat, then I walk with him up a steep road on the side of the island farthest away from where the party boats usually dock, to where he and Sudix had put Yusuf.

Coming up the hill the first thing I see was mounds and mounds of dirt piled around a big hole. I could hear noises coming from it.

I look down into the hole to see Yusuf, his back bent low, sorting garbage into small piles, and it was obvious that Calu and Sudix had followed instructions to a T.

"Have him collect every plastic bag, every discarded spoon, fork, plastic cup and plate that those people from the boats drop on the beach. Have him do it at night, on his knees. Have him put it all in a big hole, and then have him sort it all, piece by piece, into piles, down in the hole. And all the time, he has to recite these *hadiths*. He has to pray for a clean heart, pray to stop his addiction to the weed and all that other stuff that was messing up his mind, and had put him in trouble with Sandfly in the first place. It's either that, or we tell Sandfly that he isn't under our protection any more."

At night, after he was done, before he crawled into his cot, Calu and Sudix were instructed to pray with him. Talk to him. Listen to what he had to say about his task. No matter how much Yusuf might cuss them, they had to treat him with respect.

You could call it psychological reasoning if you want, but really, it just go to what the old people use to teach us. Soft words turn away wrath. At least with some people. No matter how many soft words Haji use with that government, they were hellbent on harassing us. So sometimes, you have to use other measures. Anyhow, knowing what kind of bad-john Yusuf thought he was, I figure that Calu and Sudik musta get a lot of cussing out, and I expect him to do the same to me. But when Yusuf turn his face to look up at me, he was smiling. He offer me the greeting, and when Calu tell him to come up and eat with us, he say "No, Brother. I want to finish the work first, then I will eat. *Shukran*."

Well, wonders will never cease. I know Calu and Sudik could do good work, and it wasn't the first time they'd had to train somebody, but I shoulda known they would work their special mojo on him. Haji know that too. That's why they had the assignment.

Some people might look on these men as bad-johns, but I know from experience they have soft hearts, Calu especially.

I could see him warming soft candle and Vicks to rub Yusuf's knee caps to ease the pain. And Sudix? He's a story man. Many nights when we had was to train in the bush, Sudix would keep us up telling stories. We would get so engrossed in them that we would forget about pain, about mosquitoes, about wet socks and damp clothes. I tell you, he knows some of them old-time stories to make your blood curl. Then you end up laughing. Before you know it, is morning and you ready to climb through the bush without even feeling the stinging nettles hit your face.

Back in the house, I asked Calu if he thought Yusuf was sincere. I could see, by the changes in his face, that he really want to say yes, but he was being cautious. More than once, fellars had come to the mosque, undercover, and especially in the early days, before we learn how to test people, we get fool. We learn the hard way to be careful. The other side musta learn new tricks too, so I could understand Calu wanting to be careful about Yusuf.

Trust is the most important ingredient in a movement like ours, and if you can't put your head on a block for a man, then you could only take a drink of water from him after he take a sip first.

"I could say he's coming along with the language good-good.

He has a good brain. First day or so he put up a lot of resistance, but Sudix talk to him. You know how he is. Now we don't have to tell Yusuf the prayers. He know them by heart."

He take a deep breath before saying more. "I watch him when he thinks nobody seeing him, and so far, I can't say I see anything to make me real suspicious. Every now and then I could see in his eyes he still debating with himself what to do, but so far, so good. He still has a long way to go, though."

I tell him they might have to hold off on the training because we would have more important things to do soon, and he say Haji had tell them to get ready.

As we go toward the next hut, I remember asking Calu something that just flow out of my mouth. I didn't even know I was thinking it, but maybe, deep down, I was. It was only natural, and I know, with Calu, I could ask that without feeling shame.

"You not frighten?"

He give a little laugh, all the time shaking his head. "Sometimes. I can't lie. Sometimes I does wonder about after. Not so much about how it will go down, but what about after. Haji doesn't talk about that much."

"You think some of the others know?" I ask him.

"I sure hope so. Supposing, eh. Just supposing something, God forbid, happen to him? Who we should listen to if that happen? That is really the kind of thing I worry bout. I make my peace with God already about what I have to do, but I wish Haji would talk more about afterwards. What bout you?"

"I know he's planning to call a council before the end of the week. Maybe then he'll tell us."

"I know bout the meeting. But you ask if I get frighten. What about you?"

"Like you. Sometimes. Especially when I think about what might go wrong. What if something happen to me? Ma will take care of Shaquille, but I want to see my son grow up, yuh know? I want to teach he how to play cricket and football. I know we not suppose to have any doubts, but man, I'm human, yuh know? And this is a big-big thing. Massive! Is not like 1970. Them fellars didn't know what they was doing. They just follow-fashion the Americans with their Black Power thing. I know Haji's a smart man, but he's not the one always calling the shots. You know what I mean?"

"Yeah," Calu say. "We going to have to pay the piper one day. That's for sure. But how? That's a question I have to ask in the meeting. Is time somebody tell us."

"Some things Haji keeping close to his chest," I tell him. "Maybe is best we don't know. If we trust him, then we have to go with the flow."

"I trust in Allah," Calu say. "Otherwise I wouldn't be here."

We reach the door where Sudix was waiting for us, so the conversation stop. Is not that I don't trust Sudix. I would put my head on a block for him. But for me, talking to him wasn't as easy as it was talking to Calu.

"What all-yuh looking so serious bout?" Sudix was looking from me to Calu. "Something happen?"

I tell him Calu was just explaining to me about how far Yusuf come. "I thought I would get cuss too bad, but he actually smiling."

"Yeah, well," Sudix take out the cinnamon stick he was always chewing. "You have to remember what ole people say: 'All skin teeth eh laugh'."

Calu was laughing at Sudix for using the old time saying, but he come up with one himself to show us he agreed. "Many times monkey say 'cool breeze' when is pepper sauce on his body."

That was how the two of them operate. Always trying to outdo one another. That made it easy for them to stay together on the island.

But those ole-time sayings carry a warning to be careful round Yusuf. If his conversion was coming quick-quick, that was a sign.

A part of me want to believe that he had really changed for the best, that he wasn't pretending. Sometimes fellars like him just need the right kind of attention for them to see that their lives worth more than the few dollars they could get from selling dope. Regardless of what people say after the coup, Haji make a big-big-difference with a lot of those fellars. To this day, some of them have shops, they doing trades – shoemaking and things like that – and plenty of them get a piece of land to make garden so they could be self-sufficient and still sell some in the market. So we do a lot of good. But this is Santabella, you know? We learn from the British. Is like Shakespeare say about Julius Caesar, "The evil that men do lives after them. The good is often interred with their bones."

When he did come out of the hole, Yusuf made sure for me to see him wash, then kneel down to pray, facing in the right direction, on a mat Calu tell me he made himself from coconut branches. He could recite them in good Arabic, as Calu say, so that impressed me. At least I could make a report about that to Haji, Ahamdullilah.

I noticed how Yusuf was eying the boxes from Grenada when we put them in the boat, but he don't ask any questions, so I don't have to tell him no lies. I woulda been curious too, if I was in his shoes. I woulda wanted to know why Sudix bring the boxes there and not straight to Santabella, and what they had in them that make them so heavy. Is just natural curiosity.

At one point, Sudix slip on a stone, and he nearly drop the box he was carrying on his head. Calu shout out to him to watch he didn't cause the provisions to roll down in the sea and swim back to Grenada, but I don't know if Yusuf believe that it was Grenadian ground provisions in the boxes, especially since we wouldn't let him help carry them down the hill.

He could probably sense we didn't quite trust him. We didn't let him help because we didn't want him to know for sure what was in the boxes. We had to follow what Haji tell us to do.

If I'd known that was the last time I going to see Yusuf alive, I would have tell him I was proud of how far he come, but only Allah knows how life will go from one minute to the next. I hope he get his reward in Paradise.

The next morning, I leave him with Calu on the island, and Sudix went back with me to Santabella.

Haji want us back soon, so we start out early-early, long before sun come up, not really because we so worried bout the sea patrols. We know them guys not very vigilant. How you think so much drugs come into this country?

From Maracas, Las Cuevas, Los Iros, all over the place, fellars bringing in loads of drugs to poison the people, and the Coast Guard can't catch them. We use to say they too busy guarding the coast; they should watch the sea instead. A waste of time that Coast Guard. The army too. They need training real bad.

I let Sudix take charge of the boat so I could relax my mind a little bit, look up at the stars for a while, and think about Beatrice.

I wonder how she would feel about me after. I know that woman, Miss Ann, was trying to poison her against we Muslims. Whether things went right or wrong – and I had to believe that Allah, the Merciful, the Beneficent, wouldn't make us fail – Beatrice might turn away from me. I wish I'd had more time for her to get to know me, and Haji. Sister Fareeda coulda help too, since they had went to school together.

My mind starting to feel like the sea, heaving up and down, wondering and worry bout Beatrice, Shaquille, even meh mother. She know something was up. I couldn't tell you how she know that, but she did. Some of the older people have insight, you know. I woulda like to tell her what was going down. Have her pray for me. But we had strict orders not to talk to anybody about the plans, so I had was to bite my lips round Ma.

Then I start figuring how I could get a chance to run up Rosehill before nightfall, stop by Beatrice house and take her some mango Julies. That would make her see I liked her. But maybe I should just say it plain. "Girl, I like yuh too bad." She strike me as somebody you didn't need to beat around the bush with. But it was so long since I had talk to a girl in that way, I didn't know if I would be able to do it. It take a kinda mind-set to talk like that. Long time, yes. But not since I get deep in the religion. If she take the mango, though, and didn't laugh at me, I would give her the Qur'an. Ask her to read and make up her own mind about the religion. That was one regret I had with Sandra. I kinda force her to get into the religion, but after that, I learn that everybody have to come to God in their own way and their own time.

If you read Surah 2: 221, you will learn that a good Muslim would never marry a woman who don't believe. It tell us those – meaning disbelievers, eh – will invite you to the fire, but Allah invites to Paradise. I only wish I did meet Beatrice long before, so she would get to know me, and Islam, in a kinda natural way, but man can't choose these things. It was all in the hands of Allah.

THIRTY-TWO
Miss Ann

If I had any sense, I would have given up on Beatrice. Is only so much a person can do to make another one see sense. If that one's head harder than bamboo, what you could do? I tried. I even went to Reme but that stupidy woman can't see further than her big toe.

Willy didn't give me his opinion, but I could see he was thinking Beatrice was a lost cause too. When I tell him how I see her and Melda in Clyde's taxi going down the Hill, and how they didn't even wave to me standing right there – they couldn't miss me if they had coke-e-eye. Where they going at that time of the day? On a Friday to boot. Is only the mosque they could be going. Traitors.

When I tell Willy that, all he say was that if that was what she want to do, Beatrice have a right to control she own life. Control she own life? I wasn't trying to control Beatrice's life, but if that was how he see it, I tell him I didn't want to hear one more damn word out of his mouth. Control? Control? I don't try to control nobody. I was just waiting for him to roll over and touch me, I woulda tell him that ent wukking here tonight. Talking to me bout controlling people's lives.

He'd better go and talk to Melda and Jestina about control. Both of them in it together, to get Beatrice tangle-up with that Haji and them Muslims. I bet he giving them money. When you hear the report, when the mark burst, all of them going to prison. But how I could let that happen? I had to do something.

Mother Dinah had moved her church to Moruga, so on Wednesday night I make up my mind to go and see her. Since the parlour does have to close half-day on Thursday, I figure I would close it for the whole day because I was going to take the bus. It was a long time since I travel on a bus or gone down South, so I tell myself I will just make a little excursion.

Ordinarily, I would ask Melda or Jestina to go with me, but Jestina was as scarce as flour, and Melda had her nephew, that one in the Muslims, coming to fix her kitchen cupboards, so I didn't even bother to tell her anything. Too besides, is them I wanted to talk to Mother Dinah about anyway. For a while, I thought Beatrice might like to go. She always liked Mother Dinah. Had even get baptized that time. But you never know with Beatrice. The girl too sometime-ish. She's always respectful to me, don't get me wrong, but all this Muslim business turning her head.

When I look round Rosehill, everything changing, and it start when them Muslims come and take over the school. What I wanted to know was how they could do that. How the government could just let them waltz in and take over like that. Is a lot of *simidimi* and *ratchefee* going on in this country.

Well, I figure was time to go and talk to Mother Dinah. Maybe she could help me put my mind to ease.

To get to Moruga it would take me about three hours from the time I leave Rosehill, and that was if the bus come on time. Lately, all them big bus the government buy for millions of dollars from America was breaking down left and right, leaving people stranded on the highway. Before I leave the house, I tell myself I would have to kneel down and say some serious prayers to travel safe, oui. I make sure I put on my Saint Christopher medal too, even if it was on a gold chain.

Wednesday night I bake some bread, cook up a pot of coo-coo and some meat sauce with a little bhagie to go with it instead of fish. Fish would smell up the bus too much, and I didn't want to offend the passengers, you know? I tell you, God must have been with me, because if it wasn't for that food, plus the few *puttygals* I throw down in the basket and a bottle of ice water, I would have starved in truth after that coup cause me to be stranded near a forest down South for two days. You see my crosses?

Willy didn't even roll over when he hear me leave the bedroom early that Thursday morning. He was off on Wednesday and he and Sammy had set up the whole night before playing draughts so I just let him sleep since he didn't have to go to work until the night shift. The one good thing you could say about that job with Angostura is that Willy was smelling so much rum where he worked in the bottling factory, he couldn't stand the taste of liquor any more.

It was after midday when I reached Moruga to find that Mother Dinah had gone to Manzanilla to baptize some people in the sea. The girl at her house tell me she didn't know when Mother Dinah would be back, but to make myself comfortable because she had to go and work in the garden. As she was putting on her boots, I ask if the crates of tomatoes, lettuce, ochros, and ground provisions had come from Mother Dinah's garden and was surprised when she said yes, because I had no idea Mother Dinah had so much land. And people to work it? A-A. The girl musta read something on my face.

"Haji, the imam. You know bout him, right?" the girl ask me, and I tell her yes. Then she say that it was he who give Mother Dinah the land to do agriculture.

"And he send some of his men to help us out too."

Then she say excuse me, I have to go and pray before I go back out in the fields, and the girl tie she head, splash water on she face, and gone and kneel down on a mat mumbling a set a gibberish.

Well, I had was to sit down in that hammock under that house, and fan myself with a piece of newspaper before I went into shock. That Haji was one smart man. Sammy, Mother Dinah, Melda, Jestina. All these Rosehill people, right under my nose, had turn Muslim. A-A.

He know good and well who to get his hooks into. No wonder his Muslim business was mixed in with all that drumming and Shango business. Mother Dinah was a long time believer in Rada and Shango and all that African religion that the priests talk against in the church. In the old days, it was her and Tante Vivian in charge on Rosehill. Now here she was, tangled up with Muslims practising some kind of strange thing Melda and Jestina calling Allah in the Islands. Well, look my crosses.

I could see I had waste my time coming all the way to Moruga to talk to her about those two getting involved with Haji when she herself was locked down with the man. Lord, put a hand! What

181

Rosehill was coming to? What that Haji intend to do to Santabella? Look like he want to turn everybody Muslim. But not me. Not me. That ent wukking with me. I born Anglican, and I dying Anglican. All that Allah this and Allah that not going to move me.

But Mother Dinah was a sensible woman. How she could get mix-up with those people? And if she turn Muslim, how come she still baptizing people in the sea? What kind of Muslim religion was that? They must have some special brand for the islands.

I sit in that hammock for a long-long time, racking my brain, trying to figure out what to do. I did get up so early that rocking in that hammock I fall asleep in the day like a baby. In the country, night does come down fast, and before I know it, when I open my eyes, it was making dark-dark.

The girl musta come back while I was dozing, because I see her boots, all clean , near the steps, but no sign of her. And no Mother Dinah.

I decide to eat some of the food I bring, drink a cup of water, before walking to the end of the road to catch the bus. From the Main Road to Mother Dinah's house is a good little ways, and up there ent have no street lights. Is bush two sides of the road and all kind of animals making strange sounds in the dark. Lordy, Lord. What I get myself into? Willy woulda say that's what I get for not minding my own business, but I always believe, and I believe to this day, whatever happen in Rosehill, to whomever, is my business. Is my old people, and Tante people, and Moko grandfather and all of them who turn that bush into a village. If we let them Muslims and them come and take over everything we work so hard to upkeep, what we will have to leave the grandchildren? Eh? Tell me that.

Melda and them might get blinded by all that razzle-dazzle Haji working on them, but not me. Eh-eh. I look round for a piece of paper to leave a note for Mother Dinah, but the place clean-clean. Is a good thing I didn't find anything to write on, oui, because if I did leave my name there, the police and the army mighta bust down my house too. God was watching out for me.

Anyhow, I start down the road in the dark, praying God that a big snake don't decide to cross the road in front of me. If is one thing I fraid, is snake.

The hair on my head raise a few times when I hear something wailing, but I just keep on saying Hail Mary, full of grace. The Lord is with me. The Lord is my Shepherd. Yeah though I walk through the valley of death, I will fear no evil.

I walking in the middle of the road, praying out loud.

Just as I round the last corner before the Main Road, thinking, praise God, I get there safe, a blinding light hit me in my face, and three army jeeps, full with soldiers, come pelting round the bend. I had was to jump in the canal to keep them from hitting me, and that's how I hurt myself.

Oh God, this was how I going to die? Like a dog in a canal? I could hardly move my right foot, the pain was so bad. And backpain? It was like somebody hit me whaap! in the centre of my back. I try to prop myself up, to crawl back in the road to gather my bag of food that scatter all over the place, but every time I twist my body, the pain increase. I lay back down, staring at the sky, and I ask God what I do to deserve this, eh? All my life I live to help people. The very reason I was in that forest was to help Beatrice. Is so yuh go do me? Maybe you not in charge. Maybe the devil take over the world and was playing a joke on good Christian people. And those soldiers. Where they going so fast? The only house up that road was Mother Dinah's. You see what messing around with that Haji get her? I'm sure that's where they going to search down her house and shoot up the place. Is a good thing she wasn't there. No matter that Haji turn her upside down, I didn't want bad to fall on her. You shouldn't wish people bad, because then it will only fall on you. I learn that a long time now.

But I had was to wonder if she really went to baptize anybody. Baptism on a Thursday. Thursday? Since when people getting baptized on a Thursday? It must be some kind of Muslim thing she was doing because all the Baptists I know, baptize their people on a Saturday. Oh, all that strain on my brain was making my back hurt me too bad. And don't talk bout pain in my right foot! I hear a rustling in the grass and I say is now I dead. Snake coming to get me. Oh God, oh God. Lord have mercy!

I rubbed my Saint Christopher's medal. I start calling the names of all the old people who dead to come and help me. Over and over again. And as God is my witness, the rattling stopped. It get quiet-quiet. Then, if I lie, I die, the pain in my back start to ease.

I manage to grab a piece of stick, and with that, I pull the plastic container with the food. The bottle with the water burst and one of the puttygals had roll away, but I find the other one, so at least I had some food even if I had to stay there till morning come. I open up the coo-coo, and I sprinkle some for the ancestors, and I say the 23rd Psalm five times, and I just try to sit there in the company of God and the old people, because I believe they come to help me, eh. Little did I know that while I up there, them Muslims was getting ready to burn down the town.

THIRTY-THREE
Abdul

Thursday, I went looking for Sandra by her mother's house on Nelson Street. Her mother tell me that Sandra only came there when she was hungry or need to change clothes.

"You don't know she gone through?" Miss James was shaking her head. "Bad-bad. I try with that girl. When she was with you, I say amen father, because I know you as a good man. But after she leave you, all fall down. She gone from coke-a-cola to coke. From cigarette to weed. I thought you know and you just turn your back on her. But she's my child, so what I will do? I can't slam the door on her when she wants a cup of tea or a place to rest her head. She's my cross to bear."

I didn't know what to say. Sandra hadn't come to see Shaquille in a while, but that wasn't so strange. She and my mother never get along too well, and with me so busy with Haji, I was leaving Shaq by Ma a lot more, but I hadn't realized that it was so long since I had seen her. Long enough for her to turn into a drug addict. I asked Miss James if she could tell me the places where Sandra might be hanging out.

"How I would know that, eh?" It was like she wanted to cry. Her one daughter. "I don't frequent those kind of places. You know how hard I tried to bring Sandra up right with all this badness around here."

"Is not too late," I was trying to reassure her, even if I couldn't convince myself that I could help Sandra – if she wanted help.

"I hear that the priests up Mount Saint Benedict have a programme to get people off drugs," Miss James was saying. "But is getting her there. She has to want to get clean. We can't force her. Haji don't have a programme for people like her?"

I wish I could have told her yes, but that was a ways down in Haji's programme. What you could do with young men, you can't do with young women. Still, if I could get Sandra to come and see Haji, maybe he would be able to convince her to get into treatment. He has a way with women that no other man in Santabella had.

So I promise Miss James I would do what I could, then I went to look for Sandfly because if anybody could find out where Sandra might be staying, other than Haji, it was him.

Drugs. Walking up Nelson Street, I could see how drugs had infected the community. Girls I had gone to school with, just leaning up against the wall, their clothes dirty-dirty, their eyes red like jumbie, trying to sell me their selves. Right by the corner, fellars trying to sell me coke. Right there in the open. You could tell me the police can't see what's going on? But is the police self responsible for bringing drugs into Santabella. Not all of them, mind you. But Haji have good information that at least one of the big boys on top was seriously involved in transporting major shipments from Columbia. There was no way the amount of drugs floating around Santabella could have come into the country without official help. No way.

We had people down in the compound who, in their old bad days, use to go out in small boats at night to pick up cargo and bring them back to shore. Where the Coast Guard was?

Haji had gone many times to the newspapers to tell them the stories, but them big boys in the police force have power too bad. Who could touch them? They had even killed one of our people who was on the force who they suspect had given Haji information. Shoot her down right there in the street, in her policewoman's uniform, then claimed it was bandits who do it. But we know better. We know who pulled the trigger, and who give the order.

Sandfly wasn't in his office, the little shoe shop in the back of that place on Henry Street, so I had to leave him a message. Then I went by a couple places in the People's Mall where two of Sandra's friends had stalls selling clothes, but they tell me they hadn't seen her in a long time either. I guess she was either too stoned or too shamed to let her old friends see her.

In her condition, how I could talk to her about divorce or permission to marry Beatrice? Knowing her, she would want money. Haji paid me bi-weekly, but I was putting most of that away for Shaquille. I want my son to go to university, make something big of himself. I wasn't about to give Sandra his money to spend on drugs. But I had to at least tell her I was thinking about somebody else.

It wouldn't be right for me to tell Beatrice about my feelings for her while I still married to Sandra, at least without Sandra knowing. So I had was to try my best to find her. I was getting anxious because the next day, I had a feeling we would get the signal.

I had promised Tante Melda that I would work on her kitchen cupboards, but I didn't go up on Wednesday because we had to spend most of the day praying and preparing. Then, what with having to look for Sandra, I would have to postpone going to Rosehill. That would mean I wouldn't get to see Beatrice.

I try to console myself that it was just as well anyway. After Friday, my life could change so radical, Beatrice might not want to even talk to me. Or, I could be dead. Haji had made that clear. Any one of us could die. We had to be prepared for that.

Before I become involved with Islam, I never used to think about death, but Haji make us aware that we have to be conscious of it, not only because of what we plan to do, but just as a matter of daily living.

If you become aware of death, then you live your life according to certain rules. You deal with people on an entirely different level from before. So thinking about death wasn't a bad thing since it's not possible to die without Allah's permission.

I tell myself I was ready. I'm not saying that deep down I didn't feel a little bit afraid. After all, I'm a human being, and maybe if I was born Muslim, some things, like death, I woulda accept without even thinking about it. But since I come to Islam late, I still have some beliefs from the old days inside me. Is not like Islam could whitewash you as soon as you learn to say Insh'Allah, you know. It takes years and years of studying and praying. I figure this trouble with Sandra was Allah's way of testing me, and I had to pull through. But I really would have liked to see Beatrice, to at least show her, with my eyes, how interested I was in her.

Back at the compound, I get a message that I was suppose to telephone Miss Farouka. Apparently, her daughter was in Jamaica visiting her father and had made a last minute decision to come to Santabella to see her mother before going back to Canada. Miss Farouka had to give a talk to a Women's Group meeting that night so she wanted me to go to the airport to pick up her daughter.

They say when your time comes, there's nothing you could do. That is your fate. I remember a story from one of my schoolbooks by a writer named Somerset Maugham called 'Appointment in Samarra'.

This servant – he was a Muslim too – living in Damascus, was in the market shopping for his boss when he looked up to see Death staring at him with this strange look on his face. Whoa! The servant get so frightened, he drop all the man's groceries as he ran from the market. Out of breath when he reach his boss's house, he could hardly get words out, but finally, his boss realize that what the servant wanted was to borrow a horse so he could escape to Samarra. Well, good servant that he was, the boss-man gave him his fastest horse, and the servant busted his way to Samarra where he had some relatives. Well, relatives put him up in a little batchie and the next day, he had was to go and buy some food for himself in the market. So he's there, picking through some tomatoes and thing, and you know how sometimes you could feel a person's eyes boring through you? Well, the servant looked and who he sees but that same Mr. Death standing across from him. The man nearly had a heart attack. 'What you doing here? What you doing here, looking at me like that?' he screamed at Mr. Death. 'Didn't I see you giving me that strange look yesterday in Damascus?' 'Yes,' Mr. Death tell him. 'That was my look of surprise. I was surprised to see you in Damascus because I knew I had an appointment with you today in Samarra.'

Maybe that story is to remind us that powerful as we humans think we are, we can't change fate, but try as I could, I haven't been able to accept that Ms Farouka's daughter had to die the way she did. Yusuf, well okay. But not that innocent girl. Maybe that was to teach us a lesson. Teach us that we hadn't really reached the point where we should have acted. We was too hasty. Somebody call the shots before the time was ripe, and while we believe we was doing Allah's work, it was somebody manipulating the scene, and the innocent had was to pay. Is something I will regret to the end of my days.

THIRTY-FOUR
Beatrice

Love. When I was a girl there was a story about King Edward and how he fall in love with a woman that he wasn't supposed to be involved with, and how he gave up his throne for her. In Santabella, a calypsonian had sung about it – "It was love, love, love alone/Cause King Edward to lose his throne."

I wondered if he ever regretted that decision. Turning his back on his family, on all of England for that woman. And she was a divorcee too. He choose love over duty. That's to tell you how powerful love is. He was a king; I was a small fry from Rosehill, but in a way, I was facing the same problem. All that stuff Sonny had said about us coming back home to help Rosehill, I really didn't believe. He had to say that because he knows me, but if I went to America to join him, I don't believe I would ever come back to Santabella to live because he didn't have anything to come back for. A holiday, yes. But not to live.

Moko couldn't recognize anybody. He was just waiting to die in the nursing home. Sonny didn't have any other blood relatives in Santabella so why he would want to come back? All the years I know him, the one goal he had was to leave Rosehill, leave Santabella. I'm not saying he didn't love where he was born, but it was a different kind of love from what I think Haji had for the country.

Haji. I hadn't even opened the letter from him, and to tell the truth, I was a little frightened to do so.

I picked it up three times but I couldn't open it. I was afraid that whatever he had written was just going to confuse me all the more, and my brains were already hurting. If Tante Vivian was still alive, I would have asked her to help me clear my mind. I had

190

never found her dream book and I hadn't remembered to ask Miss Ann if she had borrowed it. Tante had written little verses in the book that might have been able to help me.

To clear my head, I decide to go down to see Miss Ann to ask about the book, and just to walk a little on Rosehill before the rain start to fall.

Mango season was in full bloom. One of the things I love about Rosehill is that I could go in any neighbour's yard, pick some mangoes, cashews, plums, oranges, any fruit they had growing, and even the dogs wouldn't bark.

I slipped Haji's letter in my pants pocket, put on my sneakers, tied my head in case the drizzle turned to heavy rain, and went down to see Miss Ann. I hadn't talked to her in days, and I know she was still vexed with me. But that would pass because she loved Rosehill.

Here again, that word love come to my mind.

Miss Ann loved Rosehill, and I know that she wanted me to stay because she thought I could do something good for the children. It seemed everybody and his mother wanted me to do something to make other people happy. That was supposed to be how I lived my life?

Sammy was coming out of the track leading to his garden and we stopped to talk. He gave me some sweet potatoes and a breadfruit, and I walked with him to his house to get a bag to carry them.

"You going to the mosque on Friday?" he asked me. "I see you there the other day but I didn't have time to talk."

I tell him I wasn't sure and he said, "You mustn't pay attention to what bad-tongue people say about Haji, Beatrice."

"What bad-tongue people?" I asked him, even though I know full well he was talking about Miss Ann.

He just smiled. "You have to ask yourself how you want to live the rest of your life. Open your eyes and see what this country coming to and ask yourself if you going to sit down here on Rosehill and not do anything about it. Our old people, when they get out of the cane fields, they didn't just sit down on their hands. They get up. They walk all the way from Arouca to Santa Cruz. If they didn't have fresh water, they drink salt water from the sea, hurt belly or not. They cross over the valley where you know full well the shadow of death walk behind them but they didn't stop till they reach this place. Bush, Beatrice. Bush and big snake all over the place, but they cut the land and when they pass on, they leave it in good shape for we to use. You think the things you do for Rosehill, paying those leases, you think you do them out of the blue? No, girl. The ancestors put that in you because you carry their spirit. You and Sonny. The old ones pick you. Is the same thing I see with Haji. People might think I join up with him because of all that Muslim business, but is more than that. In him I see the spirit of the ancestors, and that mean more to me than religion. I don't have to put my business on a loudspeaker, but I want you, at least, to know – because Miss Ann could turn and twist things – Haji is a good-good man. And the Muslims, far as I could see, doing a lot of good in this hard country. But what I do, I do out of respect for the old people, and a better future for my grandchildren, Insh'Allah."

Insh'Allah? No matter what he claimed about ancestors, Haji had gotten to him too. That man know how to work people. He had a lot of intelligent people in his pocket. They probably all thought they were doing whatever for their own reasons, but he had them hooked. I could see that with Sammy.

He made me promise that I would ride down with him if I decided to go to the mosque. "The old man ent doing too well with the arthritis these days, girl," he laughed. "Sometimes I can't even count my change from them thiefing taxi-drivers."

Uncle Willy said Miss Ann had left since early morning to go to Moruga to see Mother Dinah. He couldn't talk to me for long because he had to feed the chickens and clean out the pig pen before getting ready for work. But he had to ask the usual question.

"You hear from Sonny?" I could count on Uncle Willy to ask me that question every single time he see me, and I was on the verge of saying no, but I couldn't lie.

"Heard from him today self," I said. "He send me a tape."

"Well make a copy for me, nuh girl. You know how I like American music. He put some Sam Cooke on there?"

I told him it didn't have any music.

"No music? So what kind of tape you talking about? Scots-tape?"

In between laughing at his little joke, I told him that Sonny had recorded a message, and that the be all and end all of it was that he wanted me to come to New York. Well, who tell me to say that? Uncle Willy went off.

"You see? You see what I always tell you, Bee? You never believe me, but I know Sonny. He tell me that Yankee woman didn't mean anything to him. The boy love you, Bee. Wait 'till Ann hear this. All-you getting married first, right? You know I could get a discount on the rum from Angostura, right? Just tell me how much bottles you want. Well, A-A. Is time the boy do what he say. That's meh boy, man. When you see Sonny tell you he going to do something, you could put your head on a block he's doing it. Who you going to ask to be father-giver, Beatrice? I wonder who Sonny having to stand up for him? When he coming? You know Ann. She will need time to set the fruits for the cake. All-yuh going to need a big hall because you know every man-Jack and Jane on Rosehill coming. I could get the invitations do up nice-nice for you cheap-cheap. And music, Bee. Half them steel-band fellars gone through with drugs but they could still hold their own. But you have to have some slow music for the old bones. I'm not saying I can't still ragga with the best of them but I like a slow dance better…"

Uncle Willy was so far gone with his planning for me and Sonny that I didn't have the heart to tell him that Sonny hadn't mentioned coming home to get married. In fact, he hadn't mentioned marriage to me at all. I was only assuming that was his meaning.

I leave Uncle Willy talking about killing one of the pigs for the wedding. I tell him I'll come back that night when I think Miss Ann was back from Moruga, but he was so wrapped up in his own delight that he just waved. I clean forget to ask him if he had seen Miss Ann with Tante's dream book.

On the way back up the hill, I called out to Miss Melda but her daughter tell me she wasn't home. Jestina wasn't home either, so I went back to the house.

I couldn't put it off any longer.

I took a scissors and cut open Haji's letter.

Dear Miss Salandy,
I apologize if I offended you when I offered to get you a visa to go to America, even though I was sincere. But you are the type of woman who must do what she wants to do without direction from any man. I could see this in you when you were in my office.

For my own reasons, call them selfish if you want, I would like you to stay in Santabella. But just as I had to leave, to see something of the rest of the world before I could really appreciate this country, you must feel that you need to go. It's as they say: you never miss the water till the well runs dry.

Whatever you do, I want you to know that all the things you have done for Rosehill, the people will remember. The way Mother Dinah, Sammy, and some of the other people from Rosehill talk about you, you have made your mark on the Hill. You have a revolutionary spirit, Beatrice, whether you admit it to yourself or not.

Massive changes are coming to this country, and you could be part of it. I wish I could tell you more, but if you are around, you'll see. If you are gone away, you will hear and you will understand that some of us have to stay home, some of us have to do what is right for the people. I will pray for Allah's blessings upon you, wherever you land.

Whatever you do with the rest of your life, from this day forward, know that there are people in this country who have a special love for you.
Sincerely,
Imam Haji Ben Yedder

I read the last sentence over and over. A special love for me. What was this man trying to tell me? What did he want me to think? Common sense should tell me that this man was trying to manipulate me. He knew well and good what he was doing when I was in his office, rubbing my face, getting me hot all over and then just turning away as if nothing happened. That was how he operated. That letter. He was telling me he was letting me go but

194

what he really was hoping was that I would do the exact opposite. That was his intention. I knew all that, but I couldn't change the way my inside was burning up. I read the letter again.

What was I going to hear about? He was planning something. Oh Lord Jesus Christ. What was this man planning to do? All this talk about massive changes. Abdul had said the same thing in the taxi. What kind of changes they planning to make in Santabella? No wonder the police always raiding his compound. I didn't want to get in any trouble. Love or no love, I never wanted to see the inside of a jail cell again. If it hadn't been for Sonny, I would have still been in there. Uh-uh. Miss Ann was right. This man was trouble with a capital T.

I went to bed thinking about it all, and praying for Tante to give me some clarity, and by morning, with all the dogs on Rosehill in a rampage, cocks crowing as if the world was coming to an end, I wake up with my mind clear that whatever I do, it would be for myself.

I went down by Miss Melda's house – she had gone out early – and used her telephone to call the airline. If I could get a ticket, I would leave that very day on an evening flight. I didn't have much more to put in my suitcase. I would pass and see Reme for the last. Then I would head to the airport. I wished I could have gone down to the sea to bathe for the last time, but where I was going, the same water would be there to wash the blight from my body and refresh my soul.

THIRTY-FIVE
Abdul

When I start this, I promise myself that I would tell the truth. But what I've realized is that the truth of what I know is not everything. Yes, I was one of the Haji's right-hand men, but even the right hand doesn't always know what the left hand doing, and Haji keep a lot of information to himself.

One of the rules I, and all of us who commit ourselves to the movement, had promised to abide, was to take and follow Haji's orders. When I say "orders" I have to qualify that, because if we all agree on a plan, not necessarily on how it would be carried out, but the general principles of it, then, on one level, Haji wasn't giving us orders.

Somebody has to be in control, and because it was he who washed the yampee from our eyes so we could see what was going on in this country, and because it was he who teach us the religion, a religion as old in Santabella as the first Africans who they dragged unto these shores, long-long before them Indians arrive, well, it's simple mathematics why we would listen to him and do what he tell us.

That doesn't mean that I know what was going on in all quarters. I didn't know every chapter and every verse. I didn't open the boxes Sudix and I brought back on the boat from down the islands, but that isn't to say I didn't have an idea what was in them. And I have to admit that I was ready to lose my life if that was necessary.

I hadn't seen Shaquille for a couple days, so Haji tell me I could go, but if I had time, I should try to come back to eat.

I had wanted to talk to him about Sandra to see if he could put somebody on to finding her, maybe bring her down to the compound for a few days where some of the women could try to detox her, but he was busy-busy with everything, and a lot of overseas phone calls. Besides all the men had assignments, so I just file it away for later.

As soon as I walk in to my mother's house she tell me Tante Melda ring up to ask if I'm not coming to do her cupboards again.

"You should know better than to promise that woman anything. Now is my poor soul she's going to bother until you do those cupboards. Never mind that my own kitchen needs fixing. Hers come first. Nothing change with that woman."

To tell the truth, right then and there, Tante's cupboards was the last thing on my mind. I just wanted to play with my son for a while, put everything else out from me. But my mother know me, so all the while I was in the house playing with Shaquille, reading him a story, she was looking at me in a strange kind of way.

When I finally sit down at the table to drink some tea, she start to tell me about some dream she had been having all week about a lot of men in white garments, like the ones she makes for Haji and the rest of us, how she can't see their faces, but they were all in a building, a round building, and how somebody lock the doors from outside and set the place on fire, and how she wake up screaming my name because even though she couldn't see the faces, she knew, in her heart that I was in the round building burning up.

"The only round building I know is the mosque," she tell me. "Try your best to stay away from down there for a few days if you can, son. I frightened for you. My heart beating fast-fast when I get up. I know something going to happen. Them policemen not going to leave Haji alone. They against him too bad. You have Shaquille to think about. You know I getting old. If something happens to you, who going to take care of him? Sandra is no use, you know that."

To keep her from going on and on about the dream, I tell her about Sandra, and good woman that my mother is, she say if I could find her, she would be willing to take her up Mount Saint Benedict to try to get clean. "Somebody have to reach out to that girl. She's not bad, you know. It's just those drugs in her system

197

poisoning her. Poor girl." Then she start up again about the mosque.

"Try. Try to stay 'way from there. You know me and my dreams. God does send you signs, Abdul, but young people like you don't pay attention. When something going to happen, especially something big to affect a lot of people for good or bad, God will send you signs, most times in your dreams."

Just to make her laugh, I tell her, "Oh yeah? Then how come your dreams didn't tell you I meet a nice-nice girl?"

"Is about time." She was smiling. "All you do is work and work. She's Muslim?"

"Not yet. But she's been to the mosque and I think she's coming back."

"Who is her family? Where's she from? Don't get involved with no chupidy girl, eh. She have any children?"

"All these questions! I only talk to the girl a few times. But you know her. Her name was in the papers not so long ago."

"Well if her name was in the papers, she's either a big pappy or she do something bad. Where you meet her?"

I really didn't want to tell her any more about Beatrice. Besides, I had was to get back to the mosque so I get up from the table and give her a hug. "Wait till you meet her. I betting you five dollars you'll like her."

"You going by the mosque? I know you. When you want to avoid me you always trying to bet me something. As if I does gamble. But please, Abdul. What you have to do there so important? You can't stay from there for a while? I just have this bad feeling…"

"I thought it was a bad dream," I told her.

"You know what I'm trying to tell you. It come to me. That vision come to me. And since then, this bad-bad feeling take over. Be careful, do, Abdul. And tell Haji, I say for him to be careful too. I think he trust a lot more people than he should trust. That Bilal? My blood never take him. Haji needs to keep a close eye on him. You too."

One thing about Ma, when she first meet you, if her blood doesn't take to you, that is it. I couldn't tell her that she was right about Bilal, but she was. They say keep close to your friends and keep your enemies even closer. We know long time that Bilal make a deal with the devils. Haji had that under control.

I leave Ma still worrying in spite of all the assurances I give her. Miss Farouka's daughter's plane was coming in later than expected because of bad weather in Jamaica, so instead of going up to the airport to wait, I stop by the compound.

Sudix was there with a few other men going over some information Haji had given them before he had to leave. On a side table was a feast Sister Fareeda and the other women had prepared for us to celebrate the end of the special fast. It was like Eid.

When Haji come back, he didn't even stop to eat. He just indicate for me to come to the office. He lock the door, and tell me to sit down. But he didn't go behind his desk. He pull up the other chair next to me.

For a minute or two, he just sit there, quiet-quiet, breathing deep and slow, looking down at his hands. Then he give a little sigh, a little kinda half-smile before he start talking.

"Whatever happens tomorrow. No matter how things turn out, I want you to know that I always believed I was acting in the best interests of the people."

"I never doubt that," I tell him. "I…"

"Hear me out," he raised his hand. "I see you as my right hand man. I might not always have treated you like that, but not a man in this place have the kind of sincerity you have, Abdul. In some ways, you're a better man than me by half. Your faith is simple. Mine? Mine is complicated by a lot of things that I can't talk about. I believe, yes, but that belief get tied up a long time ago with certain people who had agendas but not the faith, even though they pretend they had it. You know what's going to happen. You know why, or at least you know why I say it has to happen. But there's a price to pay for everything on the face of this earth, and before the sun come from behind the hills, I want you to know that all the plan we plan, things might not work out the way we want it. Man could plan; God un-plans. No matter what, though, I want you to know that I trust you more than any man on the face of this earth."

Shaking his head, he take another deep breath before adding,

"I wish I had made some better decisions in who we have as friends, but, at the time, I didn't have any other choice. You play with the hand you get. I just have to believe that Allah will see us through to a good end."

Over five years I in the movement, and that was the first time I see Haji looking like that. It was like he was carrying the weight of the whole world on his shoulders. Not like Atlas. Broke-down. The man look like he age ten years since I see him earlier.

I sit there, feeling sad, listening to him. It was like he was saying a kinda farewell. Maybe he realize that no matter how it turn out, after tomorrow, life was never going to be the same, and maybe it was going to be worse. Maybe he was wishing he coulda put it off. But the time was bound to come. Was a lot I still didn't understand, especially about the overseas contacts. In time to come, I would have to sort it out, but right then, I just wanted him to know that I was ready to go to the wall. But before I could say it, he changed the subject.

"You see Shaq?" he ask me.

I tell him yes, but I didn't say anything about Ma and her visions.

Then he get up and look at me. "If I've never said thank you, I want to say it now. Thank you, my brother." He reach out to shake my hand but without thinking, I just put my arms round him. He didn't move away. We stand close like that, he patting my back as if I was the one needing strength. Then he ask me to tell Sudix to come in as he went to sit down behind his desk.

Just as I put my hand on the door knob, I hear him say, "If you get the chance, you should marry that girl Beatrice. Both of you would make a good team."

When I leave them to go to the airport, he and Sudix and some of the others were still locked in his office, talking. All the way up the highway, I couldn't get his words out from my mind. I had this funny feeling that he was trying to tell me to read between the lines, but why? Everything was in place. I would never believe that he would run out on us. Cock will get teeth before that happen. But his mood was what you would call sombre, you know? Maybe the weight of what was going to happen was sinking in, and he finally realized we couldn't turn around, so that caused him to feel a certain amount of sadness.

I myself was feeling the same way. I wouldn't say I was doubting what we had to do, but, as I say before, I would be lying if I didn't say I was frighten. Not for myself, but for my son, and for how Santabellans might react.

For all the years those corrupt politicians using the people for their own good, you'd think the masses would welcome change, but that might not be true. They could talk a blue streak in taxis; they could call in to the radio stations and write letters to the newspapers to complain, but when it come to actually doing something, taking action, I didn't believe we could count on them. That's why the politicians could take advantage of them for so long. They know the only time we mass-up is at Carnival. Wining down the streets. All the rest of the year is ole talk.

That had to change. Haji have a lot of faith, well, not faith so much, but he really believed that people was feeling so repressed, all they need was somebody showing them a way, and they would follow. I wasn't so sure. But we had was to make the move.

The police was getting ready to raid us again. In fact, Haji had give certain information to Bilal. When he pass that on, we couldn't stay still. Besides, some of the big boys in certain parts of the Regiment start putting on the pressure, telling him it was time to act, and that give him the confidence they would be at his back. That's why I was so surprised about what he had to say to me. Maybe he find out something that day that tell him he was just a pawn in somebody's chess game.

Me? I would have never put my trust in anybody but God. Not in them army men. They wasn't like us. In Santabella, is not so much about race, or skin colour. The struggle is really about class, fuelled by religion. We have men in this country could be black like tar, but because they went to Saint Mary's College, they think they in a totally different class from the rest of we.

A lot of them fellars on the other side who promised to join up with Haji, well, they went to schools like that. He didn't. He was a poor fella who come up hard; went away on his own dollar; get educated, and come back to help the people. Them big fellars resent people like Haji. They look on him and we as upstarts; as if we don't deserve the best in we own country. Is only for them.

Sometimes, I think Haji must have got so wrapped up in the fact that he was up there in the same league with big men in the country – because so many people come begging him for help – he believe they had the same principles as him. I see and I know, but I couldn't tell him he was wrong. Watching from the outside, I could see it. I don't think he could see it, and even if he did, the course was set. It didn't have no roundabout for him to turn off on.

I think Haji believed that the sufferers and the strugglers in Santabella would rise up and follow him, but there again I had my own set of worries. I used to read a lot of books, and when I look at uprisings across the world, all the poor people usually do is burn down their neighbourhoods, break store windows, and take whatever they could carry.

Is true, Haji has been teaching them good principles for years, but he couldn't reach everybody, and too besides, when poor people see opportunities to full up their fridge, you think they remembering anything about revolution?

So these things keep bothering me, that's why I say I was frightened. Haji looked like he was feeling the same way. But I start feeling better when I get the call that the regiment was raiding the base in Moruga.

I had was to laugh because things was going down just as Haji tell us. Bilal had passed the information that we have weapons stored up in Moruga. I could imagine the army searching through the boxes of vegetables and not finding a single gun.

It was well after midnight by the time the plane with Miss Farouka's daughter arrive from Jamaica, but I had put my time waiting to good use. Some of our people work up there at the airport, and Haji had given me some equipment to drop off for them.

By the time I reached Miss Farouka's house to drop off Yassi, it was one o'clock in the morning. All the way down Yassi was carrying on, upset that one of her bags hadn't arrived. I would have promised her that I would go back up to the airport on Friday to get it for her but I couldn't do that. She just keep on complaining that she had some presents for her mother in the bag and she was afraid the airport people would thief them.

"Come on," she pleaded. "You know Haji is always so busy on Friday. They say the bag will be on the four o'clock flight. You could bring me up after Juma. Come on, Mister Abdul. Please."

She always called me Mister Abdul. A nice, respectful girl. But I couldn't promise her I would bring her to get the bag because of what might be happening. I just laugh and tell her that I would tell Haji about the bag and she wasn't to worry, we would get it for her.

I wanted to go home and sleep because it would be a while before I would be able to close my eyes if Haji give the word later that day, but I say let me take a look for Sandra in town. See if she was hanging out in any of the night clubs.

At the third one I tried, bottom of Charlotte Street, she was there, leaning against the wall, her eyes red-red like rookoo. I tell you, I nearly went into shock to see how thin-thin she was. Dry and hard like a piece of bamboo. A cigarette stub burning her fingers and it was like she wasn't even feeling the pain.

She didn't want to hear anything from me. I try to get her to come into the car with me, but she refuse. She start to cuss me, my mother, Haji. That girl's mouth was a cesspool.

A lady selling newspapers and dinner mints nearby tell me, "You see what drugs doing to our young women?" She said she knew Sandra from since she was small – that's why Sandra hang out close to her stall at night – and her throat had gone dry from trying to talk to her, to get her to stop.

"I give her a little something to eat every day, because she doesn't even think about food. Every cent she makes goes to the drugs."

I was afraid to ask her how Sandra was earning money, so I just give her a few dollars I had in my pocket and asked her to pass them on.

What else I could do, eh? My heart hurt me for Sandra and for Shaquille, because I know one day he would start asking serious questions about his mother. What I was going to tell him?

When you looked around Santabella, is thousands of young people just like Sandra wasting away their lives on dope. They not bringing it into the country; they not making big-big money from it, and that is just one of the things Haji wanted to change. These young people had no hope. They so blind on drugs, they couldn't see any future for theirselves. Somebody had to stop the downward slide poor people on in Santabella.

Instead of going to my place, I went to sleep with Shaquille by my mother's house. I just crawled up in my son's bed and hold him for the three-four hours I could rest my eyes before I had to get up and pray.

THIRTY-SIX
Abdul

I was glad Ma wasn't going to come to the mosque that Friday. There was going to be a big cricket match between Santabella and Sri Lanka, and traffic would be slow for hours all day in the area near the compound. Besides that, she had a headache, she tell me, from worrying about that dream.

"I know you and Haji and the rest of them fellars want to do something for this country," she tell me. "But people might not be grateful, Abdul."

"We not looking for gratitude, Ma," I try to console her. "But we can't just sit down and let this country go down the drain. Look how much drugs taking over the youths? Somebody need to put a stop to that."

Then I tell her about Sandra, and she started worrying about Shaquille. "You mustn't tell him that, you hear me?" she warned. "You must never tell him that about his mother. Children have a strange way of holding theyself responsible for what their parents do. I don't want that put on this boy. Come, let me kneel down and pray with you. I don't understand all that Arabic prayers, so I will just say my own prayers. Is the same God we talking to."

That was the one and only time my mother ever kneel down and pray with me since I was a little boy. It was a blessing.

As I was leaving, the news came on the radio that the army had raided Mother Dinah's place the night before, and they were still in the process of digging up the fields where, on good information, they knew that certain persons had hidden weapons they intended to use to disrupt the peace of the nation.

"You see what I telling you, Abdul?" Ma said. "Please do be careful."

"Everything is in Allah's hands," I tell her.

Shaquille was still asleep when I leave the house but I'm glad I kiss my son on his forehead.

At the mosque, Haji lock the door on a small group of us. He tell us that this was the last opportunity to walk away.

"Nobody will give us our freedom," he remind us. "We have been waiting hundreds of years in this country for that and it hasn't come. How much longer we should wait? People have to make the change they want. In South Africa, Ireland, Palestine, all over the world, suffering people stand up and fight. If we don't do something to ease the pressure on our lives, who we expect to do it for us? Look at Haiti? The petit bourgeoisie in Haiti living high off the hog, but the poor have to run to the sea and even if they reach America, they getting locked up. The great African American writer, James Baldwin, wrote once that the poor are always crossing the Sahara. Well, there is an oasis at the end. I believe that. If you believe that, you'll stay."

Nobody get up and leave.

We pray again, and then I get the surprise of my life, because no way in Heaven I would have believed that was where Haji had put the weapons. Time and time again, the police had raided us, but the mosque itself was sacred ground. They would dig up the yard, and search down the other buildings, but they never violate the mosque. It bother me that we might have been defiling the mosque, but this was a struggle for survival.

After we went over the plans for the last time, we prayed again. Then we went back outside. By the time people started coming to Juma, the place look as normal as ever.

People say that the Haji's wives had was to know what he was planning, but I can't believe that. If Miss Farouka did know what was going to happen that Friday, no way would she have had her daughter come to Santabella. No way.

Right before Juma, she pulled me aside and asked me if I would go up and get the bag for Yassi. "Times like this I wish she had a driver's license. The girl's harassing me." She was laughing, but

I know how Yassi could be. When she wanted you to do something for her, she never let up until you say yes.

I asked Miss Farouka if she had told Haji about the suitcase and she said she hadn't spoken to him that day. He had spent the night at Zhara House.

I tell her if he give me the word, I would go to the airport. But I know that with what was going to happen, that suitcase was the last thing Haji would be concerned about.

I was wrong.

Right before he went into the mosque, he pulled me aside.

"I want you up at the airport," he tell me. "Yusuf came over last night. He'll take your place. You be at the airport. Keep your eyes open. Report to us what they doing up there."

Yusuf? Yusuf was to take my place at Parliament House? Haji could see the questions in my eyes.

"He needs to prove himself. You? I don't have any doubts about you."

I asked him if Calu had come over because I didn't see him at the mosque.

"Calu has his own responsibility down the islands," Haji tell me. "Don't worry about Calu. When we start out, don't go through town. Take the road over the hill."

"You think I should take Yassi with me?"

He give me her airline ticket and the chit for the bag. "She's going to stay with her mother. They'll be safe. Don't worry."

Haji is not a man given to hugging and all that sort of thing, but he hold out his arms and give me a hug. "Whatever happens, we making history today. This country will never forget us."

We exchanged the peace, and he went into the mosque.

I looked around to see if Beatrice had come but didn't see her. I ask Sammy and he tell me that he had talked to her the day before and he was hoping she would come down with him, but when he went and knock on her door, nobody answer.

I was glad that she hadn't come even though I really wanted to see her. Maybe after all this… but I didn't want to speculate on how she would feel about me. I just had to pray to Allah that she would want to be with me.

Sammy tell me that my Tante Melda was vexed that I hadn't

come to do her cupboards. "I tell her I will do them for her. You have a lot of responsibilities down here. So don't worry yuh head about that."

That was how people in our movement work. We all know one hand can't clap. It's a pity the rest of the country didn't see it like that.

THIRTY-SEVEN
Beatrice

Reme couldn't stop crying, she was so happy that I was leaving. She kept telling me, "Walk good, Beatrice. Walk good. God opened a way for you. Remember to thank him every day of your life. And don't forget your old mother, eh?"

"Ma, you not old. Stop talking like that. As soon as I find myself, I'm sending for you. Maybe even by Christmas. But it's getting late. I don't want to get caught up in that Friday traffic leaving town and miss my plane."

I had to pull away from her because the taxi was waiting to take me to the airport. Last thing she called out was for me to send her a television, a colour one.

Traffic going back into town was really bad because of the cricket match. It was like the whole of Santabella had taken the afternoon off to go to the game. When we passed by the mosque, Juma had just finished, and people were pouring out the gate.

I imagined Haji was back in his office with his people. Abdul must be there too, taking care of business as usual.

It was strange, but once morning had come and I had made up my mind, I wasn't feeling any sorrow or regret in my heart. It was as if a big load had fallen from my shoulders or a screen from my eyes.

I wished Haji and Abdul and Sammy and all of them the best of luck, but maybe they didn't depend on luck. For them, it was always Allah.

By the time we got to the airport, it was nearly four o'clock.

I made it through security and was looking to buy a magazine in one of the shops right before going through to the gate when a lady came out of the back office to tell the clerk that she had just heard that Muslim man on the radio declaring that he had taken over the radio station and his people was in charge of the country.

Oh my God!

A coup!

I dropped the magazine and ran toward the gate, praying to God that my flight to Miami was still going to leave.

They were boarding people fast-fast. I shoved my ticket into the girl's hand and ran across the Tarmac to that plane.

We were up in the air when the captain came over the intercom to say that the city was in flames.

I prayed all the way for God to keep my mother safe, and I prayed for Rosehill, especially for Miss Ann, Melda, Jestina, Sammy, Uncle Willy and all the rest of my family.

I prayed for Abdul because he seemed like a good man, and for Haji. But most of all, I asked God, Allah, to take care of all the people in Santabella.

What would happen to them? Haji had brought Allah to the islands. I just hoped it was going to turn out to be a good thing, but I was worried.

I was still crying inside for my country when the plane landed in Miami airport.

THIRTY-EIGHT

Miss Ann

All night I stay in that canal, my leg getting stiff with cramps. I thought I was dead for sure. I never pray so hard in my life. I remind God about all the good I do in this world. I couldn't believe he would let me die like that.

I had to plug up my ears to stop from hearing the animal noise coming from the bush. I couldn't stop the mosquitoes though, and by foreday morning my arms and legs had big red welts on them. Them mosquitoes had a field day on me.

I never see the army pass back so I had to figure they were still digging up Mother Dinah's place, doing what only them and they God knows. I was praying they would see me when they pass by, but I couldn't keep my head up.

When I finished eating the coo-coo, I put the plastic bowl on a piece of stick. I figure as soon as I hear anybody passing, I would raise the stick. Maybe they would see me and stop.

And that's how the old man find me. Mr. Pashule he tell me was his name. Coming up the road early-early to go to his garden, he see me waving the stick and was he who save my life.

He put me in his donkey-cart and take me back to his house for his wife to take care of me.

When I ask him if he had seen Mother Dinah, he said she had gone to do a baptism and she didn't usually come back for two days. You could tell me why that damn girl hadn't tell me that? But is so some of these young people is in this country. Chupid-chupid.

Miss Pashule tie up my ankle with some aloes and make me lie down in their hammock because she tell me the bus wasn't going to come until afternoon. I tell you, is country people who will save this country. They have good-good hearts. If I did fall down in the road in town, you think I would be here talking like this? But those country people treat me like family. I have to remember to send them a nice rum cake when Christmas come. Miss Pashule give me two aspirin, and she tell her little grandson to push the hammock, and is so I get some sleep.

I feel somebody shaking me and, when I open my eyes, was the old lady leaning over me to say that she had just heard on the radio that the Muslims take over Santabella. Well look my crosses, nuh.

"They playing all kind of calypsos on the radio," she say. "And the Imam come on to say he want everybody to stay calm, that he wasn't going to hurt the people, but the people not listening. They burning down the town. Robbing and stealing. They even burn down the police headquarters. Is a whole big mess. I just hope they don't come up here. I see the regiment flying up the road last night. If them Muslims come up here, is war for so. What this world coming to?"

Mr. Pashule come back into the yard right then to say he had was to leave his garden because the army officers set fire to the fields and run everybody off.

"They leave a few men up there but the rest of them jump in their trucks and head out to the airport through the back road. Is a mess in truth. They search me down even though I tell them I ent have nothing to do with them Muslims."

He was bleeding in his forehead where they had hit him with a gun. Poor man. Miss Pashule cleaned the cut up with Dettol. He really need to get some stitches but we couldn't go anywhere.

I use their telephone to try to call Melda to give Willy a message, but the phone line gone dead. I only hope he lock down my parlour before them hooligans break in and tief all my things.

Santabella is Africa now? We having coup like them Africans? You see what happens when Black people get mixed up in Indian thing? What we know bout Muslim? Bout Islam. Bout Allah and all that. That Haji. You see? You see what that man do? I warn them time and time again that man was up to no good. A blind man could see he was trouble from the start. What he want to go and take over the country for, eh? I hope Melda and Jestina and that Sammy happy now. They could put on long dress and walk about town with their head covered. Not me. Not me. Haji will have to shoot me first.

Allah in the islands. Eh-heh. The country burning down. Lemme see Allah help them now.

"Miss Pashoule, if the roads block, I might have to use your donkey to get home, oui. I just hope my poor little parlour ent get ramsacked. Lordy-lord. Put a hand. Put a hand, master."

It take two days before I could get home because you could hardly get transportation. Is Charmers come up to get me. Jestina send him. I never see Mother Dinah after that. I hear the army mash up her place and she went Grenada. Beatrice leave too. She get away just in time. Tante Vivian must still be watching out for her. The government try to punish we in Rosehill because they say we side with the Muslims. Up to this day, the children ent have a decent school to go to.

That Haji mess up a lot of people's lives, oui. They have his arse in jail. I don't care what Sammy and Melda and Jestina say about all the good he do. I hope he stay there 'til he rot.

THIRTY-NINE
Abdul

I had just reached the airport when it start. I never got Yassi's bag because the authorities close down everything. Only one or two planes were able to take off before the army arrive. They barricade everybody in the terminal, cordon off the car parks, then block all the roads in and out of the airport. I let Haji know what was going on.

He was at the television station. He was waiting for the people from the Regiment, the ones who had promised to help, to come up from the base.

I and some fellars were off by ourselves in a corner of the airport, waiting to see what Haji want us to do, but he had to wait for the Regiment guys because we didn't have enough men to do everything.

Six o'clock come and Haji call to say that the regiment side still hadn't come. Then he tell me the saddest news. Yusuf had got shoot down at police headquarters and worse than that, some policemen had gone to Miss Farouka's house, bust down the door, and killed Yassi. I know that would send Miss Farouka mad. Her one daughter.

I never thought I would hear Haji crying, but I know he was.

Seven. Eight. Midnight come and no Regiment. I had a feeling all along that them big boys wasn't going to do what they tell Haji they would do. All they wanted was for we to do the grunt work for them. Clear the bush, right? Maybe get we-self kill. Then they could come and take over.

I coulda tell Haji that's how it was going to be but I keep my suspicions to myself. He learn the hard way that not everybody in this country have the same agenda, even when they put their hand on a Bible and swear.

The worst part of the whole business was what the people do. They run amuck in town, burning, thiefing, left, right and centre. That is what we sacrifice for? For bandits to run up Belmont with a microwave on their heads? For women to ramsack the stores for a few panty? Maybe they think Haji just want to give them the chance to get some freeness. In a way, that is the mentality of a lot of people in Santabella. *Let me see what I could get without paying for it.* But somebody have to pay. Somebody always have to pay.

Next day, the army come out in full force and start shooting people on the street. They put a ring of soldiers round the airport, the Parliament building, and the television station where Haji was. They shut down the broadcast antennae so Haji couldn't communicate with the people.

The last time he call me from the station was just before he was going to come out. The fellars at the parliament building had tell him that one of the ministers get shoot. He wasn't dead, but Haji say he don't want any more killing. We wasn't supposed to kill anybody. That might sound strange because we had guns, but we wasn't supposed to shoot first.

After we talk, I went in the toilet at the airport to wash my face before I start praying for Allah to keep him and the rest of them safe in the hands of the infidels.

That was nearly a year now. They holding him and about two hundred of the members down the islands, but the lawyers say is a good chance they will get out soon. Haji was smart. When he realize that the Regiment wasn't coming to help, he made sure that the PM and the ministers in Parliament sign an agreement not to prosecute. Nobody hold a gun to their head for that. Just talk. The British lawyers we get say this is ironclad, so is just a matter of time before Haji and them get let out. Is the government side playing games, getting the case put off every time, so we people could stay in jail.

I hear from Calu now and then. He's overseas.

I never get arrested. They pull me in for questioning, but

nobody ever see me with a gun in my hand so they had was to let me go. But for the rest of my life, I will feel responsible.

Yes, we made history in truth, but what we do was wrong.

Haji might never admit that in public, but he bound to be thinking so. Yassi, Yusuf, both of them dead. A lot of we fellars get shoot by the police and now have to walk with one foot. Everything at the compound get mash up, even the school. Everything fall down. All for what?

Ma was right. Santabellans didn't appreciate what we do. Oh, I'm not saying all the people hate we. A lot of them don't, but they put their hands over their mouth when they talk, while the rest of them bad-minders writing letters to the newspapers calling for the government to hang Haji and the rest without trials.

I hear we make international news, but it was a one-day wonder.

The day after the coup, Saddam Hussein invade Kuwait, and the world forget about Santabella. Maybe that was a good thing, but sometimes I wonder if certain people overseas set us up as a distraction. The intention was never for us to give up so easy, but to this day I believe Yassi getting killed like that cause Haji to call the truce.

I decide to tell the story because we coming on the first anniversary, and I still feeling the weight of what we do every day as God send. We had a lot of good reasons to do it, but we shoulda do it different. Maybe some people get lucky fighting fire with fire, but too many innocents lost their lives in Santabella over what we do, and I can't see what we accomplish.

I go and visit Haji once a week to tell him how things going at the compound. Is not much left of what we had, except the mosque. Some of the faithful, mostly the women and children, still come to Friday prayers. I try my best to carry on, and every once in a while, one of the imams from down in the country will come.

We all just holding strain until the cases they bring against Haji wend their way through the courts. We know that he will walk out a free man one of these days because what he do, he do for Allah. Allah is especially merciful to those who act in his behalf.

Haji's wives? Not one of them leave. Not even Sister Farouka.

216

She lose her one daughter and that woman still stay strong with Haji. That is love father. I could only pray that, one day, Allah will grant me the same.

Tante Melda tell me Beatrice went Miami. I think about her sometimes, wondering how things coulda been different. I wish I'd had a chance to tell her how I was feeling. Tante Melda say she will get her address for me and I'll write to her. Who knows? Maybe one day I will meet up with her over there. We'll lie down on the beach in Miami and look up at the stars and hope they keep shining bright over Santabella.

In the meanwhile, I'm doing the best I can to take care of my son, and my old mother, and I still have my faith. Ahamdullilah.

ABOUT THE AUTHOR

Brenda Flanagan was born in Trinidad in 1949, the twelfth of fourteen children in an impoverished family. Her father was a barman, her mother a laundress. Brenda Flanagan recalls having a hunger for involvement with the wider world and dreamt of being a writer. She started writing poetry at the age of ten and by thirteen she was singing calypsos and earning money for it. However, at the age of fourteen she had to leave school to help support her family, by then only parented by her mother. She worked for a time in a factory, then was taken on as a trainee reporter of *The Nation*, the newspaper of the then ruling People's National Movement led by Dr. Eric Williams.

In 1967 she left Trinidad for the USA, working initially as a domestic servant. Marriage and motherhood deflected her plans to study, but by 1975, then a single mother, she began undergraduate studies at the University of Michigan. There she won prestigious Hopwood Awards for her short stories, a novel and drama.

She is the author the prizewinning novel, *You Alone Are Dancing* (Peepal Tree Press). Her collection of short stories, *In Praise of Island Women and Other Crimes* will be reissued by Peepal Tree in 2010.

Brenda Flanagan teaches creative writing, Caribbean and African American Literatures at Davidson College, North Carolina. She is also a United States cultural ambassador, and has served in Kazakstan, Chad and Panama.

David Dabydeen
Our Lady of Demerara
ISBN: 9781845230692; pp. 288; August 2008; £9.99

The ritual murder of a mysterious Indian girl and the flight of seedy drama critic from his haunts in the back street of Coventry to the Guyana wilds to find out more about the fragmented journals of an Irish missionary in Demerara are brought together in a hugely imaginative exploration of spiritual malaise and redemption.

Curdella Forbes
A Permanent Freedom
ISBN: 9781845230616; pp. 210; July 2008, £8.99

Crossing the space between the novel and short fiction, this collection weaves nine individual stories about love, sex, death and migration into a single compelling narrative that seizes the imagination with all the courage, integrity and folly of which the human spirit is capable.

Earl Long
Leaves in a River
ISBN: 9781845230081; pp. 208; November 2008; £8.99

What brings Charlo Pardie, a peasant farmer on an island not unlike St. Lucia, on the edge of old age, to leave his wife, family and land and take himself to the house of Ismene L'Aube, known to all as a prostitute? And what, three years later, takes him home again?

Anton Nimblett
Sections of an Orange
ISBN: 9781845230746; pp.152, June 2009; £8.99

In this collection, characters migrate between stories, (just as they migrate between Trinidad and New York), being sometimes at the fringes, sometimes at the centre. Writing with equal empathy about the lives of gay men, heterosexuals, young and old, country folk and urbanites, Anton Nimblett is a singularly attractive new voice in Caribbean writing.

Geoffrey Philp
Who's Your Daddy? and Other Stories
ISBN: 9781845230777; pp. 160; April 2009; £7.99

Whether set in the Jamaican past or the Miami present, whether dealing with sexual errantry, skin-shade and culture wars, with manifestations of the uncanny, or with teenage homophobia, Geoffrey Philp's second collection confirms his status as a born storyteller.

Patricia Powell
The Fullness of Everything
ISBN: 9781845231132; pp. 240; May 2009; £8.99

When Winston receives a telegram informing him of his father's imminent death, his return to Jamaica is very reluctant. 25 years in the USA without contact with his family has allowed mutual resentments to mature. Told through the perspectives of Winston and his estranged brother, the novel explores the power of past hurts and the possibilities of transcending them.

Raymond Ramcharitar
The Island Quintet
ISBN: 9781845230753; pp. 232; June 2009; £8.99

In these sometimes seamy, often darkly comic and bracingly satirical stories, Ramcharitar reveals Trinidad as a globalised island with permeable borders, frequent birds of passage and outposts in New York and London. His characters scramble for survival, fame and fortune in an island struggling to come to terms with both its history and its present.

Ed. Courttia Newland & Monique Roffey
Tell-Tales Four: The Global Village
ISBN: 9781845230791; pp. 212; March 2009; £8.99

With contributions from Olive Senior, Matt Thorne, Sophie Woolley, Adam Thorpe, Catherine Smith and twenty others, this collection of stories from the UK-based Tell-Tales literary collective touches on love, sex, death, war, global warming, immigration and crime in sometimes dark and sometimes funny ways.

CARIBBEAN MODERN CLASSICS

Spring 2009 titles

Jan R. Carew
Black Midas
Introduction: Kwame Dawes
ISBN: 9781845230951; pp. 272; 23 May 2009; £8.99

This is the bawdy, Eldoradean epic of the legendary 'Ocean Shark', first published in 1958, who makes and loses fortunes as a pork-knocker in the gold and diamond fields of Guyana, discovering that there are sharks with far sharper teeth in the city.

Jan R. Carew
The Wild Coast
Introduction: Jeremy Poynting
ISBN: 9781845231101; pp. 240; 23 May 2009; £8.99

A sickly city child is sent away to the remote Berbice village of Tarlogie. Here he must find himself, make sense of Guyana's diverse cultural inheritances and come to terms with a wild nature disturbingly red in tooth and claw.

Neville Dawes
The Last Enchantment
Introduction: Kwame Dawes
ISBN: 9781845231170; pp. 332; 27 April 2009; £9.99

This penetrating and often satirical exploration of the search for self in a world divided by colour and class is set in the context of the radical hopes of Jamaican nationalist politics in the early 1950s. First published in 1960, the novel asks many pertinent questions about the Jamaica of today.

Wilson Harris
Heartland
Introduction: David Dabydeen
ISBN: 9781845230968; pp. 104; 23 May 2009; £7.99

First published in 1964, this visionary novel tracks a man's psychic disintegration in the aloneness of the forests of the Guyanese interior, making a powerful ecological statement about man's place in the 'invisible chain of being', in which nature is a no less active presence.

Edgar Mittelholzer
Corentyne Thunder
Introduction: Juanita Cox
ISBN: 9781845231118; pp. 242; 27 April 2009; £8.99

This pioneering work of West Indian fiction is not merely an acute portrayal of the rural Indo-Guyanese world, but a work of literary ambition that creates a symphonic relationship between its characters and the vast openness of the Corentyne coast.

Andrew Salkey
Escape to an Autumn Pavement
Introduction: Thomas Glave
ISBN: 9781845230982; pp. 220; 23 May 2009; £8.99

This brave and remarkable novel, set in London at the end of the 1950s catches its 'brown' Jamaican narrator on the cusp between black and white, between exiled Jamaican and an incipent black Londoner, and between heterosexual and homosexual desires.

Denis Williams
Other Leopards
Introduction: Victor Ramraj
ISBN: 9781845230678; pp. 216; 23 May 2009; £8.99

Lionel Froad is a Guyanese working on an archeological survey in the mythical Jokhara in the horn of Africa. There he hopes to rediscover the self he calls 'Lobo', his alter ego from 'ancestral times', which he thinks slumbers behind his cultivated mask.
Denis Williams

The Third Temptation
Introduction: Victor Ramraj
ISBN: 9781845231163; pp. 108; 23 May 2009; £7.99

A young man is killed in a traffic accident at a Welsh seaside resort. Around this incident, Williams, drawing inspiration from the *Nouveau Roman*, creates a reality that is both rich and problematic. Whilst he brings to the novel a Caribbean eye, Williams refuses any restrictive boundaries for Caribbean fiction.

Visit www.peepaltreepress.com for safe on-line ordering and a wealth of information about Caribbean writing.